déjà
Vu

SUSAN GILES

déjà vu

Matador
9 Priory Business Park,
Wistow Road
Kibworth Beauchamp
Leicester LE8 0RX, UK
Tel: (+44) 116 279 2299
Fax: (+44) 116 279 2277
Email: books@troubador.co.uk
Web: www.troubador.co.uk/matador

ISBN 978 1784620 776

British Library Cataloguing in Publication Data.
A catalogue record for this book is available from the British Library.

Typeset by Troubador Publishing Ltd, Leicester, UK
Printed and bound in the UK by TJ International, Padstow, Cornwall

Matador is an imprint of Troubador Publishing Ltd

Also by Susan Giles

The Primrose Path

Chapter 1

The disclosure came as a shock. But that was not surprising. It could not have been anticipated. And it wasn't every day you learned something of that nature about your partner. But Catherine thought there was no substance to it. Anna was merely being mischievous.

Catherine Cox did not rate Anna, personally or professionally. On the first count, she was a gossip, a troublemaker – a woman with loose morals. On the second, it was accepted that her position in the Company rested solely on the generous auspices of her grandfather. Someone had once quipped that setting the IQ mean at 100 to ensure nobody registered a minus score failed to take Anna into account. But nepotism ruled the day and in the wake of a carefree adolescence, and a growing tally of rejected suitors, a job was found for her. But that was incidental to Catherine: her job was not at stake. Her partner was.

Anna had pursued him from the start, from the moment she joined the Company. She had always dressed provocatively whenever he was in the office, low necklines, figure-hugging minis, sexual innuendo – she had made her availability patently obvious. 'But of course, Alex, if you want me to work late, I'd be quite happy to. I could bring us sandwiches. And it doesn't matter how late I stay. I've *nobody* at home waiting for me.' But even if there had been somebody waiting for her, it would not have mattered. A bonk at work would do very nicely, especially if it was Alexander doing the bonking.

That he hadn't responded to any of the invitations, Catherine knew as fact. And whenever she had raised the subject with him, he had always laughed, told her that Anna was just a kid and would eventually grow out of her childish ways. 'When she finds the right *boy* for her,' was a perennial line of his.

But it wasn't that simple. If Anna wanted something, she *had* to have it – and that trait extended to men. And men were inherently promiscuous, their genes were programmed differently to women's – it was evolutionarily proven. Chip away at the trunk long enough and the sap will eventually rise. No matter how faithful the man, given the right set of circumstances, you were in trouble.

And it was difficult trying to reason with her, hard to make her see that chasing another woman's man was wrong. In fact it was impossible. Her desire for conquest overshadowed ethics and morals in equal measure. She had a diagnosable psychological condition, maybe even a treatable one, but Catherine was no psychologist.

She held Anna Symonds's stare. The party was to celebrate Catherine's birthday. There was nothing more to it than that. She and Alexander had planned it. His proposal had been to keep it business only, just a few colleagues, financial friends. At the time she had agreed, hadn't thought his suggestion particularly odd. But in view of Anna's revelation, that had changed. It now appeared unusual, suspiciously so. Nevertheless there was no doubting but that it was a birthday party: greeting cards on the mantle; gifts on a coffee table – someone had even attached birthday balloons to the railings outside the apartment. But there was a confidence to Anna's expression, the impatient blue eyes, as sharp as a buzzard's beak, the lips quivering ever so slightly, as though about to deliver the punch line of a joke. Catherine's gaze narrowed. 'Are you sure?' she asked.

Anna Symonds smiled. It was a knowing smile, well-practised. 'Oh, yes, Alex is going to run the new branch the Company is opening in the States. He will announce it later, you wait and see.' Her expression pretended puzzlement. 'But I thought you knew. Everyone else does.'

Perhaps it was true. Catherine sipped her drink, a subterfuge to cover her rising uncertainty. The Company's expansion plans had been discussed weeks ago. They were common knowledge. But there had been no mention of Alex in them – at least, none that she was aware of. And Alex had not said anything, and surely he would have done, if it were true?

Catherine turned instinctively towards her partner. Alex was pouring a glass of wine for Brenda Willis, who had just arrived with her husband Joe. She saw him hand the drink to Brenda, his expression welcoming, the open smile softening the ruggedness of his physiognomy. Catherine became aware of her heartbeat. If Anna thought she was going to cause trouble between them tonight, she had better think again. She turned back to face her rival. 'Yes I did know... really,' she fibbed. 'But don't let on: Alex wants it to appear as if it's a surprise to me.' Studying Anna's suddenly crestfallen face, winking, she added: 'We're going to have our own private celebration later.'

'Well that's hunky-dory then,' Anna Symonds replied coolly, waving to her latest acquisition, a muscle-bound hunk named Tarquin, who was sitting forlornly on a sofa, temporarily abandoned, nursing a glass of orange juice. She started towards him. 'See you later then.'

Catherine watched Anna threading her way across the

room: the long blonde hair brushing tanned shoulders, the six-inch heels, the hourglass figure cocooned in the blue Armani mini, and that deliberate little wiggle she affected for any man who might be watching – and of course they all were. But golly, what she wouldn't give for a figure like that. She watched Anna Symonds slide into an impossibly tiny space on the sofa. Dieting for a year would not get her in there.

'Happy birthday, my dear – very best wishes to you.'

Catherine turned towards the voice. She saw that Brenda Willis was holding out a gift-wrapped box. 'Oh, thanks.' Catherine surfaced from her reverie. 'Thank you,' she said, smiling as she accepted the present.

'Me, too,' Brenda's husband Joe said, kissing her on the cheek. 'By the way, you look gorgeous this evening.'

Catherine flashed him a good-natured smile, thanked him for the compliment. Earlier, putting on her face, doing her hair, trying on different outfits, she had felt okay – even a bit more than that. But now, having just matched herself against Anna, her confidence was floundering. 'And you look like James Bond, Joe,' she teased, smiling again.

'I know it,' he responded seriously. Then, grinning widely, he added: 'Pussy Galore is always saying the same thing.'

Brenda laughed, scoffed at her husband's joke. 'Not with that stomach,' she said. 'But yes, you really do look lovely, my dear. I noticed you when we were talking to Alexander.' Her gaze took in Catherine's silk blouse. 'Red is definitely your colour.' She paused, before adding conspiratorially: 'You will have to watch him tonight you know.'

Catherine had no worries on that score. Her eyes briefly scanned the room. She saw that Alex was now loafing against the living-room door, the posture accentuating the bulk of

4

his shoulders, revealing the muscularity of his buttocks. Her gaze lingered on the taut muscles… and her pulse quickened. He caught her stare and grinned, seemed to read her thoughts. She smiled back, experienced the flush of her heartbeat. No worries. She was the one who would need to be watched.

Tearing her thoughts from later, she unwrapped Brenda's present. It was a silver charm bracelet. 'Oh, it's lovely.' She looped the bracelet round her wrist, hugged her friend, thanked Joe. 'I'll put it on now.' She shot a glance towards Anna. 'I have a feeling I'm going to need all the luck I can get this evening,' she added, fastening the clasp.

Brenda also glanced at Anna. 'I've told you before, Kate,' she said, '… a thousand times.' She touched Catherine's arm affectionately. 'Don't let her get to you. If you do, she will ruin your happiness.'

Brenda Willis had worked for the Company for over twenty-five years, and knew everything that was going on, or about to go on. She was Catherine's best friend in the office, her confidante. She was also a family friend. With Catherine not long out of university, and with little work experience, she had been instrumental in getting her a place on the Firm's internship scheme. A confidence not misplaced; for now, just three years later, and from her modest beginning, Kate had risen to become one of the top investment managers in the business – and that included the whole of the City's financial sector.

Catherine nodded absently, toyed with her new bracelet, thinking, pondering the turn of events. Brenda had not mentioned anything about Alex's promotion, so surely it was a story of Anna's making, an invention intended to cause trouble – yet Anna had been so convincing, so certain of her facts. 'Brenda,' she began thoughtfully, 'Anna mentioned something earlier about tonight being merely for Alex to announce his promotion. Do you… do you…? Is it true?'

Brenda's expression sagged visibly, and the hazel eyes darkened. Catherine studied the look, searching for clues, waited patiently as her friend now sipped her wine. After a while Brenda lowered the glass from her lips. 'You… you know my opinion of that minx.' She paused to wave across the room, before adding: 'Oh, there's Elizabeth. I must quiz her about the revised interest rate, before I forget.' And with that she was off, all but spilling her drink as her hasty departure caused her to bump into a sofa.

Catherine turned to Joe, only to see him heading for the buffet.

That something was afoot Catherine was sure, and Brenda knew what it was. All that muddled prevarication confirmed it, running off in the middle of a conversation like that. Indeed, she knew all right. In retrospect, they all did. Catherine hadn't twigged before but it was obvious now. Everybody had wished her a happy birthday, kisses, hugs, the usual stuff. But there was more to it than that. Those smiles that appeared normal then now seemed odd, conspiratorial – the earlier innocuous glances seemed now underpinned with meaning.

Anna's story about Alex's promotion was true then. But no one was going to enlighten Catherine. It was to be a secret, until Alex announced his surprise, his birthday surprise.

But why arrange it like this, she asked herself, and in front of everybody else? Did he just assume that she would accept it, that she would go with him? They'd been together for three years, and had often talked of working in America. She had been particularly enthusiastic. 'A meritocracy, a land of opportunities,' she had told him. So maybe he thought she would jump at the chance. But going over there would mean giving up their London life and friends, this Chelsea flat. She wasn't particularly against the idea, in principle, but it needed discussion, mutual discussion, not just a pre-emptive announcement.

Then something else occurred to her, another possibility. If he had been offered a top job in the States, perhaps there was no role for her. Maybe his intention was to go out there alone... or with somebody else from the Firm.

As if possessing a will of its own Catherine's gaze wandered across the room to Anna, who was still sitting on the sofa, wedged against Tarquin. She appeared distracted, her mind elsewhere, fingers absently drumming on her boyfriend's inner thigh. Clearly, she was waiting for Alex's *revelation*, hoping to gain some sexual leverage from it.

Catherine's stare moved on to Tarquin, whose manner bespoke of a concentrated mind. And who could fault him? she mused. Those fingers were getting closer and closer. Despite the circumstances, her mood lightened. Whatever else was planned, at least Alex was safe tonight.

Alexander grinned smugly at his reflection in the glazed kitchen door. Holy smoke this was going to be some bombshell. What precautions he had taken to ensure that, particularly after the boss had let the cat out of the bag by sending that public email. Silly bugger was getting too old, too forgetful. That slip had almost ruined the whole shebang. Luckily for him Kate was visiting a client that day and hadn't got around to checking her emails. That piece of good fortune had given him time to persuade IT to wipe it from her account.

But what was so smart about his planning, so satisfying, was that he had managed to string it out to coincide with her birthday. How sweet was that? Okay, he'd only had to sit on the secret for three days but with office gossip being what it was those three days had felt more like three weeks. Yes, his lovely lady was about to get the surprise of the century.

He watched her moving amongst their friends, laughing, sharing a joke, a kiss here, a hug there – the perfect hostess. Sure it was a cliché but that didn't make it any less true. He was lucky to have her as his partner, the luckiest man in the world. Sure, another cliché. But once again it was spot on.

He recalled their first meeting. The Company was expanding and had taken on several recruits. Catherine was one of them. Alex made an emphatic nod of his head – a raw recruit he had immediately fancied seeing in the raw. Anyway, arrangements had been made for all staff to go on a so-called "bonding" weekend in the Lake District, where they'd been expected to take part in team-building activities. To be honest, he had thought it a bit bloody silly. But Jack Symonds had been taken with the idea, had decided that it would reinforce the morale of the Company's personnel, help the newcomers gel into the corporate infrastructure, and so they'd all been required to go.

Catherine was hopeless at the outdoor activities: cycling, rock climbing – zilch; orienteering – well, she came out top at map reading, not so hot at the hiking bit though; canoeing – all right until she tried to get out of the thing, then she got her backside stuck, which was perfectly understandable. God, they should have given him extra points for the effort he put in helping her out – up to his knees in water, freezing water, prising first one cheek then the other, over and over, until she popped out, like a champers cork.

But in the theoretical exercises they'd done in the

evenings she had excelled. In one they'd had to imagine they were survivors of a plane that had crashed in clear conditions a hundred miles from the North Pole, with rescue being twenty miles southwest. What survival equipment should they take with them? They had all agreed about bolstering their clothing and making snowshoes out of salvaged bits and pieces of the plane, but they had laughed when she opted for a star map and they chose a compass, until the instructor told them you couldn't rely on a compass that near to the pole.

And that talk she gave on Keynesian economics versus monetarism – brilliant. Even the Chancellor of the Exchequer would have been hard pressed to match that. Well, he couldn't have. But her trousers... criminal; he had all but burst out of his. Every time she'd turned round to the whiteboard to write down a bullet point. Good God! Talk about fluid mechanics. He was already hooked by her intellect, but that backside landed him in the keepnet, clinched the deal.

Mind you, another side of her nature had emerged on that weekend away. It was while they were playing a particularly stupid game – teams of four working on doing a jigsaw puzzle, one puzzle per team. What a bloody waste of time. It was supposed to encourage teamwork. He smiled to himself. Team building, it almost ended up causing a riot.

Catherine was the captain of one team, had volunteered, had put herself forward. Fine, good on her, until the instructor said: 'Off you go.' And they had, all hands to the pump. It was like watching half a dozen octopi making love – more moves than a tin of worms. It was a shambles; a terrible mess; total confusion – squabbling like kids. They still hadn't completed the frame when everyone else had finished. Clearly, as team captain, she was to blame: she should have organised who was

9

working on what, somebody doing the straight bits, somebody sorting prominent colours... And, of course, someone else organising, coordinating, bringing all the elements together. The other captains did it that way, including him. The problem was obvious: she was a loner – a competitive loner at that.

But worse was to come, for she had sulked for the remainder of the evening, hardly spoke to anyone – and all over a bloody game. Somebody called her a bad loser, which nearly cost him an eye. Competitive, hated to lose – and she hadn't changed. He grinned. She was all right now, being a team player, especially when they were in bed – still competitive there though, particularly where games were concerned. His grin broadened. And of course there would be plenty of games later, fun and games, when they got down to celebrating, properly... when *he* got down to celebrating, *properly*.

He glanced around the room. It looked like everyone was here, so no point in delaying any longer.

'May I have your attention, please?'

Catherine turned her head in the direction of the gravelly voice, the sonorous timbre that commanded attention. She had seen it turn heads at meetings, focus minds on the agenda. Politicians went to speech doctors to acquire voices that carried authority, public speakers and actors, too. But Alex had it naturally – he did not have to try. She saw that he was standing in the corner of the room, by the door that let into the kitchen, his down-turned palms performing the traditional quietening gesture.

'Hush everyone; I've got something to say.'

He caught her gaze and beckoned her to him. For the briefest of moments she considered not co-operating. She knew what was coming next – Anna had seen to that. But no way was she going to give that conniving creature an opportunity of another triumph. Aware of the other woman's envious gaze, she sauntered across the room and stood beside Alexander King, chief investment strategist of Symonds and Symonds Investment Bankers.

Catherine gazed up into his tanned face. The jawline was square, tilted now in confident mien as he surveyed his audience, the nose straight, the hair almost black, parted in the middle, the eyes attentive – and the brows… dark but not brooding. He could pass for a young Hugh Grant… but more masculine. Her stare settled on the wide mouth, the lips, firm, capable… And the smile that told any woman all she needed to know.

She felt Alex's arm encircle her waist, protective, reassuring, felt him draw her against his side, and experienced the flip of her heart at the touch, the sexual heat of his muscular frame as it squashed the softness of her hip. He worked out in the gym three times a week, swam regularly, cycled. And he had stamina: he had run the London Marathon for the past five years, all in times under three hours, which was exceptional for a man of his size and bulk. He was totally fit – she could vouch for it. A picture of his buttocks, taut, motive in the mirror above their bed opened in her mind, the delight of syncopated rhythm.

'Hush, please,' he began. The hubbub quickly subsided and the room became quiet. 'Firstly, I'd like to thank you all for being here… on this auspicious occasion.' He coughed, glanced round the room. 'Indeed, we are gathered here tonight to celebrate an achievement, a landmark, something truly momentous…' Catherine prepared herself to hear confirmation of Anna's news, resolved that, when it came, she would not look at the other woman. She glanced at Alex. 'We all get older,' he was saying. 'It's a fact of life – can't be avoided. And no woman welcomes the milestone that is her fortieth birthday… and Kate is no exception.' General amusement

11

came from the room, and Catherine realised that promotion was not his topic. She was. He was talking about her birthday. Perhaps, then, she concluded, Anna's story was made up.

He turned to her. 'Sorry,' he said contritely, 'couldn't resist the temptation, even of a hackneyed old chestnut like that.' Just for a moment, Catherine was puzzled... Then she realised the extra decade that he had added to her age. He was an inveterate practical joker, and responsible for most of the risqué emails in the loop at work. She caught his gaze. 'In fact I can't resist temptation full stop,' he continued. He bent his head closer, so that only she would hear what he was going to say next. 'But it's that little naïve look that you adopt at some of my jokes – that turns me on no end.' He brought his head even closer. 'Listen,' he whispered, 'how about leaving them all to it and going straight to bed?'

Another image came into Catherine's mind... and the longer it remained there, the more her face reddened. She turned away, to catch Anna Symonds's green expression. She stared straight at her, hoping her own glowing cheeks would convey some sense of the question that Alex had just asked her. Ten minutes ago she was angry with Anna, envious of her looks and figure, ready even to ruffle that blonde hair. But now, standing at Alex's side, bathed in his aura, she saw Anna as inconsequential, a woman of no substance.

'Seriously though,' he began again, addressing himself to the room, 'you all know tonight has a joint purpose, that is everybody except for my lovely lady. I've kept her in the dark – not that that's always the best way – so as to maximise the profit of my investment.' He placed his arm round her shoulder, as though they were mates, buddies sharing an in-joke, and gazed down at her. 'How do you fancy living and working in America?' he asked.

Catherine flinched. So Anna hadn't lied. Even though she had accepted Anna's story as fact, Alex's corroboration nevertheless hit her where it hurt. He had been promoted. He had been offered the American job – and his plan was that they went over there.

And she would relish doing so – of course she would, if everyone else hadn't been informed first, even Anna. It was a lifetime's opportunity. Catherine stared down at her hands, thinking. Alex hadn't told her, not a thing, not a whisper. And he must have known for some time. Suddenly she felt betrayed, let down. He had taken her acceptance for granted, as if she were no more than an underling. He was making decisions for her, decisions he had no right to make; he hadn't even bothered to consult her about her own future.

And she did have an independent future. She managed several large corporate accounts, was procuring others… pension funds. She had won the Berryman account single-handed, had managed every aspect, every minutia of the transfer the same way. Catherine blanched in chagrin. Indeed, after the directors had all but surrendered it to Lloyds, she had stepped in and recovered the situation. She was senior enough in the Firm to have been asked her opinion.

'That's settled then,' he said over her silence. He nodded resolutely, his mind clearly savouring the fulfilment of their move. 'That's settled,' he repeated, 'done and dusted.' He then went on to tell her about their promotions – emphasising the plural – how she would take an instrumental role in setting up the new branch, how her flair for capturing new accounts would rake in the dollars, how they would travel, Washington, Boston, New York… Wall Street. 'What a team we'll make,' he ran on excitedly. 'Alex and Kate; King and Cox. Watch out Chase Manhattan!' Then he kissed her…

From the maelstrom of her mind, Catherine heard the applause from the room, heard Bill Thomas from Administration tell Alex to leave some for him, that congratulations were for everyone to give. The job was a plum, a reward for their efforts, their success. She should have been overjoyed, thrilled. But she shouldn't have found out like this – been the last to know.

She ended the kiss. No, she shouldn't. If they wanted her as an equal partner out in the States, setting up the new branch from scratch, then the Company should have consulted them both – together. Before he went throwing promotions across the Atlantic, Jack Symonds should have shown her the common courtesy of eliciting her opinion. She was miffed, and getting angrier by the minute.

Alex settled himself on the sofa, stretched his legs out straight and crossed his ankles. Ably assisted by a little alcohol, he was pooped. Catherine was okay. Just look at her, busy, focused, clearing up the aftermath of the celebrations – and all after preparing the buffet (most of the afternoon) – and then, this evening, welcoming, chatting, accepting congratulations with the grace of a royal. Yes, she had enjoyed her party. And soon they would be in bed. He wouldn't be too pooped for that… bushed afterwards perhaps.

He poured himself another whisky, brushed a surreptitious hand against the conduit in his trousers. 'Kate, leave it for the morning.' He patted the space beside him. 'Come and have one for the road… the highway to heaven.'

Catherine carried on with the clearing up, placed a tumbler on the tray that was balanced in her left hand.

Alex continued to observe her. He saw that she had assumed her inscrutable face, the one he knew well from the boardroom, when somebody or something had upset her. 'What's the matter, Catherine?'

'Nothing.' She picked up a champagne flute, set it on the tray beside the tumbler. 'Nothing's the matter,' she said, reaching for another glass.

But Alex knew that something was wrong. He had already noted the miniscule tremor of her hand as she collected the glasses, the tremble that signified a pent-up emotion – and the way that she'd said 'nothing's the matter' told him that something was. She was holding back, waiting for the right moment. He didn't like arguments. They hadn't had a serious disagreement in the past three years, but he sensed they were about to have one now.

He stood up, took the tray from her hand and placed it on a coffee table, then turned back to face her. 'Yes, it is,' he said, holding her gaze. 'Something has upset you,' He caught her hands in his. 'Tell me what it is.'

'It's nothing.' She glanced up at him, almost diffidently, he thought. 'We can discuss it in the morning.'

Alex held her stare. Her gravitas was making him feel uncomfortable. It was almost as if she was waiting for him to confess to a misdemeanour. But he hadn't done anything wrong; the party had been a great success, everybody had enjoyed it, everyone had said what a great time... Then he had it. 'Oh, God, Kate, it's the Anna thing again, isn't it?' He sighed. 'Because I've told you before that–'

'It's not actually her,' she interrupted. 'I–'

'So there is something,' he cut in, giving her no chance to explain. 'I knew there was. What is it?'

'I don't like being the last to know,' she said, starting to turn away to go back to clearing up.

He held onto her hands and prevented her from

completing the manoeuvre. Now that she was in front of him, up close, he could see that she was tired. It had been a long evening, and he knew that she had drunk more than usual. In truth, she hardly ever drank much, red or white wine at dinner, a beer when they went down the pub, but it was her party, and she'd had their promotions to celebrate too. 'The last to know what?' he asked, guiding her back to face him.

'The last to be told about your promotion.' Her eyes darted spiritedly between his. 'The last to know that I'm part of the deal, or expected to be part of it.'

Alex's tension eased. So that was it – next to nothing. He would soon get it sorted. But she was clearly upset, taking it seriously. Nevertheless, it was still only an insignificant matter, a trifle. He released her hands and took a step back. 'It was meant as a surprise,' he said quietly, shaking his head. He ran his fingers through a shock of thick black hair that had fallen across his forehead. 'Catherine, I thought you'd be so happy. Crikey, I've been itching to tell you, ever since Jack put the proposition to me – and I don't know how I've stopped myself from doing so. But I wanted to keep the news back for your birthday. I thought it would be the greatest birthday present ever.'

'It wasn't a surprise anyway. I already knew – obviously not as long as everyone else, but I already knew.'

Anna. Realisation hit Alex like a dig in the solar plexus. She had told Kate. He grabbed the bottle of whisky from the coffee table, splashed a shot into his tumbler and, raising it to his lips, swallowed the liquid in one go. 'Anna!' The word came out as an expletive. He measured himself another drink. 'Everyone in the office was sworn to secrecy; they all agreed the birthday surprise idea was great… working in the States. That is, in the light of all we've… you've said about living and working over there.' He paced the floor, dumbfounded, shaking his head. 'But I should have known that she would spoil the surprise, that she would try to stir up trouble. And she waited until this evening to do it.' He took a considered slug of his drink. 'Yeah, I should've known. It was obvious. What a bloody fool to trust her.'

'Then why did you invite her, if it was so obvious? I for one didn't want her here.'

'Oh c'mon, we could hardly leave her out. How would it have looked? Besides, she's been working in Brenda's department for the past month.' Alex sighed. 'We wouldn't have been able to keep it from her.'

'You kept it from me,' Catherine accused. She folded her arms. 'But of course with Anna being Jack Symonds's granddaughter, you wouldn't have wanted to jeopardise your promotion.'

Alex started laughing, only to become serious again when he noted his partner's unchanging expression. He said: 'Jack is the consummate professional; you know that − business first, second, and always. Okay, he dotes on her. But to suggest that he would change his mind about someone's promotion just because his granddaughter hadn't been invited to a birthday party is hilarious.'

'Okay; point taken.'

'Kate, if I'd had any idea...' She started to speak, but he indicated that he wanted to finish. '... just the merest suspicion, that she was going to let on, then she wouldn't have been here tonight − believe me.'

Catherine spread dismissive hands. 'I don't care that she was the one who gave away your secret. Knowing the full facts now, I would have been disappointed if it hadn't been her. But the matter goes deeper than office tittle-tattle: it's a question of professionalism. By accepting on my behalf you were taking me for granted. It looks from here as if you thought my opinion didn't carry any weight, that it was of no consequence to you and your ambition.'

Alex could see that Kate was frazzled, wound up like a clockwork toy. He had to unwind her, otherwise he would end up being the frazzled one – later, in bed. He took a thoughtful breath. 'Only because of what you've said about America – yes, I did take that part of it for granted. And anyhow it was only a tacit acceptance, prior to our discussion of the offer. My position was that the final decision would be yours. Certainly, if you'd been against it, I would have argued, tried to persuade you, but I wouldn't have gone without you, if that's what you think.'

'But I'm on the same seniority level in the Firm as you,' she persisted. 'Yes, my acceptance may rightly have been assumed, but professional etiquette dictates that we should have been consulted together.'

Alex sighed and placed his hands on her shoulders, decided against pointing out that his position was senior. That wasn't important. But he knew Catherine. Trying to placate her wasn't going to get him anywhere, not in her present mood. She was going to fight her corner every inch of the way, even though her corner was a nonstarter. He decided to change tack, to put it to her straight, tell it like it was. 'So you feel professionally slighted,' he said evenly. 'But, hey, c'mon, you're a grownup girl: you know how the financial sector works. Sure, by and large it's a man's world, but you've done okay in it. So why so uppity now?'

'I've worked hard to get where I am,' she retorted, pushing away his hands as he started to knead her shoulder muscles. 'The Company should have treated us as equals.'

He looked at her, his gaze immediately softening at the emotion in her voice. 'You're probably right,' he agreed. He shrugged his shoulders, noting Catherine's attention switch from his face to the ripple of muscle beneath his sports shirt. No worries. Their disagreement wouldn't undermine his plans for later: she wanted him as much as he wanted her. 'But you know Symonds and Symonds Bankers,' he went on, 'the quintessential English establishment firm, traditional... conservative... old school tie...'

'Chauvinistic,' she put in, taking advantage of his pause as he searched for the appropriate words.

'Again, you're probably right. But with your astuteness, you doubtless realised that by the second interview – but you took the job all the same.'

'I needed it,' she said. 'I was a junior. I was going nowhere at Barclays.'

'That's beside the point.' Alex poured himself another drink. 'But look at it realistically. In terms of the integrity of the Company, the interests of our clients always come first – we work hard to ensure that. Before recommendation, we research all potential investments, not just for their profitability, but also for their long-term stability, their ethical credibility.' He held her gaze. 'Did we get involved with buying sub-prime mortgage debt? No. Did we dabble in futures? No. Did we massage interest rates for our benefit? No. And, finally, did the Government need to bail us out? No. We're a solid, dependable firm...' He paused, allowing her time to digest the veracity of his argument, before concluding: '... if a little too staid, a little too square for some of our feminist employees.'

She stared up at him, scowling. 'You were doing all right, until your penultimate word,' she said sharply. 'But that's infantile and, moreover, downright untrue.' She turned away and went back to clearing away the debris of the party.

Alex knew that if he didn't act decisively this silly squabble was in danger of escalating, if it hadn't already done so. He placed his empty glass on the coffee table. 'You don't need to do that now,' he said, taking the drinks tray from her hand and placing it back on the table. 'Leave it for the morning.' He pulled her to him, held her against his chest. 'It's late: let's go to bed.'

She struggled, attempted to free herself from his embrace. 'I'd rather do it now.' She pushed at him. 'Let me go! There's nothing worse than getting up in the morning to be faced by the mess of the night before.'

'I know it's Saturday tomorrow,' he said, restraining her struggles, 'but I'll phone the cleaner – she will be glad of the overtime.'

'Please let me go,' she repeated. 'Besides, it's not fair to ask someone to come in at the week–'

He silenced her protestations with a kiss, felt his hackles rising at her invigorated attempt to break free.

A wet gurgle came from her throat as his tongue forced her lips apart and entered her mouth. He had never coerced her before – she was such a sexual being – but her resistance, far from being a dampener to his desire, which it should have been, was in fact adding to his ardour, inflaming him more. Already he had a hard-on. He did not want to stop – he couldn't stop.

Alex experienced her now, all wriggles and squiggles and squirms, but he held her fast, his lips moving on hers, his tongue sparring with hers. Her breasts were squashed against his chest as he wrestled with her – he could feel the nipples, hard, like thimbles. He knew she was up for it, that she wanted him. So why was she fighting – surely not over a stupid misunderstanding? He knew he could overcome her resistance, her refusal. She loved it when he kissed her like this. His dominance was the prelude, the jump-start, to the most passionate of lovemaking – and was he going to give her some of that. Good God how he loved her though.

Somehow she managed to get her hands between their bodies, flat against the rock hardness of his chest, the muscles that were now working as he tried to control her writhing body. Another push and she pulled her mouth from his. 'That's right,' she gasped, clenching her hands into fists, 'try to win the argument in the typical male way.' She swung her head away from his fresh attempt to kiss her. 'It might work with Anna but it won't with me.'

Alex held her at arm's length, angry. 'Don't be so bloody infantile, Kate. You know you're talking nonsense, so why persist with it?' He returned her stare. 'I love *you*,' he said, his voice throaty with desire. 'If you think that anything I've done was wrong, then I apologise.' He paused, breathing hard. 'Whatever you think, everything I've done was done with the best intentions, with your happiness in mind.' He paused again, feeling his simmering passion ready to erupt. He took a gulp of breath. 'I love you, Catherine,' he said simply, pinning her arms behind her back.

'No, Alex,' she said. 'No–'

He silenced her plea with another kiss, experienced her weakening resistance as his kiss plied her libido. He became aware of her femaleness, the aroma of female arousal – a heady, intoxicating mixture that never found him wanting. He felt his erection straining against the taut material of his trousers. He was in purgatory. He loved her so much, wanted to possess her body. His head started to swim; he felt lightheaded, felt a sudden giddiness, an overwhelming desire to penetrate her, to fulfil her, to show her how much he loved her. She thought Anna was the male idea of perfection. How bloody wrong she was. Any real man would give his right arm to make love to her. And he was going to – now.

'No, Alex. Please...'

He started to unzip her skirt, heard a button ping and fly across the room as he pulled the waistband of the garment down on to the swell of her hips. He felt her try again to push him away, but it was an effete movement, carried no conviction. She was telling him no but meaning yes. She wanted to be taken; she wanted to be taken against her will, and fucked.

He jerked her skirt down over her hips, still kissing her to silence any remaining protests. Not that there were any now. She was kissing him back, turned on, gagging for it. His kissing had done that. You couldn't beat a good snog to get a woman going – same for him, too. Aware of the increasing constriction of his fly, he commenced to unbutton her blouse, pulling urgently at the silken material as his spiralling passion sought respite in her body.

In moments he had her standing before him, clad now only in her underwear – the creamy flesh of her breasts threatening to spill from her brassiere... her cleavage... and the protuberance of her rump that bedevilled his wits. He had never loved her so much, never desired her so wholeheartedly. Then he removed her underwear, scooped her into his arms and carried her through to the bedroom.

Chapter 2

Catherine lay on the bed, where Alex had placed her, and waited for him to undress. She had made a decision, a pragmatic one: she had decided not to resist. What was the point? He was going to do it – full stop. He intended to have his way and there was nothing she could say or do to prevent him. But once he'd had what he wanted, she knew that he would be ashamed, that he would regret what he had done. Men were like that, once their lust had been sated, their reason returned. Ultimately, the moral victory would be hers.

And this way would be quicker, over and done with sooner – and would also be less traumatic. Lie still for a while, switch off, and she would be herself again in no time.

Just look at him though, fumbling with his clothes. He was in a hurry, almost falling over in his haste to get it off. Catherine felt disgusted. It would serve him right if he did fall over, if he disabled himself… if he caught his foreskin in his zip.

He had once done that. They had been on holiday, walking the coastal path on Lundy Island, and he had gone behind some bushes to relieve himself. Suddenly, she'd heard him cry out – a real howl of pain it was. Fearing that a snake or some other wildlife had bitten him, Catherine had gone to his assistance… and had found him doubled over, grimacing like a baby, trying to free his trapped part. It had taken her ages to extricate him, teasing the zip gently free…

and all the time his plaintive meowing. And then he had wanted her to kiss it better. Indeed, she hoped he caught himself… good and proper. She observed him now, hopping around on one leg, unbalanced as he tugged frantically at a trouser leg.

She had seen such antics in films – usually French farces. This was more of an English tragedy: the intelligent male being outwitted by primitive instinct. Catherine all but laughed – me Tarzan, you Jane.

And now he was getting into a panic with his underwear – a simple garment that should have been easy to remove had outfoxed him. If he pulled that way anymore, he would give himself a wedgie. While she knew it unlikely, she was nonetheless hoping that her quiescence would bring about an early return of his senses, that seeing her lying here, unresponsive, might dampen his ardour. Averting her gaze as his erection sprang free of his pants, Catherine doubted that it would.

Alex flung his briefs on to the bedroom floor then sat down on the bed. 'Don't be bloody childish, Catherine,' he said huskily. 'I've done nothing wrong. My surprise was meant well.' He combed his fingers through the bob of her hair, attached his stare to hers. 'I love you… and I know you love me. Nothing has changed that. You're absolutely and utterly irresistible.' He switched his attention to the soft mounds of her breasts, caressing, fondling, kneading. 'I've been looking forward to this moment all day – and I know you have, too.'

'Surely *this* isn't what you've been looking forward to?' she said coolly. 'I assume you were anticipating making love, not–'

'For God's sake, Kate,' he broke in, 'love is what I meant. I love you; and we will be making love.'

She glanced at his face. He looked tired, exasperated, frustrated, and not a little inebriated. But shortly she would be the injured party, obliged to participate. 'It takes two to do that,' she said.

'I love you so much, Kate… But…' He faltered, and she saw that he was on the cusp of becoming emotional. 'But I wish that you weren't so bloody stubborn.' Then he stood up and turned to face her.

She became closely aware of his tumescence, rampant, hovering above her as he thrust himself forward – as he presented himself to her. He was near enough for her to see the throb of his fervour, the glisten of his enthusiasm. In normal circumstances she would have been with him, taking part, doing her things, the things he so enjoyed. But nothing about tonight was normal. Holding her arms at her sides, she looked away.

He surveyed her supine body, mumbled something incoherent. Then, cupping a breast in his hands, he sucked a nipple deep into his mouth, commenced to gnaw on its sensitivity.

Catherine stared at her reflection in the mirror above the bed, saw passion – unwelcome desire – awaken in her eyes, and tried desperately not to gasp in delight as he nursed on her. She could give in now, join in. Despite what he had already done – what he was now doing – a part of her wanted to. She had made her point, and it really was little more than a misunderstanding, exacerbated by Anna. But, she reminded herself, he had been prepared to force himself on her earlier. If she hadn't acquiesced, he would have done so, however much she had fought him. He was doing so now, by default. 'Please make it a quickie,' she said indifferently, glancing pointedly towards the clock. 'If you really must do it, at least be quick. I'm feeling really tired just now.'

He raised his head and stared down at her, his eyes sad. She could see that her remark had hit its target, had cut deep. Catherine thought that perhaps she had been too direct, too offhand. Alex was sensitive, had a soft side. He could easily be hurt. Her thoughts piled high. She started to waver once more. And she did love him – and he loved her. She began to frame an apology. But before she had chance to utter it, his expression changed, became fixed, and she heard him say: 'All right, Catherine, if that's how you want it.' He climbed on to the bed and knelt beside her. 'But you'll damned well enjoy it all the same.'

That did it. His declaration provoked her, instantly. Her emotional seesaw tilted back the other way, taking with it her hesitancy. 'No I won't,' she said, yawning. 'I can't imagine that I'll enjoy being forced to have sex. I–' She all but squealed as, unseen, he brought a hand up between her thighs and commenced to meddle with her nether flesh. Her heartbeat went up like a sky rocket, and she felt herself go slick beneath his pliant fingers. Catherine's purpose fell apart. She wanted to be loved, needed to be loved; her body demanded it. Her heart told her to capitulate, to end their battle. That was what she should do. But, determinedly, almost masochistically, she fought off her feelings. Let him do what he liked, she resolved that he would not see even a suggestion of pleasure, a flicker of emotion on her face. A minute ago she had been on the point of giving in, of loving him back. Catherine wasn't anymore. She would be emotionless, as cold as a cadaver. 'I won't enjoy it,' she reiterated.

'We'll see,' he said evenly.

She felt him part her legs, experienced the vulnerability of her exposure. For a moment she thought of kicking out at him, but immediately reverted to her original decision. He intended to do it. So why fight him? He hadn't pulled the duvet over them, and she could see his eyes roaming her body, flaring like those of an alley cat – a physical indication of his determination to back up his assertion. But, Catherine decided, he would not succeed. He would lose this one.

He penetrated her then and, holding himself at arm's length, commenced the sex act. She had never liked the detached posture, the remoteness that distance imposed. She preferred intimacy, kissing, caressing, his body pressed on hers. He knew that. But detachment suited the present circumstance. The farther away he was the better. It would make disregarding him easier. 'Don't fret,' he said sarcastically, staring down at her. 'It won't take me long. Then you can have your sleep.'

'If I drop off before you've finished,' she said, as casually as she could manage, 'don't forget to pull the duvet up when it's over.'

'You won't sleep, Kate.'

In spite of herself, Catherine found his words, his assertion, his pig-headed self-confidence, a turn-on. Sexual submission was in her nature. Moreover, he was good in bed, knew how to rouse her interest, knew what she liked and how to please her – but not this time. She closed her mind against the delight of him reciprocating inside her, tried to anaesthetise the capacity he had for attending to her needs. Her libido wanted her to respond in kind, to move with him, to take part. But, denying its dictate, she yawned once more, clamped rigid arms against her sides, taut, tense – in another scenario a nervous patient awaiting the dentist's first move. Then she closed her eyes.

'Oh no you don't,' he snapped. 'If you want to refuse me, at least have the courtesy to show me the courage of your conviction. I want to see your resolution... before I break it down.' He paused. 'Open your eyes.'

This was a game to him... That's what it was, a childish masculine game. Who did he think he was – a real-life Heathcliff? How infantile. She almost laughed out loud. 'I wish you would hurry up,' she said. 'Then we can both get some sleep. It's been a long day.' And with that she took on his stare.

She saw that his passion had been replaced by abstraction... remoteness. Like her, he too had numbed himself to the immediate pleasure of sex. It was almost as if he were performing by rote – an automaton that had been programmed to carry out mundane domestic tasks. For the look on his face, he could have been doing the vacuuming, or a spot of DIY. He looked ridiculous... even a little scary. Yet for all his assumed distance, his blank expression, she could see that he was determined to win. Poor Alex – would he never grow up?

'Look in the mirror.' His words were a command, part of his game. She saw the amused glint in his eyes. He thought the duel was on. Silently she stared into his face, saw the stressed muscles of his jaw, the gritted teeth of his concentration. 'Do it,' he hissed. 'Do it now.'

'Act your age, Alex.'

'Afraid of losing – is that it, Kate?'

Yawning again, she glanced over his shoulder, to the mirror in the ceiling. It had been his idea to have the thing placed there, and it fitted into many of their games, innocent games, fun games, games that they both enjoyed – unlike this ridiculous charade that he was playing out now. He loved to gaze at her reflection, when she was on top, and he had invented names – hilarious titles – for some of her positions, like *The Shaky Shanghai Spiral* and *The Bossy Burmese Bounce*. He said that it turned him on, to see and feel at the same time. It worked for her too. Catherine determined that it would not do so tonight. It would be absolutely awful, degrading, to be pleasured against one's will – as if one had no cerebral control over one's emotions, no kerb over one's bodily functions, like an animal… like a man. 'There's no chance of that,' she said. 'None.'

'Really?' he asked, immediately increasing his pace, changing something that she had previously experienced as a canter to something that now felt more like a gallop – so that she thought herself being ridden as though in a steeplechase.

'Yes, really,' she put in quickly, between bucks.

'Then all you have to do is wait until I'm finished, don't you? Whenever that may be.' He winked at her. 'But it will be after you, be assured of that.' He repeated his outrageous gesture. 'But keep looking… if you can.'

Catherine remained silent, ignored his taunt.

'That's right, Kate,' he said evenly, 'concentrate.'

'Grow up, Alex,' she responded, reflecting an earlier sentiment.

'I am,' he said.

Now she gazed at his reflection, the bedside lamps making the flurry of action into a kaleidoscopic whirl. She saw the lean muscular thighs, the taut buttocks, the working muscles rippling the tanned skin with each change of direction. He was like a human dynamo, a perpetual motion machine – relentless. She saw her own limbs, white, splayed wide by the tensioned torso, her flesh shaken by the mechanistic movement. And the interplay, the interchange between what she was seeing and what she was feeling – a growing awareness of herself and of what was being done to her… a heightening of sensation. No… No, it mustn't happen.

She conjured up a picture of Jack Symonds, his gaunt, old-man's face, with its crinkled loose skin, for her the antithesis of sexual desire. But no sooner had she done that, than it faded from her imagination, to be replaced by an impression of Alex, his expression pent with passion, and telling her how much he loved her. She evoked another image, a goblin from the nether world, a repulsive, ugly troll who was going to eat her alive. But, aided and abetted by the mirror image, even that faded from her mind, to be replaced by a vision of Alex. It was an image that, this time, she found she could not chase away, and in it he kissed her... and she felt his lips moving on hers... felt his hands caressing her body, heard his voice: 'I love you, my darling.' She knew then that she was about to succumb, but she vowed that he would not know it. He would not know that he had given her pleasure.

She dropped her gaze from the mirror... to see that Alex was studying her face, scrutinising her with all the focus of a scientist examining a newly found specimen under a microscope. Was that amusement in his eyes? Was he mocking her? Did he know?

'How is the magic lantern show?' he asked levelly, bouncing a glance off the tell-tale burgeoning of her nipples. 'Is it entertaining or merely a distraction from the proceedings?' And with that he changed his rhythm, mixing up his tempo, so that she could no longer dance to his hitherto mechanical tune. Catherine all but cried out in despair as a flurry of shallow strokes was followed by a deep lunging stab, then more shallow strokes, another deep thrust, over and over, on and on... until, unable to resist him any longer, she felt her pleasure dome liven with all the fun of the fair.

As her climax came, as pleasure became bliss, she bit a metaphorical lip and stared unblinkingly into his returning look. *Kiss me,* her errant heart cried out. *Tell me that you love me.* She wanted that, and more. But with one final exercise of will, she denied him any knowledge of his victory.

She experienced the slackening of his pace, as he drew to a halt. He was still ramrod-stiff inside her – unspent. Catherine felt hot, her face flushed, her limbs languid. An involuntary tremor took hold of her body as a final pulse of pleasure thrummed her sex. And then, with him still holding himself at arm's length, still holding her stare, she felt him inflict another lunge. For a moment, she thought he was going to join her in climax. But she was wrong, for it was a single thrust, a spiteful jab – a murderer finishing off his already lifeless victim with a superfluous stab of his knife – and the accompanying grunt that rammed his message home. She saw the look in his eyes. He knew… and he was telling her so.

He knew.

And it was then, in that insightful moment, that he did something unexpected – that he took her by surprise. For, still denying himself his pleasure, he withdrew abruptly from her body, hopped silently from the bed and started off across the room. Catherine could see plainly that he was unfinished. Feeling herself abandoned, annoyingly so, she stared after him, watched his long, athletic stride take his lithe body into the ensuite. What was he doing? A puzzled frown crept onto her face. Why hadn't he completed? Why go in there? Her frown intensified. Or had that been enough for him? Had winning been all he required?

He had not begun that way. He had wanted to make love to her – and that was how he had started… She checked herself. No, that was how he *thought* he had started. Yes, that was right, but then along the way, his thinking had altered, had moved away from simple lovemaking to a determined effort to humiliate her… to punish her. She mentally flinched. Her rejection must have hurt him more than she could ever have imagined.

But she'd had a right to refuse him. Just because she was his partner, that they lived together, didn't mean that she forfeited her right to say no to sex. Their quarrel had nothing to do with that. He had wanted to celebrate by making love; she had not – end of argument.

Catherine pulled the duvet over her, drew her knees up, her mind a maze of emotions, veering first one way then the other. Her body felt bruised, raw from the satisfaction it had given. What a fool she had been to allow herself to be drawn into his game. He had deceived her; he had tricked her into playing that to mitigate his sexual assault. She castigated herself, regretted her gullibility. But she had fallen for it. That hurt. But he had known that she would fall for it. He had used her. And that hurt more.

Now she lay in the bed and listened to him shower, heard the splashing of water in the cubical, imagined him soaping his body, his tanned skin shiny, the water running in rivulets down his limbs, the flexing muscles as he washed. Her thoughts turned then to earlier events, how he had tried to convince her of his good intentions, his exasperation – and then later how he had very nearly become weepy. Of a sudden, even though she had been used, her temperament exploited, she nevertheless now experienced a need to make up, a feeling that she should make the peace between them. She accepted that she might have overreacted after the party, rejected his explanation out of hand, without proper consideration. Everybody said she was stubborn, refused to listen. There was some truth in that. Maybe… maybe, she thought, when he came back to bed, they could talk, discuss their differences… and later make love properly, like lovers, without playing games. Yes, they could. She would try to–

But then, instantly overriding her thoughts, emanating from the bathroom, came a low mournful sound: 'Ahhhh…' She listened intently as the cry continued, as it went on and on, seemingly without end. He could almost have been crying out in extremis, crying out as some terrible calamity overhauled him. But she knew better: she knew what he had done.

Determined to blot out the cry that still reverberated in her mind, Catherine held her hands to her ears, clamped them there. Even in her imagination, she did not want to hear his pleasure, his release, his ecstasy – an ecstasy that should have been hers, too. Then she felt the duvet being drawn aside. She half-opened her eyes, to see him getting back into bed. She had been right: he had finished himself – he was sexually replete. And then his cry echoed again in her mind, a clarification of what she had just heard. Annaaaa… Anna. He had been thinking of her; he had imagined her body as he did it. Anna.

Catherine's soft breathing, interrupted by an occasional restless sigh, told Alexander that her sleep might not be entirely peaceful. He stared up into the mirror, focused his gaze on the tousled head, now turned away from him, and let out a sigh of his own. God, but her obstinacy had frustrated him tonight. All that discussion, the toing and froing, the telling points he had made, and then her refusal to accept the obvious. Surely she realised he had meant well, that he had only wanted to please her. It was as if she had deliberately misunderstood everything he had said – or had ignored it. Stubborn to the final whistle, that was Kate.

He glanced at her, as something like a sob escaped her lips. Perhaps he had been too demanding, playing a game like that, imposing himself on her. He supposed that it was a selfish thing to do. But she had played along with it. He may have issued the challenge but she had said that she would not enjoy it and that was tantamount to taking him on, which, in turn, had triggered his competitive instinct, had incited good-natured rivalry, who would enjoy the other first. The game was probably inappropriate for her mood though. It might have been better to have played something less domineering, less aggressive. But it was no worse than many of the games they played, the majority of which Kate had invented. He loved her imagination, her inventive flair. Anyhow, she'd enjoyed it – finally. Sure, she had tried to hide it under that deadpan expression of hers, that inscrutable look that she used to such good effect in business dealings. That must have taken a considerable effort. But old Alex had known: those giveaway signs that no woman could hide. Yes, she had enjoyed it – a lot. Holy smoke, her palpitations had all but brought him off too, had almost ended the game in a dead heat.

She had lost though, and he knew there would be repercussions. Catherine was not a good loser. He would pay for his pleasure in some way. It occurred to him then, belatedly, that he should have let her win. If he had done that, they'd be at it again now. He would have been up for it, she would have seen to that. Kate would have raised his game, re-peppered him. He wondered what she might have chosen. Something she knew he particularly liked. *Tawny Owl...* Maybe... No, *Puppy Dog*. Magnanimous in her victory, she would have allowed him his favourite. Alex closed his eyes, imagined… He saw her on all fours, her rump raised in that puppy-dog posture that she was so good at, puppy-dog eyes looking over her shoulder, appealing for her master's approbation, maybe even a puppy-dog whine… Alex all but choked on the imagined scenario. Oh, why hadn't he had the sense to lose? 'Alex, you imbecile,' he blurted out.

But of course it might not have been puppy-dog night tonight. She might have gone for something else, something entirely different… an imperial role… Maybe she would have been Catherine the Great and he the Russian serf, subservient, kneeling at her feet, kissing her toes, then moving higher, Kate calling the shots, issuing the orders. He glanced at the door to the ensuite, tested his semi-flaccid state. Whatever it'd been, it would have been infinitely better than this. He flopped back onto his pillow, repeated his self-rebuke.

Alex decided that he might as well go to sleep – he was pooped, all that booze – try again in the morning. He reckoned she would have calmed down by then. He switched off his bedside lamp, turned onto his back, closed his eyes, shuffled himself comfortable, and relaxed… But almost immediately, unable to gloss over his stupidity, he turned the light on again. He glanced at the head on the pillow next to his, let his glance linger. You had to make allowances with Catherine, be patient. She was, mathematically speaking, a genius: statistics, accounts, balance sheets – you name it. And boy what a memory for numbers – a bit like the character in the film *Rain Man* – she could recall six-digit telephone numbers by the hundreds. Formulae too: her party piece was to recite the figure for Pi to over one hundred decimal places. The average was three. Brilliant! But with people, it was a different story. No under-the-surface understanding. What most people knew instinctively, she had to work out… and then she usually got it wrong – like tonight.

He observed her recumbent form, stroked her plump little arm affectionately. He had thought he'd been doing right in making their promotions a surprise, assumed it would add to her delight. He'd taken it for granted that she would be thrilled by the news, overjoyed, and that a night of passionate lovemaking would follow. He had certainly misjudged that one.

The trouble was he'd been so bloody horny. He had watched her all evening, the sway of her hips, the jiggle of her ass as she'd gone about the apartment – and without doubt, one hundred per cent certain, she had the sexiest, lustiest ass of any woman on the planet, an ass to die for. He had visited quite a few internet sites that specialised in booty, but none of them had anything to match Kate. He reached across the bed and, holding his breath, carefully pulled back the duvet. Even in sleep, lying on her side, her buns were big and rounded, plump hemispheres of creamy heaven. Careful of not waking her, he poked a finger into her soft flesh, sighing inwardly as he watched it disappear to the knuckle.

Encouraged by her lack of reaction, he placed a finger on her tail bone, held it there, his mind suspended in awe. If only old Leonardo had painted an arse like that instead of wasting his time on the Mona Lisa… a highlight here, a shadow there, pick out the curves… maybe a crimson handprint on the right cheek… Falling too far into his reverie for his own good, he moved his finger down into her botty cleavage… only to snatch it back in response to a reflexive quiver.

Alex lay back on his pillow, stared up into the mirror. That there was more to her arse than its size or shape, or even motion, he was well aware. Ratio, proportion, those things were important too. They were the things that made it all work, brought it all together. A big arse with a thick midriff was no good. But look at her waist: tiny – twenty-three inches. He knew. He had measured it enough times. And her hips, he had measured there too, a bit lower down to include her bum – thirty-eight. Ratio... Ray-she-oh! Sighing, he replaced the duvet over her shoulders. God, but he loved her though.

He loved her sincerity, her intelligence, her liberalness; he loved her whole wonderful personality – apart from her stubbornness. Although, to be fair, that had often served her well, particularly in professional situations, like that time she'd defeated him – and others – over the inner-city construction project. They had wanted to go with the corporate option, a plush office suite, but she had taken the affordable housing route. And she'd been right: it was needed, and the site was perfect for it, had all the amenities, the infrastructure, to hand. He'd seen that later, as had the other managers. She had saved the Company from criticism, had averted backlash over that one. In the face of so much opposition, it would have been easy for her to have crumbled, given in, but she had stuck to her guns and in the end she'd been proven right. Correction: he loved her stubbornness. It was part of her makeup. She wouldn't be *his* Kate without it.

Alex pulled back the duvet again, feasted his eyes. He was still feeling randy, still up for it. That session in the bathroom was just a tide-me-over. It was no way like making love. He ran a gingerly hand over the exaggerated parabola of his partner's hip, down her outer thigh... and thought about bringing it round and up on to her sex. If he rolled her over, gently, on to her back, carefully parted her legs, not too much... started to... But she was bound to wake up.

He had done that once, early in their relationship. No particular reason. Well, he had seen a video on the internet. Of course, he had taken it easy, minimal foreplay, entered her slowly, little by little, supported his weight, then leisurely strokes, not too fast, not too deep, hoping that by the time she came to she would be sexually aroused, too far gone to complain – like in the video. But she had woken up early all the same. Alex shivered. He would never forget what followed. Befuddled from sleep, she had stared up at him, questioning eyes – for ages, it seemed. It was as if she were trying to make sense of where she was, what was happening to her. Then her expression had changed. He had never seen that look on her face before – a forlorn look, as if something she believed real had just been taken from her. Then, as wakefulness had come further to her, she had started to cry – real tears. It had taken him ages to placate her. Later, she told him that she'd been having a dream. Alex thought that his lovemaking might have caused it, had got her subconscious engaged on a love theme, triggered a sexual fantasy. External stimuli could do that, could have that effect on sleepers, on people asleep, apparently. Then maybe she'd awakened, before her time, thwarted – hence her disappointment.

Once more Alex shivered. No way was he going to try that again. Anyhow, on top of what he'd already done, she would probably cut off his balls. Swallowing dryly at the uncalled-for thought, he replaced the duvet over Catherine's shoulder. He could wait until the morning – get up early, clean the flat, bring her breakfast in bed… lunch too, if she was up for it.

Alex stretched his legs out straight, slid a hand under the duvet. Bloody Anna, letting on like that, she'd ruined his night. He bet if Brenda Willis had been the one to let the

38

secret out, then everything would have been all right. Kate would have been okay with that – and all would be fine in their world. And Catherine actually worried that he would sleep with Anna. God, was her self-esteem really that low? Compared to Kate, she was a nonentity, intellectually challenged. And she had no figure. Okay, her tits were passable but she had no arse. Certainly she was pretty… in a magazine model way, but she had no personality. And look at her this evening, on those high heels, wiggling around as if she had ants in her pants. But she had nothing to wiggle. She had the backside of a man – and Alexander King was not gay. Certainly he was not. He liked women… women with big arses.

Unable to prevent himself, he pulled back the duvet yet again, cast a lingering gaze over Catherine's body. Women like that. She was a Botticelli masterpiece; a work of art – evolution's safeguard for the survival of the race. And her skin, like silky velvet, flawless, Ferrari smooth. He leaned over Catherine's torso, for she was turned away from him. And look at those tits, ballooned by the squash of the mattress, perfect for a tit roll – he could vouch for it. Holy cow he was hard again. Maybe, if he was ever so careful… took his time… gently does it… No, he was too young to be gelded.

Alex hopped out of bed and scampered across the carpet to the ensuite.

Chapter 3

Catherine pushed herself upright, swung her legs over the side of the bed. Her mind was made up – she had a plan. She intended to show him that she was not a sexual commodity, merchandise to be used whenever the mood came upon him. When he woke up, he was in for a surprise.

She glanced over her shoulder at the recumbent Alex, sleeping like a baby, his sleep untroubled. Dreaming of Anna, she expected. He was lying on his side, with his left leg forward of the other. She saw that his penis lay along the thigh – flaccid. No, he wasn't dreaming of Anna. Given that he was circumcised it would be easy to carry out. If she held the glans firmly in her left hand, stretched him a little, for tautened skin would sever easier, and then drew a knife in a firm cutting stroke, it should be decapitated in one go, in one slice. A carving knife would do the business, sharp, with a nice long blade. Catherine thought that any prolonged hacking or sawing would be inefficient, and cause him a lot of pain. She did not wish for that. But if performed correctly, it would be no different to a surgical removal – as in the nineteenth century, before the discovery of anaesthesia.

There was a report of a woman in America who did it. Apparently, her husband came home drunk and raped her, and so she lopped off the head. There were obvious similarities here. And, like the American woman, who was cleared of blame on the grounds of temporary insanity, she guessed that she too would be acquitted along similar lines. Catherine pictured the judge, the bewigged upholder of justice, then heard his verdict: 'The defendant acted under great duress, while the balance of her mind was temporarily disturbed. Case dismissed.'

She fetched a carving knife from the kitchen, tested its edge with her thumb – almost cut herself doing so. This would do it, she was sure, quick and clean – one stroke. Taking Alex in her left hand, she pulled him tight, perpendicular. Once cut, she imagined that the remaining segment would spring back, recoil like snapped elastic. She held the knife in her right hand, selected her spot... And at that moment it moved, a little pulse, immediately followed by another, then another. And at the same time, Alex gave out a somnambulant sigh, an exhalation of unmistakeable pleasure. Catherine released him and placed the knife on the bedside table. Men! That part of them never slept.

Would it be better, she asked herself, if she were to cut off the balls? For with just the head missing, the erectile faculties would still be intact, some pleasure could still be had. If, on the other hand, she castrated him, there would be no more hard-ons. He would have his dick... but be for ever flaccid. How frustrating would that be for him? He could conjure up his vision of Anna – but nothing would happen. She pictured him in action, rubbing frantically, impelling his lazy lob, perspiration flying from his brow as he tried in vain to work himself into a lather. It was certainly an idea to warm to.

But of course with no testicles he would probably have no sexual desire at all. Anna could walk naked into his office, parade her slim figure in front of him, and he would turn an indifferent eye, have no interest in the proceedings. For him it would be as if an androgynous manikin were strutting its stuff. Catherine thought for a moment. Perhaps she should cut off just one ball.

Whichever piece of him she decided on, if indeed she did decide, there would be some pain involved – that was unavoidable. She knew the body went into shock at such events, which had an anesthetising effect. She was also aware that down there was filled with nerve endings, so there was bound to be some degree of discomfort. But once endorphins started to circulate, he should be all right.

Pain or no pain, Alex would be leaping about, shouting, cursing, searching desperately for his severed balls… or penis. That would be best, she thought, his dick, for it was more symbolic… and also gave her a better chance of avoiding punishment. Castration would infer that some thought had gone into the process, while beheading would suggest spontaneity, as if her emotion had got the better of her and, unthinking, she had looped it off. Yes, she concluded, it should be the penis. Despite her drastic contemplation, Catherine all but smiled as she imagined the look on his face, panicked concentration as he hunted for it, sheets being ripped from the bed, shaken, every crease, every fold examined. She saw him on his hands and knees, scampering round the room, like a dog, sniffing out his missing dick – for it was his whole world, his *raison d'être*.

She would need to be quick though: hold it and cut immediately, otherwise it would start to erect, as it had just now, which would mean more bleeding, blood gushing out all over the place. And with nothing to fill, it would go on doing so – unless shock caused a lowering of the blood pressure… which was likely. But, she decided, speed would be essential, all the same.

Catherine picked up the knife, reached for his penis... then withdrew her hand again. Even with reduced blood flow, and no matter how swiftly she acted, it was bound to be messy – blood over the sheets, over the carpet... all over her. Too much thinking was making Catherine squeamish. She glanced at her hand, opened the palm, saw it gory, rivulets of blood staining the creases. And then, as if in a nightmare, she saw something else there, squirming snakelike, alive... a blood-stained roll of excised human tissue, an autopsy specimen – Alex's dick. She tried but failed to suppress a spontaneous shudder. No, she decided, she could not do it. She would stick to her original plan.

She replaced the duvet over the sleeping Alex, then walked through to the living room, cast an appraising eye around the area. Not too bad, she decided – mostly glasses, paper tableware, napkins... and birthday wrap. And thank goodness nobody smoked any longer. It wouldn't take her long to sort out. Then she would do the washing up, tidy the kitchen.

At the window, she drew a curtain aside, and peered down at the silent mews, four storeys below. The flat was set in a Georgian terrace. Originally gentlemen's town houses, it had been converted in the 1960s, then updated thirty years later. It was right in the heart of Chelsea, just off the King's Road, with views south towards the river. You could see the pretty Albert Bridge. 'A sought-after penthouse suite,' the estate agent had informed them; 'bound to increase in price; an absolute solid investment.' And he had been right, for in the three years since their purchase, and despite the depressed economic conditions in the country, its value had risen by fifteen per cent. Of course, with their financial knowledge, they had known the agent was not exaggerating. But even with their good salaries and bonuses, they wouldn't have been able to afford it had not Alex's parents stumped up a hefty sum to aid the purchase – and still the mortgage was frightening.

A couple came into view, walking along the mews, hand in hand, taking an occasional hug. They looked "together". Catherine glanced at the carriage clock on the mantel. It showed two-thirty. She guessed they were going home from a late-night party. Perhaps they would make love later – lovers making love, caring, sharing, unlike the sort of love she'd had imposed on her. The couple disappeared from view, and the street was empty again. It just went to show, she thought, you could never truly know another person's mind, never really understand what made someone tick, under particular circumstances.

She recalled his taunting: *Look in the mirror. How is the magic lantern show? Show me the courage of your conviction.* How ridiculous – farcical. And his facial expression, ruthless, tyrannical, a modern-day Heathcliff, that had been a pathetic piece of theatre – and his concluding spiteful lunge... unpleasant... unusually vindictive. And then, to cap it all, going into the bathroom and masturbating like that – calling for Anna. That had been deliberate. He had done that as a provocation, and to belittle her. That was unworthy of him. It was the unholiest side of the entire episode, reciting that hussy's name. If he had not done that, she felt that she might have been able to forgive him.

But afterwards there was that moment when she'd thought he was ashamed of his behaviour, for she had heard him cry: 'Alex, you imbecile.' He had said it twice. Was that contrition? Had he been sorry for what he had done? Yet soon after that, he was prodding at her with his finger, like a

44

horse trader testing the resilience of an animal's flesh before buying. And he thought she had been asleep. Lucky for him he hadn't tried anything else – he would have woken up with his voice in a higher register if he had. He still might, if she changed her mind. But of course, he hadn't needed to try anything else, had he? He had satisfied himself in the ensuite, wanking, fantasising about Anna. Well, why fantasise when he could have the real thing? She wouldn't stand in his way.

Catherine turned angrily from the window, scooped several party remnants into her arms, started to carry them through to the kitchen. No, she thought, this wouldn't take her long to do. She paused, glanced round. Then she would go to bed – on the sofa. Alex would not come in to the living room tonight. He was only a light social drinker and the amount he had consumed would keep him comatose for a good while longer yet. She would get a few hours of uninterrupted sleep.

Alex yawned and stretched, gave himself a few moments to gather his wits. Bloody headache, felt like a jackhammer was at work behind his forehead. But it was a good party... until Catherine threw a wobbly. Damned Anna, he would give her a good dressing down Monday morning. Directing his thoughts to more pressing matters, he turned to Catherine, only to discover that she wasn't here. He glanced at the bedside clock: 8:15. Quarter past eight, Saturday morning. God, she hadn't got up early to do the housework, had she? He had more important things on his mind than that. And he had suggested they get the cleaner in.

Sighing in exasperation at his partner's early rising, he climbed out of bed, then glanced down at his own early rising. Holy smoke! He cranked his head towards the closed living-room door. 'Catherine, come back to bed. Leave the clearing up for later.' After a little while, receiving no reply, he put on his dressing gown and walked through to the living room.

Alex found the space immaculate. He glanced around. You could shoot an ideal-home commercial in here. Catherine had done the lot, the whole kit and caboodle. He became aware of a voice coming from the kitchen, singing. And now she was doing in there. She sounded happy, in an upbeat mood, last night's row forgotten – nice tune, too. In spite of his headache, Alex grinned. If he played his cards right, they would soon be back in bed for a morning of hot lovemaking. God, he could already feel her in his arms. At once chirpy, he winked at his tented bathrobe, then started towards the kitchen door.

The kitchen was at the front of the apartment, facing south, with good natural lighting – and good views. They could work in there and watch the river traffic. He was a better cook than Kate and did most of the cooking. Back in March they'd had friends round for the boat race. You couldn't see the rowing from here – that started at Putney – but they'd had lunch here, then down to the river to watch the race, and afterwards back here for drinks... and teased Kate, because Oxford had lost. You had to be careful though, you couldn't take it too far: her dislike of losing extended to her alma mater – sulking like a kid, when their friends had gone. He was a lucky guy. Alex thought of the morning ahead. Yes, he certainly was.

He pushed opened the door and stepped inside. 'Catherine, there's no need to do this now. Let's go back to bed, I'll cook breakfast later...' Then he realised that he was talking to himself.

Not a little stunned by the unforeseen circumstance, he gazed about him – like the living room, all was immaculate. Even the early-morning light, slanting in through the open window, could not pick out a speck of dust or a ghost of a stain on the granite worktops, the shiny appliances, the breakfast bar. From condiments in the rack, to saucepans on the shelf, to coffee mugs on the ledge, everything was set out in regimented alignment – the way Catherine liked it. She had cleaned in here as well. Alex went to the lonely popup television and switched off the device. If they called that singing, they had no taste in music.

In a moment he took two paracetamol tablets. Bloody long time since he'd had a morning-after headache like this one. Those should clear it up though. He dropped another tablet onto his tongue – better safe than suffer. And he would need a clear head later to plead his case, sweet-talk Kate… Mind you, it would be a mistake to be too indulgent. The quarrel wasn't his fault. He placed the tumbler on the draining board, then returned to the living room.

'Catherine.' He paused, waited for her reply. 'Kate, where are you?' He paused again, listening.

Receiving no answer, he walked round the apartment, stopping here and there to call her name. He found no trace of her. 'Catherine, are you hiding from me?' The flat wasn't huge but he walked round it again, just in case.

Alex returned to their bedroom, sat on the edge of the bed, thinking, bewildered. Kate wasn't here. She was not here – nowhere in the apartment. All at once his heart started beating faster and a sick feeling arose in his gut, for it occurred to him then that she might have left, that she might have walked out on him. But no that surely couldn't be; a simple misunderstanding; a silly squabble. She had gone out to get something, that was all. No worries. He relaxed. Then he saw the note on his bedside table. He had missed it earlier. He removed the knife that was holding it in place and started to read:

Alex, I've decided to take myself off for a break. I apologise for leaving without discussion, and I hope that you understand, but this morning I did not feel that I could cope with another row like last night's. I think it's better, if we spend some time apart before we discuss it. I need to be by myself for a while, to think and to sort things through.

I have some holiday owed me in lieu of those weekends that I put in on the Berryman account, and there is nothing in my in-tray that will suffer from my absence. In any case I have taken my laptop, and will keep up to speed on things. I know that I should have informed the Firm in advance but, anyhow, no doubt they will attribute my sudden holiday to female capriciousness. Perhaps you will square it with them for me.

I will be in touch as soon as I feel able.
Catherine.

Alex noted the absence of an endearment. But that was typical Kate. When she was upset, even the smallest thing mattered. There were no concessions, no in-betweens. He picked up the knife, glanced at it. There was some meaning in that, albeit one that only Kate would know. She could have used almost anything to keep the note in place, but she chose a knife. He took it to the kitchen and placed it in the cutlery drawer, then returned to the bedroom.

He sat on the bed thinking, trying to assemble his jumbled thoughts. Nothing made sense to him, seemed real

– except his headache. He felt let down, treated unfairly. From his standpoint, not only had he done little wrong but he had also been denied a chance to explain, to argue his case. Alex decided that women were complicated, their motivations unfathomable – Catherine's especially so. He wondered then if she had written her message in here, when he was asleep, while he was lying naked in the bed. After further reflection, plus a meticulous examination inside his bathrobe, he went back to the kitchen and transferred the knife from the cutlery drawer to the washing-up bowl.

Back in the bedroom, Alex read the note again and, in spite of his changed mood, managed to summon up a smile at Catherine's overt jibe at the Firm's chauvinism. Reading between the lines, he didn't think the circumstances sounded too serious: she would be coming back. It wouldn't take her long to see that his birthday surprise had been well-intentioned. Yeah, he thought, but they'd had a serious quarrel, their first – and Kate was so sensitive. If she imagined herself ill done-by, she was quick to take umbrage. And she always overreacted.

He recalled a verbal assault on a colleague who had volunteered some advice on a presentation she was giving – semantics really, nothing attacking the gist of her argument. Under it, the poor sod had withered, had looked devastated, and hadn't uttered another word all meeting. Her research was sound and Richard's points were trivial, so there had been no need to go in so hard, so scathingly.

Weighing up his options, Alex fetched his mobile from the dressing table. If he spoke with her now, then perhaps he could sort things out. Or was it too soon? She was obviously upset about last night. It might be better to give her some time to herself, as she'd requested, before phoning, let her reflect on events, get everything into perspective. But on the other hand, by not acting, by letting things go on, the misunderstanding might fester, might become embittered. She might even think he didn't care that she'd left. Alex did not want that. Making a rapid decision, he rang Catherine's number. After a few seconds' delay, he heard her phone ringing, muffled by its position in the drawer of her bedside cabinet.

Suddenly angry, he cancelled the call. How bloody perverse, leaving her mobile behind so that he couldn't contact her. But perhaps she had just forgotten to take it with her? Catherine? Not a chance. She'd left it behind, deliberately. Anyway, he knew where she was. He put in a call to Brenda Willis.

'Hello.'

'Hi, Brenda, it's Alex. May I speak to Catherine, please?'

There was a pause, before he heard Brenda say: 'Isn't she with you?'

So that was their game – the old incommunicado trick. Alex was onto them in a flash. But they were friends… and he knew that Brenda was some kind of quasi-relative. It was obvious which side she would be on. He wondered then how much Catherine had told Brenda about last night… Well, there wasn't much to tell. He decided to play it cool. 'No, she went out just now and I assumed she was coming your way. Then something cropped up and I–'

'Is anything wrong, Alex?' Brenda's voice cut in.

'No, no,' he said quickly, anxious now – in case Catherine really wasn't there – not to alarm Brenda. 'It's nothing pressing, nothing that won't wait until she gets back.' Then, with an exaggerated compliment, he rang off.

Alex decided to check on what clothes – if any – she had

taken with her. That might indicate how long she intended to stay away.

Pursuing a resolute path round the apartment, he attempted a definitive list of missing items: probably a couple pairs of jeans, some skirts... Well, her red one with the squiggle design wasn't here. But it might be at the cleaners. What about T-shirts, he asked himself, tops, cardigans? A fawn one wasn't here... maybe. Alex nodded at a sudden triumph: her Barbour jacket was missing... and a pair of trainers... Ah, and it looked like a couple pairs of sandals had gone, too... possibly. Why did women need so many shoes? They had the same number of feet as men. Sighing, he gave up. When this was all over, he determined to take more interest in her clothes and not confine himself solely to how good she looked in them.

On a sudden whim, he thought that it would be interesting to find out if she had taken them with her. Knowing that might indicate something, might give him a clue about her long-term intentions. It probably would not though. Besides, it was really none of his business. He scowled. Wasn't it? And he knew where she kept the key, if she hadn't taken it with her, or hidden it before she left.

He skirted round the bed to Kate's bedside cabinet and opened a drawer. Yes, there it was, right at the back, nondescript as any key could be. The other drawer, the one the key opened, had to be kept locked, Catherine said, because she was afraid the cleaner might accidentally find them.

In a moment or two Alex pulled back the bottom drawer of the cabinet three or four inches, to expose a plain frontispiece. He slid that aside and there it was, another drawer, another lock. Feeling a little bit like a schoolboy about to put his hand into the sweetie jar, he unlocked the secret drawer and pulled it open.

He cast a critical eye over the collection, knew immediately which one was missing. To be honest, he had not expected any absentees. Her decision to leave must surely have been an impulsive one, spur-of-the-moment. There couldn't have been much time for planning, for deciding what to take with her – let alone one of these. But if one was to be taken, he knew which one it would be. Top of the range did not do it justice. It had all the usual features you would expect, plus a unique low-frequency sound-wave system. It was made by a specialist company in Germany... bespoke – *Vorsprung durch Technik.*

He would never forget the first time they had used it – during one of their games, a role-play that had almost ended in disaster. The scenario was that Catherine was a suspected foreign agent, while he was an MI5 operative. She had known ISIS sympathies, had travelled in Syria and Iraq, and her Twitter account showed her as being a left-wing activist – anti-establishment. He was the shadowy government figure, operating on the margins of the law, charged with extracting information from her... whichever way he could.

Obviously he wasn't going to use any rough stuff; that wasn't his style. He knew that some players did, in a certain kind of game. But Alex wasn't one of them: his approach was more subtle. He was aware that gameplay situations could escalate, could get out of hand. Once in character, a normal person could lose his sense of reality, could become fanatical in pursuit of his goals. It was surprisingly easy. He knew somebody who had broken his wife's arm in a simulated rape. Yeah, believe it or not, that was a popular scenario with gamers, even for a husband to become a voluntary cuckold, to play dumb while another man enjoyed his wife. But whatever your kick, the thing to remember was to play safe. Sure, you had to believe in the storyline, immerse yourself in the plot, suspend belief in the everyday, the here and now, just as you do when reading a novel. But you had to do so safely, have a pre-agreed safe word, a word that a participant could use if she felt threatened, or was in pain. Both he and Kate were good at it. And that was why they got so much pleasure from their role-play.

Anyhow, he had interrogated her and things were going fine – no confession. So he had stepped up the pressure, stripped her naked, introduced a psychological element – the bad policeman, nice policeman routine. Threating – a slap across the rump, the promise of a harder one to come. Cajoling – a kiss on the reddened arse, the gentle application of an emollient. But no way was Kate going to crack that easily. Her competitive nature would not allow it. But of course that was what he wanted, what the game demanded. Secret agent Cox was going to be fatigued into submission. And that's where the device came in.

Suitably exasperated by her intransigence, he had hogtied her, trussed her up like an oven-ready turkey, limbs drawn up and folded like drumsticks. Then he had given her another chance to confess, to divulge her information – planned acts of terrorism, info on her associates. And when she had refused him, changing his tactics, he had threatened her with untold Western decadence. She had reminded him of the *Kama Sutra*, told him she was an exponent of its teachings, inured to anything he might do. And so he had commenced to insert it… little by little… until it was all the way in. Nice. Then he had set it going, just a gentle purr to warm her up – to move the game forward. Yep, everything was cool. No problem.

Looked tremendous from where he was standing, like an excavation drill burrowing down between two sand dunes, and with all the controls at his fingertips.

'All right Mata Hari, if you won't come clean, let's try a different approach, shall we? Tell me your views on female circumcision.' *Genital mutilation, you mean.* 'Do you see it as being a cultural ritual, a religious obligation, or something else?' *I think that it was conceived by men as a means to stop women from being unfaithful.* 'How come?' *Take away the pleasure, remove the desire.* 'I see that you haven't had it performed on you?' *No.* 'But if you remain intransigent, I will have no choice other than to do just that.' *You had better get on with it, then.* 'I intend to… at some future point. But no need yet. For the present a taster will suffice. I've acquired some Botox, enough to ensure that you get no sexual enjoyment for the next six months… at least.' *Allah will be my incubus.* 'Even he can't raise the deadened. But don't worry: I'm going to allow you one final orgasm.' *That's awfully thoughtful of you.* 'Isn't it? But please remember that it will be your final climax for some time.' *You had better make it a good one, then.* 'Don't doubt it. And anytime you feel like talking, just go right ahead and spill the beans.' *I won't do that.* 'You'll spill all right. I guarantee it.' And that's when he had switched on the special feature.

Nothing much had happened at first – the gentle purr had increased to a hum, got a bit louder, risen an octave. Fine: that was the sort of thing he had expected. But then, after a short delay, the humming had cut out, to be replaced by an altogether different sound, resonant, tangible, almost physical in nature, something not unlike the flap, flap, flap of a helicopter's blades. Alex had suspected a malfunction. But no, it turned out that he hadn't spotted that it was set at the highest level, together with the simultaneous operation of all the other functions. He had meant to start low and work up. Anyway, he wasn't to know. The maker's claim was that it mimicked the biophysical properties of an orgasm. And it did... in spades. On full power, poor Kate's eyes, bulging like golf balls, had all but popped out of their sockets. She had gone orgasmic, instantly – hyper-orgasmic.

And her eyes weren't the only items to bulge. He'd seen stuff on the internet where women engorged bits of themselves using vacuum tubes. But with Kate it had occurred naturally. Her clitoris had come up like a miniature penis, a faithful replica – glans, shaft, the lot. He had never seen anything like it before. And it went on and on. Her toes curled up and she shook and trembled all over – like someone getting electric shock therapy. "*By the roots of her hair some god got hold of her.*" And all the time her clit, ticking like a metronome, stiffly turgid, waggling like the tip of a finger – a schoolmarm scolding him for his dreadful deed.

Alex paused to adjust himself, to get his mind in order.

But as if that wasn't bad enough, the spiral of ridges on the surface of the device seemed to be causing it to revolve. They were intended as additional pleasure-giving features – nothing wrong in that. But let loose on full power, and they were acting like a giant screw thread, burrowing the thing in deeper and deeper – too deep for safety, let alone comfort. It looked at one time as if even the rubber flange at the base was in danger of being sucked inside.

After a while of watching, it had started to scare him. Kate obviously wasn't going to come down from where she was at. Neither was she going to surrender, forfeit the game, even if she were able to, which, by this time he doubted. The effects just went on and on. If he hadn't realised his mistake, sussed that she was all but speechless, and turned it off pronto, she might well have suffered a coronary... or even the displacement of her internal organs. He shook a reminiscing head. There should have been a health warning on the thing – learning by experience was too dangerous.

But they had learned, eventually, after much patient practice... and judicious experimentation. They certainly had. But, yes, little wonder that she'd opted to take that one with her.

He flopped onto the bed, gazed round the room. His headache was taking a long time to go. It was making him irritable. And he felt dehydrated – obviously dried out from all that alcohol. He gazed at his mobile – his "useless" mobile. There wasn't much pleasure in being thwarted. He didn't like unresolved issues, particularly when he was impotent to settle them.

Then he recalled that Catherine had taken her laptop with her, so he could email her if he wanted to. He picked up his phone, thinking. After a little while he tossed it onto the bed. No, he decided, he wouldn't – not yet. Better to give her more time by herself... if that was what she wanted. Anyway, he knew why she'd gone. Yeah, he knew why. You couldn't pull the wool over Alexander King's eyes.

Chapter 4

Catherine edged her car through the Saturday morning traffic onto the Hammersmith flyover. The sun was behind her, the M4 motorway lay ahead. It was a good day for driving, for leaving the city behind – a perfect day for putting her troubles in the rear-view mirror.

She hadn't been down there for ages, ten years in fact. It was sort of taboo – at least, so it had become, in her mind. But of course it wasn't really like that – not any longer. She was over it. Even so, Catherine knew that there was bound to be some sadness involved in visiting, even after all this time. But she was prepared for that. She was ready to test the healing power of time. Many people regarded her as being emotionally tough, uncaring, indifferent to sentiment. What did they know? She was as sensitive as the next person – more so than most. Just for a second it occurred to her to go somewhere else, but just as quickly she rejected the idea. That would be childish, and she'd had enough of that sort of behaviour from Alex. Don't worry, she scolded, everything will be fine.

Following the assault, her initial idea had been to stay with Brenda, just for a day or two, until she had worked through her problem. But was that wise? she had asked herself. For when Alex found out where she was staying, he was certain to call, try to persuade her to go back with him. Catherine did not want that pressure, that further upset. And so she had reconsidered, decided on *there* instead. She was certain now that her choice of destination was the right one.

Catherine banged an impulsive fist on the horn as another motorist cut across in front of her, mouthed a swear word at the grinning reflection of the male driver in the other car. Why, she wondered, did they always think such behaviour clever? Just for a second, she thought of retaliation, of going after him, giving him a taste of his own medicine. Instead, regaining her purpose, she signalled left and took the slip road to the services, found a vacant spot and parked her car. Her journey had barely begun, but there was a matter to attend to before she went any farther.

Pulling her bag across the passenger seat, she took out a mobile phone – the one purchased earlier this morning. She smiled: new phone, new SIM – new Catherine. She was determined that her time away would be exclusively hers, unshared, except for one person. Then she keyed in Brenda's number.

'Hi Brenda, it's Catherine.'

'Oh, hello Catherine, didn't recognise the number–'

'No, it's a new one,' Catherine interrupted. She paused. 'I've something to–'

'Alex phoned.' Brenda broke back in. 'He… he appeared confused, he seemed to think you were with me. I told him you weren't, but I don't think he believed me… What's going on?'

'After the party we had a row,' Catherine began; 'things got pretty heated… and… and he became aggressive.' She gave her friend a condensed version of the past twelve hours leading up to her departure, occasionally pausing to listen to Brenda's disbelieving interjections – and her heartfelt promptings. Following a repeated one, she brought the mobile closer to her lips. 'No, I'm not going to the police,' she responded decisively. 'That's out of the question. I'm going away for a few days. I'll give you a ring once I'm settled into a hotel.'

The idea of reporting Alex to the police had never occurred to Catherine, neither during nor after the assault. It wasn't the kind of thing to do. She always administered her own affairs, found her own way through a problem. What was the point of putting oneself through a process of personal questioning, and a possible court appearance, when he would almost certainly get away with it? He was her partner: a domestic dispute had gotten out of hand – end of case. That was how the system worked.

'Look, Catherine,' Brenda was saying, 'I don't think… I really don't think it's wise you going off like this in your… in your present frame of mind. Why don't you come and stay with me and Joe for a few days? We've got the spare room, and we can talk, sort—'

'Thanks,' Catherine replied briskly. 'That's really thoughtful, and I appreciate the offer, but I don't want to be a nuisance.' Brenda started to protest, but Catherine went on: 'If I stayed with you, Alex would be sure to find out… And it wouldn't be long before he paid a visit.' She paused. 'I don't want to involve you, Brenda. It's better this way.'

'It's down to you,' Brenda replied. 'You know that. But the birthday-party surprise, your promotion, really was… well, just that, a surprise. Alex had kept the secret for days.' She paused, and Catherine heard her friend's sigh. 'When you asked me about it last night, I know I should have said something, especially as I realised you were on edge about Anna. But he had been like a kid at Christmas… and your question was so unexpected, and the announcement so near... and... Oh, I feel stupid–'

'Then you shouldn't,' Catherine cut in. It seemed to her that Brenda also thought the whole affair little more than a prank. Anxious to disguise any unintended irony, she said: 'That description better suits me.'

'She needs her backside tanned, causing trouble like that. You just wait till Monday. I'll put her right, that I will.'

'You will do nothing of the sort,' Catherine said resolutely, watching a passer-by drop a cigarette butt onto the bonnet of a nearby car. 'It will only make her think she has scored a victory.' The fag end glowed for a second or two, then went out in a curl of smoke. 'Brenda, say *nothing*.' Anna had outwitted them all, Catherine decided, but she must not be given the opportunity to gloat on it.

'All right, dear, it's your decision. But I think–'

'Brenda, leave her alone.'

Brenda let out a grumpy huff. Then: 'He thought you would be delighted, that you would be over the moon.'

'And I was... to a point. But that's not why I'm leaving, is it?'

'No, of course it isn't. I realise that. But I just wanted to add that making the announcement at your party was my idea.'

'And it was a good one.' Catherine paused. 'But after what he did, I just have to get away, be by myself for a while.'

There was a short silence before she heard her friend say: 'You haven't said where you're going, Kate.'

Catherine was ready for the question. 'I would be more than happy for you to know,' she said. 'But sooner or later Alex will ask you where I am – he has already assumed that I was with you – and, for the time being, I would rather that he knew nothing.'

'I wouldn't tell him… I would not.'

'I know that, Brenda. But I would prefer that you could answer his question truthfully.'

'To be honest, after his behaviour towards you, I would be quite prepared to lie through my teeth.'

'I would rather that you didn't have to.'

'Okay, dear. If that's what you want.'

'Thanks, Brenda.'

After she had rung off, Catherine pulled down the sun visor, flipped the cover up from the vanity mirror. She twiddled with her fringe… contemplating. She'd often thought of going blonde. Mousy was a bit… well, mousy. It was all to do with image. In the business world that she inhabited, blondes were usually considered intellectually lightweight – not taken seriously. Even in today's supposedly more enlightened times, she knew that to be true. But of course, she reflected, there were precedents, patterns that upheld the prejudice. Undeterred, Catherine pulled a face at her reflection, allowed her mind's eye to drift.

In a little while she started the car, drove down the slip road and accelerated on to the motorway. It would take her most of the day to reach her destination – a stop for lunch around midday, something late afternoon, and she would be there by early evening. Catherine snuggled her frame into the seat and drove with the flow.

Following an hour of composing, editing, restructuring, correcting, checking, plus a modicum of fine tuning, Alex appraised the final version of the email:

Catherine, your refusal to communicate is silly. How can we resolve anything like this? I admit I acted impulsively.

I'm not denying that. But you are not entirely blameless yourself. For surely it was obvious that my news was intended as an innocent surprise, nothing more. (All the later unpleasantness originated from that misunderstanding.) It was obvious to everyone else, Brenda included. In fact, it was her idea. Of course, in view of your running off, and with the benefit of hindsight regarding Anna, I wish that I'd told you earlier.

With regard to the fact that the Firm did not consult you personally about our promotions, well we have already discussed that, and I think we agreed on why it happened that way.

I understand if you feel aggrieved, even hard done by, but you have made your point, and I ask now that you come home. Or, if you prefer, why not phone me so that we can discuss this matter like grownups?

With love,

Alex

Yes, he thought, that should do the trick, make her think, stop her feeling sorry for herself. And it was succinct, to the point. He particularly liked his reference to Brenda's involvement. That would count in his favour. He wasn't good at this sort of thing – apologising, but his plea was reasoned, honest... balanced. He had pointed out that she had to shoulder some of the blame, and he had shown regret for the part he had played. And he had included an endearment. There was no tit for tat with Alexander King. He was not petty.

Alex moved the cursor over the send button, hovered... Perhaps there was scope for further conciliation, a bit more contrition... And at that moment the door to his office opened and someone entered the room. He didn't look up from his computer. He had a meeting scheduled later with Daniel Samuels from Accounts and assumed the accountant had called in early to discuss the agenda. 'Hello, Dan. Grab a seat. I'll be with you in a jiffy. Just gotta–' Then the overpowering aroma reached his nostrils. Chanel No. 5, he guessed. It was Catherine's favourite. But she never used it to excess, unlike his visitor, who must have tipped it on as if trying to disguise a bad smell. He hit the send button, checked the email had left, then looked up from the computer screen. 'What can I do for you, Anna?'

He had intended to bawl her out for opening her big mouth at the party. But what would that achieve? Nothing other than reveal his annoyance, give her the impression that she was important, that she had outwitted Kate. And so he had changed his mind. In any case, snide behaviour was best ignored.

'I was just passing and thought that I'd call in and say hello.' She shifted her weight from one foot to the other. It was such an aggrandising movement that it took her bust, held like a powder keg by the silken material of her blouse, several moments to settle down.

By and by Alex came back to himself, raised impatient eyes. 'I'm expecting a colleague, Anna, so I'm afraid–'

'Oh, I realise you must be busy, Alex, your new appointment to organise, tying up accounts here, but I... Well, that's it... Being so busy, I thought that I'd see if there was anything I can do to help.'

'The move's not for another six months. And, besides, Catherine will do most of the organising. She's great at that.' He stifled a grin at the effect his words had had on her hitherto buoyant expression. The poor girl looked nonplussed. It was almost as if somebody had crept up behind her and attached invisible weights to the corners of her mouth – happy clown, sad clown.

Anna plumped herself down on the chair opposite his, then manoeuvred it back from his desk, affording him an unimpeded view of her lower limbs. He watched as she made a show of tugging fruitlessly at the hem of her miniskirt. That the move was designed to draw his gaze to her thighs was obvious. Her legs were touchingly ajar and he reckoned that the merest wriggle would raise her skirt enough to show him her panties, if she was wearing any. Rumour had it that she… Don't go there, Alex, he told himself; don't be drawn into the trap.

Her stare roamed the office. 'I hope you don't mind me asking, Alex,' she began, bringing her gaze to bear on his, 'but is Catherine all right? She's not in today and… and, I mean, there are a lot of summer colds going around at the moment.' She paused to rearrange conspicuous legs. Alex saw that the rumour was incorrect – at least for today – and that her knickers were white… Then he noticed the loop. For a moment he thought it was something else and started to look away. But then he realised what he was looking at: the withdrawal cord of a… She was wearing a vibrating egg. He wasn't wrong. He knew. He had got one for Kate. They were worn inside the pussy and operated by a remote control device. Great for the bedroom. But at work… The horny bitch. He suppressed a smile. They were also fun for a tease on a night out, particularly when somebody else had the remote control. He remembered one time whetting Kate's appetite at Shark's.

Once more Alex saw Catherine's questioning eyes across the table. She was sitting next to his friend Greg and clearly afraid that he would hear the thing going. But they were actually pretty silent, especially when in situ, or you kept the setting low, which he had done – no worries. Even so, Kate hadn't looked best pleased: out with friends, in public, embarrassed in case she... Nevertheless, she had taken him on: through starters... the main course... pudding... Kate could concentrate, block things out. And you wouldn't have noticed, even when, over coffee, he had upped the ante, had turned up the vibes, talking as if nothing was going on. You would never have guessed what she was incubating.

He raised his gaze from Anna's crotch. 'I thought at the party,' she was saying, 'that she seemed under the weather, you know, a bit moody, as if she were going down with something. And I wondered if she's okay.'

'Absolutely tiptop,' he replied jauntily, playing on her false concern. He watched as she tried unsuccessfully to hide her disappointment. 'Tiptop,' he reiterated even more jauntily. 'Why, she's so far ahead of the game that she's taking a few days off before starting on structuring the setup out there. We'll need some local talent, people with connections. She's putting out a few feelers, looking for the right guys.' He grinned at her. 'The Americans won't know what's hit them.'

Anna got up off the chair. 'All's hunky-dory then.' She turned on a high heel and started for the door.

He watched the galloping gait – in no way constrained by the gossamer material of the mini – and the prancing buttocks, as lean as those of a male athlete... and just as muscular. He flinched. No way Jose, not if his life depended on it. You could crack walnuts between– Alex's train of thought promptly derailed as Anna suddenly swung round to face him.

Shit! He bet she thought he'd been ogling her ass. Well he had been looking, but not in that way. He now registered the little smirk of satisfaction that had spread across her face. Yeah, that's what she thought. Conceited bitch.

She showed him a seductive smile. 'If you don't mind, Alex, I might call on Catherine sometime in the week.'

'Fine,' he said, absently reaching for a folder. 'But you had better phone first. Kate mentioned that she might visit a client up in… up in Manchester, and she will probably have to stay over.' The last thing he wanted was Anna calling on him unannounced.

'Oh, I will. And don't forget, if there's anything I can help you with, anything at all… especially if Catherine's going to be away overnight.' She opened the door. 'You know where I hang out.'

Alex knew where she hung out all right: in the office next to her grandfather. That was one of the problems of course: even though business was old Jack's chief focus, you still couldn't afford to belittle his granddaughter. He loved her like a Catholic loved a virgin. Nevertheless, despite her grand connections, she was only an office junior, and likely to stay one if merit meant anything. She was often called on when someone needed a bit of typing done, or shorthand. She was reputedly pretty good at that – longhand too, when required. At least Mike Popham in Human Resources had ranked her right up there with the best. Maintaining a straight face, he said: 'You'll be top of my list, Anna.'

'You're always top of mine, Alex,' she replied, winking. 'The other investment managers are okay to work for but I prefer someone whose requirements are more demanding. I like…' She pouted her lips provocatively. 'I like to have my potential stretched.'

He wondered if potential was the right word – not if

she'd meant it the way he thought she had. Her sexual potential had long since expired. He pretended to appear thoughtful. 'If you're looking to progress your career,' he said, 'Catherine has a number of clients whose accounts are especially complex.' He nodded encouragingly. 'I'll tell you what, when I get home tonight, I'll ask her if she wants any help. How's that?'

Anna slid round the door. 'See ya, Alex,' she said, dragging her leg suggestively against the woodwork.

Alex returned his attention to his computer screen, removed his thoughts from occupational hazards. He had better get a move on, otherwise Daniel Samuels would be here before he was ready. He clicked on a file... and just then an alert arrived from the computer server. Catherine had just blocked all emails sent from his account. Shit! Well, at least she had read his message. So she knew that he was concerned enough to contact her – of course she did. She also knew that he cared and, furthermore, that he was sorry for his part in the misunderstanding.

Chapter 5

Catherine strolled along the quayside in the afternoon sunshine. Colourfully clad holidaymakers wandered here and there – different but the same. She saw that crates of fish were being unloaded from a trawler, cod, whiting, pollack, conger eel; they were all here, just like before. Even though she hadn't been down here since, it was still familiar – almost as if she had never been away. She paused to watch another fishing boat come into the harbour. A fisherman was standing in the prow shouting orders to a man on the waterfront. The man recovered the end of a hawser that had been thrown ashore, carried it to a mooring bollard, then started to secure the vessel. A derrick on the boat was being readied; the assembled crew were preparing to unload the catch. The scene was workmanlike. Her eyes returned to the fisherman… lingered. Everything was as she had left it.

Moving on down the quay, she shrugged off her cardigan, folded it into her bag. The town had other ties for her too. When she was a child, family holidays had always been spent here – same town, same guest house, same weeks of each summer, final one of July, first one of August. Her father had been a man of routines and her mother had always gone along with him, never complaining. Catherine had grown up like that, wishing her mother would venture an opinion of her own. 'Maybe we should try somewhere different this year, John. France would be a nice change… or Italy.' Unthinkable.

Perhaps, she mused, that was why she herself put so much store in having her own freedom, in being her own woman – an unconscious rebuff of her mother's subservience. It was likely. Such a trait could be "inherited" that way – it was certainly not in her genes.

Some girl friends of hers saw living with someone as tantamount to losing one's independence, which had been her concern too when moving in with Alex. But it hadn't worked out that way. Sharing, doing things together, had been integral to their relationship – so too had been individual freedom. It was a question of balance, and they had got it just right. Goodness! Catherine gasped as she witnessed a cat scamper across the wharf and grab a mackerel from a crate that had been left unattended on the quayside. What a cheek. Smiling, she watched it turn and make off back across the wharf, its ill-gotten gains held firmly in its jaws. But yes, theirs had been a genuine symbiotic relationship, two people sharing for the benefit of both. Trust was of course also important – and they had had that. She had trusted him, until last week, until his assault.

'He's famous for it.'

Catherine surfaced form her reverie, glanced briefly towards the voice, saw a man in nautical gear observing her from a nearby skiff. Surely he hadn't read her thoughts. Then she realised her gaze had been directed at the cat, which was now tucking into its meal beside a stack of oil drums.

'Does it most days,' the man went on. 'All the fishermen know him. Some feed him scraps. But for them who don't…' He glanced at the cat. 'He doesn't take that much.'

She followed his gaze. 'What's his name?' she asked.

The man grinned. 'Conger.' He paused as he hopped from the dinghy on to a flight of stone steps. Then, noting her quizzical expression, he added: 'Because he'll eat anything they leave out, even tasteless old eels.'

'He was lucky today,' she observed.

'He was. Them's his favourite.'

In a moment, Catherine bid the man good day and resumed her walk along the quayside, returned to her deliberations.

She acknowledged that her trust had taken a knock, that was undeniable – a veritable brickbat. Even so, on waking this morning alone in her hotel room, her first thought had been: It wasn't all Alex's fault. She accepted that some responsibility for his actions rested with her. Perhaps she had misjudged the tension between them? When the argument began to escalate, maybe she should have been more placatory, less argumentative. He had made some points. Then later, when he started to lose control of himself, she had simply acquiesced, had let him do it. Even her protest had been half-hearted, restrained – mentally distanced. She realised now that that had been a mistake – being demonstrative might have brought him to his senses. This morning Catherine had begun to question the role she had played. Earlier today, she had even thought of going home. Then that email had arrived – arrogant concoction of rubbish that it was, an insult to her intelligence. That had put her firmly back on the offensive. *I acted impulsively...* Some euphemism! *All the later unpleasantness originated from that misunderstanding...* putting the blame on her. He hadn't mentioned the real reason for why she had left him – and he surely must know it. There was no explanation, not a genuine word of apology for what he had done. And then to finish with that phrase about *discussing the misunderstanding like grownups...* implying that her leaving him was childish. He may not be entirely to blame

70

but, despite what he might think, he was not wholly blameless either.

At the extremity of the quay, she took the path to the west cliff. She knew there were better views to be had on the eastern side of the town, where the headland jutted out into the channel, where the comings and goings of the harbour could be observed. But she wouldn't go there. The thought came to Catherine then that perhaps she really shouldn't have come here. She had questioned her choice before. Her gaze wandered wilfully across the harbour to the east cliff. One option would be to move farther down the coast: Mousehole was nice. Or she could go over to Newquay, watch the Atlantic waves. Maybe she would meet a hunky surfer.

One time, a year or two after Christopher, she had holidayed there. She hadn't felt able to come here: Newquay was the nearest she was able to manage. Catherine smiled, recalling how she had been pursued by a bespectacled American, 'searching for the perfect wave'. Sun-bleached hair, muscular and tanned, he was, apart from the glasses, the quintessential surfer. Though, like all men, he was seeking more than the perfect wave.

He was an interesting guy, all the same, at least in the sense of their shared interest: mathematics. He had studied at the Massachusetts Institute of Technology, and had made a lot of cash, he said, out in Las Vegas counting the cards at blackjack, before being rumbled and asked to leave. He had told her how the gambling scheme worked. What you had to do was remember the sequence of high- and low-scoring playing cards dealt – which was a difficult thing to do as five packs of cards were used in the game. But as the object was to score twenty-one points or lower, being able to do this obviously gave you an advantage over the dealer. Then he had tested her numerical memory, dealing from successive packs of cards and asking her to memorise the runs. Clearly his intention had been to demonstrate his ability, to show her how much better than the average he was – a bit of showing off. Catherine smiled again as his later words returned to her. 'Bloody Hell, gal, we gotta go into this together. We'll take every gambling joint in the States. And your English accent will bring us credibility, make us seem legit.' Yes, he was really in to it. She wondered where he was now.

Near the top of the cliff, she stepped off the path to allow a family to pass by. They were heading back towards the town. The children, a boy and a girl of about nine and… Catherine thought they might be twins, were waving colourful plastic windmills, trying to make the vanes spin in the still air. The parents were holding hands on the narrow track, the husband leading the way, turning occasionally to smile at his wife.

Catherine watched them disappear round a twist in the descending path. She had never had any maternal yearnings. She had been too young with Christopher; and with Alex it was all about their careers, about making money – and hedonism. They had a good lifestyle, everything they wanted. Perhaps one day though, when she was older, as long as it could be fitted in with her career. A boy first… Alexander II, following the popular American practice of naming the first son after its father… if they did go over there, which seemed unlikely now. Then a girl… Catherine caught herself: she had no desire to become a mother – ever.

Just then her mobile started to ring. Catherine came out of her musing, fished the instrument from her bag.

'Hi, Brenda.'

'Hello, Catherine. How are you – when are you coming home?'

Catherine smiled at the promptness of her friend's second question. 'I don't know yet. The weather's gorgeous and I'm thinking of staying a bit longer than I initially planned – move round a bit. You know, make the most of my time away... And I'm fine. How's work, by the way?'

'Going along,' Brenda replied. 'George finally charmed the private arm of the McDermitt account from Matersons. That's the big news of the day.'

'The big news of the year,' Catherine replied. And it was: Robert McDermitt was a leader in the construction industry – and the deal would net their firm in the region of £75,000,000 worth of business per annum. It would not be their biggest account by any means – even so, it was pretty significant. And it was a foot in the door at McDermitt: it could be built on. 'Tell him well done from me. He's been after that one for some time. I'm sure he will repay their confidence.' She paused. 'Is there any other news?'

'No, nothing out of the ordinary.' Brenda hesitated. 'I did hear that Alex went out with his old buddy Gregory Hitchins last night. Judging by his visits to the coffee machine this morning, I think they may have had a drink or two.'

Catherine smiled. She knew Alexander's friend, Greg Hitchins. They met up with him every now and then, usually for a meal, but sometimes for a trip to the theatre. He was the playboy type, suave, smooth-talking, and always had a different woman with him whenever they went out. He also had a reputation for drinking – would be a bad influence on Alex. Still, that was none of her business, now. 'It's good to hear that he's missing me,' she said.

'Why don't you come home, Catherine?' Brenda encouraged again. 'You know you can stay with me and Joe.'

'I need a bit longer yet,' Catherine replied, admiring her

friend's perseverance. 'It's still too soon… And I've received an email from Alex – an annoying one, an especially annoying one.' She informed Brenda of the email's content, concluding: 'He just doesn't seem to realise what he did to me.'

'Perhaps he's so ashamed of his behaviour that he has blocked it from his mind. That can happen, Catherine. It's… it's a subconscious response, I think. You know, when an otherwise decent person commits a heinous crime, a denial process kicks in to protect him from self-recrimination.'

'Maybe,' Catherine replied doubtfully. She thought that Brenda really should give up on those psychology books. If you delved deeply enough, it was possible to find a reason… an excuse, for all kinds of bad behaviour. 'Maybe,' she said. 'Although I think it more likely that he just doesn't regard it as serious. Some men are like that. Because somebody is living with them, they see sex as their entitlement. It's as if a woman gives up her right to say no when she moves in with a man. She becomes his property, his chattel.'

'That doesn't sound like the Alex I know. I am aware that things – bad things – can happen in the heat of the moment, but what you are suggesting is… is calculating, as if he was working out what he could or couldn't get away with.'

'Oh, he can be pretty calculating when he wants something badly enough. He…' Catherine's retort petered out. She knew she was being unfair. Alex wasn't like that. He was upfront, straightforward, in no way devious. She should acknowledge that as fact… But, she reminded herself, she was the injured party, and her case needed to be made. Ignoring her own sentiment, she went on: 'He reasoned that sex with me was his prerogative.'

Brenda sighed. 'Catherine, you're all alone – wherever you are – and after what's happened that's not a good thing. You've got nobody to talk to, no one older to go to for advice.' She paused. 'Oh, I know that you analyse people, you study them, their mannerisms, and you work situations through. And there is nothing wrong in that. It's the way you are. But when a person is by themselves, in an unfamiliar place, it's easy for deliberation to turn negative... Kate, I really feel you should come back here and stay with us for a while.'

That Brenda was laying it on, going all out to persuade, was clear to Catherine. But she had to admit that her friend was right about one thing: she did study people, and their behaviour, tried to figure out their motivations – but only because people were so arcane, so difficult to comprehend. 'Thanks for the offer,' she said. 'I'll take a rain check for now, but I may well take you up on it later.' She laughed. 'I might need a roof over my head.'

'All right,' Brenda replied. 'But I wish you would at least consider telling me where you are. Alex hasn't pressed me, and I don't think that he will. He doesn't even know we're in contact with one another.'

'He will have guessed that I've phoned you. He'll ask you some time.' Catherine shot a glance at her mobile. 'And the only reason he hasn't already done so is because he doesn't care,' she added bitterly.

'Of course he cares, Catherine. Despite what he has done, he loves you. You know that.'

'He loves me!' Brenda was beginning to sound like an Alex King apologist. 'Then what about his email? All that amounted to was an attempt to put the blame on to me... to absolve himself.'

'I agree it doesn't sound very tactful. Nonetheless, from what you told me, I think that he was genuinely trying to apologise. And you know what men are like with writing letters.'

'Then I must have told you wrong,' Catherine shot back, suddenly cross.

'Obviously I'm not as emotionally involved as you are, Catherine, but perhaps that gives me a better view of the overall picture.' Brenda paused briefly. 'However, my main concern is you. And as I said before, brooding over a problem by oneself can make matters appear worse than they actually are.'

'If they *appear* to get any worse, I'll give you a call,' Catherine said, ending the conversation peremptorily.

Dropping her mobile into her bag, Catherine started off up the path once more, strode out in a petulant gait. Tiffs with Brenda were rare. She was a peacemaker. As the saying had it, the one to pour balm on troubled waters. And she hated to upset anyone. Catherine could just imagine her now, turning back to her work, tut-tutting, mumbling under her breath...
'I do hope I wasn't too harsh with her.' Then justifying herself, assuaging her conscience... 'But she needs guidance; for all her scholarship she still needs that.' Catherine paused to remove something that had gone into her eye. Brenda was a good person, genuinely caring – just one of the many reasons why she alone shared Catherine's teenage secret.

Sporting two glasses of whisky, Gregory Hitchins returned to his friend's table. 'Darn me, old chap,' he said heartily, passing Alex his drink, 'the two of us out on the town twice in one week. It's getting just like old times.' He raised his glass. 'And here's to them.'

Alex gazed at his whisky and soda. 'Don't I know it,' he said reflectively. Since settling down with Catherine, going out drinking with the boys had lost much of its appeal. But now, with Kate away... He too raised his glass. 'We'd better make this the last one.' He took a sip of the liquid, then placed the glass back on the table. 'I want to get some work done later.'

Alex first made the acquaintance of Gregory Hitchins while studying at The London School of Economics. The Yuppie era was over – the recent stock market crash had seen to that – but for those with a crumb of foresight the world of finance was still the preferred route to prosperity. As Alex and Greg had independently realised, banks and banking were, and would always be, an essential oil for the smooth running of the economy and society – thus both ambitious young men had opted to take degrees in accounting and finance. However, as aspiring as each boy undoubtedly was, that would be the sum of their academic parallel; for while Alex got a First, Greg barely scrapped a Third; and while Alex pursued a professional career in the City, Greg drifted from one mundane job to another. In spite of his profligate lifestyle, he was currently working as a personal trainer – a position which, as he frequently boasted, gave him access to some pretty hot tottie.

Greg glanced at his watch. 'It's early days yet, old chap.' He performed a double-take on his watch. 'Surely you don't work–'

'Yes, I do,' Alex broke in. 'The markets are always trading somewhere across the globe, and I like to keep up to speed on potential opportunities.'

Greg looked at him cannily. 'Ah, I know what it is. It's your anniversary, isn't it? It's *three* whole days since Catherine made off.' He took firm possession of his drink. 'Well, don't worry, old boy. She loves you. She'll be back. But in the meantime–'

'I don't fancy yours, but mine will do just fine.'

Greg immediately shot to his feet. 'Hello, ladies,' he said, grinning rakishly. 'I trust that I'm the one who will… *do just fine.*'

Swearing under his breath, Alex also stood up. 'Hello, Anna,' he said, less than enthusiastically. Then he sat down again.

This was all he needed, for he guessed that this unplanned meeting would be anything but chance when news of it reached Catherine – and it would. Alex had sussed the lie of the land. Brenda. She was not a gossipy kind of person and, while it was possible that she didn't know where Catherine was, she was for sure a channel to her. Anna would exploit that. He knew she hadn't bought his story about Kate working from home, that she suspected something was afoot. She had a sixth sense for sniffing out another person's misfortune, and a seventh for profiting from it.

'Now let me see we've met before, haven't we?' Greg was saying. 'You're Anna, Alex's colleague.' He ran a raffish eye over her figure, hovered on the crotch of her body-hugging stretch trousers, before finally coming to rest on her cleavage. 'Yes indeed, a lass as pretty as you must stand out like a movie starlet amongst all those pinstripes. He tells me, by the way, that you are the mainstay of the Company. And your friend is…'

'This is Rosemary,' Anna said, turning briefly to her companion. 'She's up from the country for the week, so I thought I'd bring her to Muffins and introduce her to the whirl.' She eyed Alex greedily. 'And also show her what… what *eligible* men we have here.'

'Excellent,' Greg said, pulling back the two spare chairs at the table. 'Now, I hope you ladies will join us.'

Oh, you try to stop them, Alex thought wryly. He too had noted Anna's stretch trousers. He was no lip reader, but he was pretty certain the message read: "Yes please".

Anna claimed the chair closest to his, and Rosemary, a gawky blue-eyed girl clearly unaccustomed to "the whirl", sat next to Greg. Trying not to smile, Alex studied his friend. It looked as though Greg was planning to add another conquest to his tally. Well, fair enough and good luck to him, but he wouldn't allow himself to be drawn into anything that could be misconstrued. He reached for his glass, decided that after this one he would leave them to it.

'And what would you ladies like to drink?' Greg looked around furtively. 'I take it you are both old enough to do so?'

Anna giggled, then shot Alex a knowing look. 'I'm… I'm tempted to go for a highball,' she said, simpering. 'But I think I'll start with a gin martini… I'll leave the highballs for later.' She turned to her friend. 'You'll have the same, won't you, Rosemary?'

Rosemary giggled. 'Yes, please.'

As soon as Greg had left for the bar, Anna returned her gaze to Alex. 'When we first spotted you, I thought that Catherine might be *hiding* somewhere.' She paused, licking her lips. 'She isn't here, is she, Alex?'

Alex took a long pull on his drink, deliberately keeping his eyes well above the deeply plunging neckline of Anna's blouse. He hoped she didn't get hiccups. But if she did, it would make fascinating speculation: will they, won't they? His money was on the affirmative. 'No,' he replied. 'This is strictly a *boys'* night out.'

'Oh, I just adore those,' she said. 'I find the idea of competition frankly rather boring – a fucking *waste* of time… and a waste of *fucking* time.'

Just then, with Alex smiling apologetically at the shocked faces at the next table, Greg returned with the drinks. Alex saw that his friend had brought him another whisky. 'Not for me, Greg. As I said earlier, I've things to get on with later.' He turned slightly towards Anna and, raising his voice, added: 'And I promised *Kate* that I wouldn't be late home.' Returning his gaze to Greg, he acknowledged his friend's imperceptible nod. Greg was okay, caught on quick – he wouldn't give the game away.

'Don't be a spoilsport, old chap. You don't have to be sober to check on the markets, do you?' He winked at Rosemary. 'Besides, we can't allow these lovely ladies to drink alone.' Feigning concern, he shot another of his furtive glances round the area. 'Why, you never know what fate may overtake them.'

At Greg's remark, Anna clapped her hands together. 'Oh, I'm a fatalist,' she said gleefully. 'You know, like in the song "Que Sera Sera".' She gazed at Alex, openly eyeing his credentials. Then, on a deep breath, she started to sing: 'When I was just a little girl, I asked my mother what will I be…'

Trying to blot out Anna's tuneless rendition of the song, Alex took a resigned draught of his drink.

In spite of his resolve to leave the nightclub early, Alex had been unable to find the right opportunity to do so, and now, as he and his three companions descended the venue's steps onto the pavement, it was nearly midnight. Despite the hour, summer heat still hung heavy in the air – as did Greg hang heavy on Alex's arm. There would be no new conquest for him tonight. Drink had seen to that. Anna and Rosemary, giggling incessantly, clung to each other amid a maelstrom of merrymakers. Anna had removed her shoes, and now carried them by the heels in one hand.

Alex left the group and moved to the kerb. His intention was to hail a taxi and dispatch Anna and Rosemary home – to ship them off before Anna tried anything on. In her present state he knew she was capable of anything. After that he would get another taxi for Greg…

And then, as he was ruing his decision to come out tonight, Anna came weaving across the pavement. 'We'll go back to my place, Alex,' she said, dropping one of her shoes. She threw her arms around his neck. 'Rosemary will be there but she won't get in the way, I've got two bedrooms.'

Alex disentangled himself from her embrace, glanced round, hoped nobody who knew him was watching.

'Don't fight it, darling,' she said petulantly, as he dodged her attempt to kiss him. 'It's writ in the stars…' She made a drunken lunge for his crotch. 'Tonight Venus will collide with Mars.'

Parrying away her hand, he retrieved her shoe and, rather incongruously, used it to attract the attention of a passing taxi.

The taxi driver pulled over. 'Where to, mate?' Without answering, Alex opened the taxi door and shoved a startled Anna inside. Ten seconds later, he had deposited an equally stunned Rosemary in beside her. Instructions to the driver, a fistful of twenties in his hand, and he watched the taxi pull away from the kerb. Sorted – any witness was sure to find in his favour. He turned round, to see the nightclub doorman grinning appreciatively in his direction. Nice work, Alexander, he told himself. If the global economy collapses tomorrow and you need a job, there's your route into bouncing.

He returned to the nightclub steps, where Greg was now sitting, propped against a flight of railings, and looking for all the world as if he might throw up. His friend had been right earlier: it was just like old times. He walked back across the pavement, raised his arm to attract another taxi… And it was then that he realised he still had Anna's shoe in his hand.

Chapter 6

Are you all right? The words seemed to float in and out of her perception, like in a dream, being far away yet close at hand together. *Are you all right?* But it couldn't be a dream, because Catherine was thinking, aware.

'Are you all right, Miss?'

Catherine opened sleepy eyes, saw a man stooping over her, peering, inquisitive, hands resting on his knees. She saw that he was wearing dungarees over a checked shirt. It was dusk, past sunset, but a waxing moon and parabola of stars illuminated the area as though lit by floodlights.

Not a little confused by her sudden awakening, she propped herself into a sitting position. 'Yes, I'm fine. I must… I must have fallen asleep.' She gazed at the man, whose eyes were scrutinising her so closely. He had a prominent chin, square, almost comic book, and deep-set blue eyes. Then she noticed how dirty his face was… as if smudged by oil… and he needed a shave. And his hair was a mop of blond disarray, rough-hewn, as if he hadn't visited a hairdresser in months. She thought that he looked unsavoury… possibly a tramp seeking somewhere to sleep. Catherine hadn't been initially scared, but now doubts were beginning to grow in her mind. She determined to remain calm, to do nothing that might alarm him – nothing that might trigger an assault. 'Yes, I'm fine,' she repeated, shuffling away from him, backwards, awkward on her bottom.

'You had I worried fer a moment,' he said. He came

closer, hunched forward, forcing Catherine to retreat even farther into the hollow. There was, she realised, an odd aroma about him, a fishy smell… as if… as if he had been sleeping rough… in the garbage of the quayside. 'Fer a moment, I thought thee were a gonner. Then I saw thee move and I–'

'I must get back,' she interrupted. 'They will be worried.' She glanced in the direction of the town. 'I wouldn't be surprised if they were organising a search party right now.'

'Then we'll probably meet them on our way back.' He held out his hand. 'C'mon. I'll take 'e there.' He waited patiently, arm still outstretched. 'I don't mean thee any harm,' he added, shaking his head as if the very idea was absurd.

Catherine thought he seemed genuine, concerned. He was saying the right things, acting appropriately. But she was still not sure. 'It's okay,' she said. 'I don't want to be a nuisance… And I know the way.'

He grinned down at her, a broad smile, affable in its simplicity. The gesture had lightened his dour features, and she felt her apprehension start to lift. 'Don't worry,' he said. 'You won't get no mischief from I. I ain't one of yer city boys. Can't trust they, so I've heard. No, I be born and bred a Cornish man – trusty and true we be. Now, don't thee fret none, I'll take 'e down to the town. That's where I just come from, the harbour.' He told her that he owned one of the fishing boats and was on his way home when he spotted her lying in the hollow. 'I've got a little cottage down in the inlet,' he went on. 'This ain't the quickest way. But I always comes this way on nights like this.' He paused to gesture overhead. 'Often times I lie in that hollow and try and count 'em up.'

Catherine peered up at him with a curious eye, her earlier suspicion now all but dispelled by his artless candour.

He grinned – this time, sheepishly. ''Tis true,' he said.

'Trouble is though, there's so many of 'em… the Milky Way.'

Stargazing… stargazing… Catherine continued to stare, her mind shifting like a seesaw between another time and here. Then, finally convinced, she took his hand and allowed herself to be pulled upright.

He had a firm yet relaxed grip, a hold that remained briefly with her after he had released her hand. Then she realised that he had squeezed her hand gently, once he had righted her – a comforting squeeze. 'Thank you,' she said, acknowledging his kindness in the starlit evening.

Catherine glanced round the hollow, looking for her shoulder bag. 'Do you really observe the stars from here?' she asked.

'Yeah, that I do.' His gaze searched the heavens. 'People think they don't move – but they change with the seasons… like the sea.'

'I used to once.' Catherine shivered as a chill of the coming night brushed her bare arms. She picked up her cardigan, shrugged it on. 'But that was a long time ago,' she said dismissively.

He waited, smiling patiently, as she brushed several strands of broken grass from her jeans. 'Where are you staying?' he asked, watching her retrieve her bag.

'The Globe Hotel,' she replied. 'It's a little way back from the inner harbour.' She thought for a moment. The inlet he had referred to was in the opposite direction to the town. 'But you must have been walking that way,' she said, pointing along the coastal path. 'You don't want to go back to the town.'

'All modern now, but a few years back 'twas a real pub with real ale,' he said, ignoring her observation. 'I know it.'

She let him lead her back on to the path. 'How did you know that I'm not from here?' she said.

'You'd best walk behind me, Miss. I knows this path better than the one in me own garden.' He glanced over his shoulder. 'How do I know you ain't local? 'Tis obvious... I can always tell.'

Catherine guessed that it was evident. Her accent, her confusion, being up here at night, would have told him that.

As they made their way along the cliff top, and with the lights of the town now becoming a physical reassurance, Catherine began to feel increasingly confident. When he first came on the scene and awakened her, she had felt anything but. She said: 'I'm sorry but I don't know your name.'

'Chris,' he called without looking back. 'Christopher Armstrong. And yours?'

Catherine made a stumble as she avoided a bramble tendril that had grown across the path. There was a saying that lightning did not strike in the same place twice... Assisted by her earlier memories, her thinking tugged at a sentimental chord and she suppressed a sudden emotion.

When he received no reply, Christopher Armstrong drew up and turned round. Unready for his gaze, Catherine automatically bent down and clutched her knee. 'Is anything the matter?' he asked.

'No,' she said, wincing exaggeratedly. 'It's okay. My left knee often gives out... especially when going downhill... or on rough terrain.'

'You're holding your right knee,' he said pointedly.

'Yes. This one does it too,' Catherine said, rubbing the joint more vigorously. She looked up, to see him grinning at her. She studied the smile, the pursed lips, and the level stare. Catherine could not read the expression. It was, she thought, as if... almost as if he knew her. But that could not be. How could he know that she had been here before? He couldn't. She decided that

85

he was merely amused at her histrionics. 'I'll be fine when we reach the road, or level ground,' she added. She gave her knee a final rub. 'My name is Catherine, by the way.'

'And a very nice one too,' he said, nodding as he started off down the path again. Then, throwing her a casual glance, he said: 'And don't thee worry none: I knows this part's a bit steep, but you'll be on tarmac in another fifty yards.'

'I'll be all right on my own now,' Catherine said, when, a minute later, they came to the end of the path. 'It's not far.' She paused to allow him to help her over the stile. 'Thank you for escorting me back.'

'I might as well take 'e all the way, if you don't mind. I won't climb that cliff again tonight. I'll take the normal route home now.' He grinned at her. 'And she goes right past yer hotel.'

Catherine stayed her ground. She was only a visitor – no one here knew her – but a natural modesty cautioned her of being seen emerging from the direction of the cliff path at night, alone with one of the local fishermen. She said: 'I've already put you to too much trouble so–'

'Ain't no trouble,' he cut in, shrugging broad shoulders. 'Besides, you never know what's lurking hereabouts at night.' He grinned down at her again, a different gesture. 'We get all sorts down yer from the cities this time of year.' And with that he commenced along the road.

Catherine recalled his derogatory remark concerning city boys. He clearly did not think highly of urban morals. But maybe, she reflected, he was just parochial, a local lad, unworldly… untraveled. Perhaps she shouldn't have been so suspicious of him, doubted his integrity, his motive, when he had given her no reason to do so. 'All right,' she said, skipping forward to catch up with him.

Outside of the hotel, she extended her hand. 'Thank you,' she said. 'Thank you for... for ensuring my safe return.'

He took her hand in his, and squeezed it... almost timidly, she thought. Even so, once more she experienced the firmness of his grip, the feel of male skin. There was no doubting that he worked with his hands... like the other Christopher. She felt her pulse quicken. Like her Christopher. She promptly released his hand, took a half step backwards. He said: 'Best be careful if you find yerself up there again after dark. Not so much fer strangers, but there's old tin-mine workings further along, not all of it properly fenced off. Plenty of folk have come a cropper round there.'

'I will,' she said. 'But I don't intend getting caught out up there again. Tonight was enough for one holiday.' She glanced up. 'And I'll do any future stargazing from somewhere safe,' she added, laughing.

'You won't see much from here,' he said. 'Too much street lighting fer that.' He paused, weighing her with a speculative stare. 'I'll tell 'e what though,' he went on at length, 'if you want to see the stars, I'll take 'e to a place where you can do that in the daytime.'

Catherine held his gaze, unsure of what he was proposing. She knew there was no planetarium nearby.

'It's no trick. If you wanna do it, I'll show you how 'tis done. Honestly, I'm not bull– Sorry. I'm not having you on.' He stood back, smiling confidently, arms folded across his barrel chest.

Held by the sudden magnetism of his blue eyes, she continued to stare. That he was showing off to the visitor, proud of his local knowledge, was clear to her. But daytime stargazing, she wondered... 'I don't know,' she said. 'I'm... I'm not sure.' She did not want to accept but, for some reason, she was finding it difficult to refuse him outright. She was intrigued by the mystery of his invitation. And he had shown consideration... courtesy, by insisting on escorting her down from the cliff top. But it was more than that. Could it be...? No, Catherine, she told herself. If that's the reason, say no. She started to form the word.

'Oh, don't worry, Catherine,' he said, studying her face. He spread his hands, palms up. 'Don't worry: I won't come turned out like this.'

It was the first time he had addressed her by her name – and his dialect had made it into three syllables: Cath/er/ine. There was a definite earthiness in that, and she felt excited by it, disturbingly so. It was almost as if he had made her a different kind of invitation. Catherine looked down at her hands. She knew she should say no. But he seemed so innocent, so ingenuous. And she had clearly made him feel self-conscious enough to apologise for his mode of dress, when there was no reason for him to do so, for he had been walking home from his job when he found her. Cath/er/ine looked up, smiled. 'All right.'

'Well done.' He grinned. 'That be smashing.' His grin spread. 'Will tomorrow afternoon be okay?'

'Won't you be working? I mean–'

'Not then. The pots'll go out in the morning and I won't need to fetch 'em in till later...' He paused, noting her quizzical expression. 'The lobster pots,' he explained. 'That's where the money is these days. Them and taking tourists out mackerel fishing – that's easy money, that is.' He paused again, his face becoming thoughtful. 'Two o'clock... if the sky's clear? It won't be no good if it's cloudy.'

Catherine nodded silently. 'Okay, weather permitting...' She faltered. But what was she agreeing to? She hardly knew him. And what about Alexander? Experiencing a sudden diffidence, a sudden awakening of conscience, she dropped her eyes to… to uneasy hands. She looked up at Christopher Armstrong, the firm-set jaw, the beaming smile, the fixed stare… and became aware that her heart was beating faster. Perhaps it would be best to say no.

'I'll meet you down on the quay, Catherine.' And with that he was off, moving away up the street, giving her no time to change her mind.

Fidgeting with the strap of her bag, Catherine watched him go. The stride was jaunty, the arms swinging, the fists clenched. She recognised it as the swagger of a man who knew what he wanted… and probably how to get it. Maybe he wasn't so naïve after all. Perhaps that description better fitted her. All at once a picture unclosed in her mind. She saw herself, depicted as a gauche fourteen-year-old, awaiting the arrival of her first date, a mix of excitement and anticipation, but mostly nervous apprehension – and her mother trying to be reassuring: 'Don't be silly, Catherine. It's only Brian from next door.' Brian from next door… How strange, she mused, that that memory should come to her after all these years, and so vividly. Glancing then up the street, she saw Christopher Armstrong turn and wave, before disappearing round a corner. She started to climb the steps to her hotel, thinking. There was no obligation to keep the date with him. She did not have to go. In fact, she wouldn't.

Alex opened the bottom drawer of his desk, gazed incredulously at the shoe. Good God, how did women walk in these things? Must be like walking on stilts. Not that he was complaining. What women suffered in wearing them, he gained in the effect they had on arse bulge, and on arse movement – *Jello on springs*. Savouring the cinematic vision, he held onto the drawer, eyed the shoe. He would take it over to where Anna worked in a moment. She'd phoned him earlier to say that she thought she'd lost a shoe outside the nightclub. Had he noticed it anywhere? Of course he had, the silly bitch had dropped it at his feet.

She had certainly come on strong last night, had thrown herself at him – literally. Perhaps he should invite her over tonight, give her what she wanted. He was getting tired of hand jobs. She was supposed to be a pretty good lay, into kinky stuff, too – liked a good spanking, to warm her up. He could oblige there. Suddenly he saw her draped across his knees, her hindquarters bared for his attention… her scrawny haunches. He blinked and the picture collapsed. No way. He wasn't that tired of hand jobs.

He wouldn't, anyway. He loved Kate.

'Hi there, Alex, I've come to collect my shoe.'

Alex sprang out of his reverie, slammed the drawer shut in *guilty* surprise. 'I wish you'd knock, Anna, instead of creeping in like that.' He glared at her, angry, pissed off. She was wearing that silk blouse again, testing the tension of the material by the look of it. He hadn't seen the mini before… Or were they called micros? He could make out the outline of suspenders beneath the taut cloth. He liked suspender belts and stockings. Catherine looked great in them. They would look more like braces on her though.

'Why Alex, darling, you weren't doing anything that would embarrass me, were you?' She glanced down. 'I see your hand is out of sight. With Catherine away, I hope you weren't being a naughty boy.'

That did it. She may be the boss's granddaughter but there were limits. 'Listen,' he began irritably. 'You know the policy about knocking before entering someone's office.' He paused, holding her stare, his eyes drilling into hers. 'Most of the accounts in here are intellectual property. Any seen by unauthorised personnel would infringe corporate confidentiality.' That wasn't strictly true but she was too dense to question it. 'Do you know what that means?' But without giving her a chance to reply, he went on: 'I hope you do. But just in case you don't, I'll tell you: it means that either of us, or both, could enjoy a lengthy sojourn at Her Majesty's pleasure.' He showed her a knowing smile. 'How do you fancy Holloway? No men in there, but a lot of women who think they are.'

He took the shoe from the drawer and held it towards her. From the look on her face, he thought that he might have been too harsh. Well, so what. Jumped-up little office girl, trading on her connection. 'Here take it,' he said, 'and get back to your office.'

But Anna ignored the proffered shoe. 'Oh, Alex,' she said, rolling hapless eyes, 'when I'm spoken to like that... by a *man*, I simply go to pieces, my will to resist wilts.' She heaved a double-dipped sigh, causing the swell of her breasts above her half-cup brassiere to become an undulating wave. 'You don't mind if I sit down for a moment, do you?' She flopped uninvited into a chair, then crossed her legs. 'Oh, it's so unfair,' she went on. 'But it's just the way I am. It's a dominance thing, and it makes me feel so submissive... so *open* to suggestion. You know, if you were to ask me *now* to come over to your place tonight and cook you a gourmet meal, then I'd just have to say yes. I couldn't refuse.' She pouted her lips, gawped. 'Make me an offer I can't refuse, Alex.'

She was getting worse – Kate's absence was encouraging her. When Kate was around, she was never this bad, never so head-on. Alex decided that he needed to put her right, to get his message across. He placed the shoe on his desk. 'Look, Anna,' he began patiently. 'I know you think you like me, maybe even something more than that, but it's not going to happen. I have Catherine… and I love her… very much.' He paused, studying her bewildered expression. He could see that she wasn't taking anything he said on board. The idea of somebody not finding her irresistible was clearly beyond her comprehension. He said: 'You're not my type, Anna… You are not a woman I could love.'

She picked up the shoe, toyed with it, stroking the heel suggestively. 'What is love, Alex?' she said wistfully. 'Poets have exhausted their imaginations trying to describe it – but all have failed. They have only come up with fanciful notions. Perhaps it would be better if *we* were more practical. How could it then be measured, on what scale?' She placed the shoe back on his desk, shrugged a shoulder. 'Is it a bit above liking someone? Is it a mixture of affection, admiration, respect, empathy – all that sort of shit?' Her features took on a different aspect. 'Or is it straightforward sexual attraction… the kind we have for each other?' After several pregnant moments, during which Alex remained silently stunned, she raised yet another aspect to him. 'Whatever it is, Alex, it can grow.'

Alex all but caught up. Was this conversation really happening? he asked himself. Or was he dreaming? He realised then that he was never going to get through to her. He felt like booting her ass straight across his office and out into the corridor. Instead he repeated his earlier assertion: 'I could never love you, Anna.' Then he added: 'And nothing will ever change that.'

She gazed across the desk and a new expression emerged

from her repertoire. It was a shrewd look, a calculating look. 'I could be very useful to your career, Alex,' she said. 'I'm in a position—'

'My career is doing nicely by itself,' he said in a monotone. 'Why, I'm off to the States shortly...' He smiled at her. Then, bringing joy to his voice, he added: '... With Catherine.'

'There's always scope for improvement,' she said, ignoring his final comment. 'With me on your side, you sit at the top table.'

Alex yawned. 'How do you suppose the senior directors... *and your uncle*, not to mention the other stakeholders, would view that?' he asked.

She gawked at him. His question had clearly taken her by surprise – but not for long. 'Fuck them,' she shot back. 'Granddaddy values my advice.' She arranged her legs to his advantage. 'You could be CEO by next year.'

Alex had had enough. He decided that he had to get rid of her, before his desire to chuck her out became an imperative. Pushing back his chair, he stood up abruptly, almost knocking his desk into her lap. 'Get out—'

And he got his wish, for Anna leapt to her feet, grabbed the shoe and dashed from his office. He had never seen anyone in high heels move so fast. Had she finally got the message? He hoped so.

Now, through the glazed top half of the dividing wall, Alex watched her moving off down the corridor. He noted that her pace had slowed, that she no longer appeared to be in a hurry. Then he saw why: Brenda Willis was coming along the passageway from the opposite direction. Anna must have seen Kate's friend out of the corner of her eye and, in less time than it took for a praying mantis to strike, saw her chance to incriminate him. And what better place to do so than to be seen emerging from his office, with the evidence in her hand?

He watched surreptitiously as the two women paused to speak. He saw Anna hold the shoe aloft. Then the meaningful glance in his direction, the expressive smile at Brenda Willis, the imperceptible tilt of the head – lips moving. If only he could hear what she was saying. But he didn't need to, for he knew what Anna was telling Brenda. The evening spent at Muffins, drinking, dancing, having a good time, the four of them, together, when "poor" Catherine was elsewhere. And of course the lost shoe that the gallant Alex had rescued.

And now the disparaging glance from Brenda. She could hardly believe it; could not comprehend his behaviour – utterly callous. But here was the shoe, irrefutable proof. At least, he wasn't denying it. Alex decided that he would go out there, tell his side of the story, put Brenda in the picture. He took a step towards the door. Then he stopped, thinking. No, that was what Anna wanted: to create a scene, to involve more of his colleagues in the theatre. He sat down, seething with frustration.

Alex suddenly relaxed. So what? Just look at her, exaggerating, embellishing, trying to convince the other woman of his infidelity – putting the boot in like a rabid footballer. *Hell hath no fury like a woman scorned.* Brenda wouldn't pass this tittle-tattle on to Catherine. And even if she did, Kate would merely laugh it off for the fabrication that it was.

Chapter 7

Perched on the wall at the end of the quay, she watched a nearby fishing boat being unloaded. A cadre of gulls was wheeling and dipping, squabbling over oddments of fish that were being thrown overboard. Some gulls were making off for safe havens to consume their bounty. Others had chosen the quayside as their eating place, only to find that competition for food was far from over. One gull relieved another of its meal but then it too found itself pursued by others intent on taking its prize. The squawking of competing birds was deafening. Catherine thought that parallels could be drawn with the business world.

Then she spotted him coming down the wharf beside the harbour, his long stride eating up the ground to their rendezvous. She saw that he was wearing a navy blue polo shirt and grey flannel trousers, the latter item pressed to a sharp crease. A pair of blue and white plimsolls completed his ensemble. Despite his assertion yesterday, she had thought that he might still be wearing his workaday clothes – and she wouldn't have minded. He had told her about putting out lobster pots. But he looked dapper. And the hair that had been a tousled mop last night was now greased and parted neatly in the middle... just like Alex wore his.

He stopped in front of her. 'Hi, Catherine,' he said, executing a formal bow. 'I wasn't sure whether you'd turn up; thought perhaps you might change yer mind about being seen out with a sea salt like I.' He grinned, looked her up and down. 'Glad you did though… turn up, that is.' He glanced up at the sky, which was a clear azure blue. 'And we've got just the right weather fer it too.'

Catherine popped herself from the wall, straightened her trousers, adjusted her sunglasses. 'We certainly have,' she said, picking up her bag. She pursed her lips, assessed the casual apparel – the reactive shades. 'But you don't look much like a sea salt to me,' she added. 'You look more like a debonair yachtsman.' Her gaze surveyed the harbour. 'Which one is yours, by the way?'

'C'mon then,' he said abruptly, turning on his heel and marching off back along the quay. 'I'll take 'e there.'

Catherine watched, smiling, as his hasty retreat forced him to dodge around an elderly holidaymaker, who appeared more concerned for the preservation of his ice cream cone than for his own safety. Had she embarrassed him in some way? Maybe he wasn't at ease in his leisure wear, being on the quay, afraid that one of his mates would think him a dandy. Still smiling, she ran after him.

She was feeling strangely elated, walking along beside someone other than Alex. She hadn't intended to keep the appointment with him. But an update from Brenda telling of Anna's lost shoe and Alex's involvement in it had changed her mind. If he could go out and have fun, then why shouldn't she do the same? In spite of everything that had happened, she knew she still loved him. That had not altered. It would take more than a single act, no matter how wicked, to destroy what they shared. Yes, she still loved him. But having accepted an invitation from another man, and now being out with him, she did not feel guilty. A week ago, the very idea of dating somebody else would have been unthinkable. Catherine was just a little confused, pleasantly so. Anyhow, this was innocent: stargazing, an interest they both had in common. She wasn't about to hop into bed with him – not that it would be anyone's business if she did.

Perhaps, she reflected, as they walked together along the harbour side, Brenda shouldn't be informing on Alexander. It was not like her to tell tales. But Catherine guessed that her friend was doing so merely to give Kate something to think about – ultimately, to persuade her to come home. Maybe the reports were even embellished to that end. Brenda was a good soul, if a little inclined to worry.

Soon they were walking out of the town heading for the coastal path. From their direction she guessed that the telescope might be on the cliff top, if indeed that was how it was done. Catherine did not know for sure – and Christopher wasn't telling her. It was to be a surprise, he had said.

She gazed at the row of painted cottages they were passing. 'You always seem to get that at the seaside, don't you? Pastel pinks and greens and blues.'

'Yeah, now they be fer visitors and second homes,' he said offhandedly. 'They weren't like that when they were fishermen's houses – could see the Cornish granite in them days. City people changes everything. They comes down yer with their big money and pushes up the prices, and we can't afford to buy naught.' He shot her a disgruntled look, sighed. 'Everything's geared up fer them sort nowadays and nowt's left fer us.'

Catherine gazed up at his set expression, noted the sullen eyes. It was not her intention to spoil their excursion by discussing sensitive, local matters. She decided to be upbeat, point up the positives. 'But they boost the local economy,' she said brightly. 'They spend while they're here, on all kinds of commodities, particularly the people with second homes – and they rent them out. Moreover, from what you told me yesterday, you make part of your living from holidaymakers. I mean what you said about taking them out mackerel fishing.'

'All that be only in the season, the summertime. Except fer a bit of fishing, 'tis dead yer in the winter. Besides 'tis not real fishing anymore, not like 'twas when I were a lad. Then you could catch what you liked, and as much as you–' He paused, silenced by Catherine's sudden giggle. 'What's wrong?' he asked.

She had not meant to laugh. It was just that his grumpy manner seemed at odds with his personality, what she knew of it, anyway. Catherine pressed on. 'You're not old enough to remember the pre-quota days,' she said neutrally. 'And what about all the boats back there in the harbour? Why I've seen all manner of species being unloaded: cod, haddock, conger eel, flatfish…'

'Have you now. Well, most of what you saw is only half the catch.' He stopped and looked down at her, his expression brittle. Then, nodding towards the sea, he added: 'The other half's out there, floating in the ocean – dead. If we catch too much, we has to throw it back.'

He was exaggerating, of course, Catherine knew that. But despite her defence of outsiders, she knew he had a sound case concerning the part-time residency of second homes: by inflating house prices it excluded many of the locals from buying their own homes. 'You're right,' she said conciliatorily. 'And… and you fishermen don't go out fishing as often as you used to either.'

'Nah, I'm not old enough to remember the old days, Catherine,' he said, starting off up the hill again. 'But I knows plenty who are. Anyhow, we gets by; we manage. We find other ways of making up our living; we diversify, like me with the mackerel, see. And the emmets love it. Give 'em a fishing rod and they think they're out there after marlin.' He cast an imaginary rod. 'Give him some slack, Ernest. Let him run, tire himself, then reel the blighter in.'

Almost running to keep up, she focused on the rugged profile of her companion, whose lips were now set in a cool smile. Catherine recognised that he was mocking her, her and her kind. The talk of fishing quotas and second homes had inspired it. However, she also sensed that his mockery was not spiteful. He was clearly too good-natured for that. But, she concluded, there was undoubtedly an edge to his character, when his traditions were challenged... or his opinions. She had already witnessed a censorious quality in his eyes. The thought occurred to her then that he might be unpredictable. But Catherine liked that quality in a man; for a little uncertainty was evolutionary, and kept one alert. She skipped around a child's bike that was lying on the pavement. He wasn't really her type, yet she felt curiously unsettled, conscious of her femininity, aware of herself in that way. He would require watching. Her guard would need to be maintained. She came down here to sort out a relationship, not get drawn into another one.

'Mind how you go,' he said, noting her manoeuvre. His glance lingered. 'You know about my job. Now tell me about yerself.' He grinned. 'Summut tells me you ain't one of those stay-at-home women?'

Catherine decided not to mention Alex, certainly not recent history. 'I work in a bank,' she replied.

'Got no time fer they,' he said brusquely. 'Need some stuff doing on me boat and they've turned I down. If I don't get it done, I won't be able to put to sea fer much longer.' He scoffed. 'But what do they care. 'Tis all about figures, having collateral, returns on their loans. They don't care a bit about me livelihood.'

'Maybe I can help,' Catherine put in.

He stopped on the kerbside, looking her up and down. Catherine watched his gaze taking in her appearance, the Burberry T-shirt, the Alexander McQueen trainers. His stare settled on her Elizabeth and James trousers. 'Maybe,' he said, turning once more to the steepening incline. 'Maybe… if you can persuade 'em to give I twenty-five thousand quid.'

Catherine followed in his wake. Perhaps she could help him. She knew nothing about the fishing industry, or the viability of trawlers – and it was not something the Firm would be interested in taking on – but she had contacts. They would require a full assessment of the work needed, examine his accounts. But he was obviously a hardworking man, and he had indicated that he owned the boat. She paused as he helped her climb over the stile at the beginning of the coastal path. Catherine thought it best to say nothing to him for the time being. She would make some enquiries and, if anything was possible, she would put it to him then.

Presently, en route for their destination, they found themselves approaching the hollow. Catherine was still ignorant of where journey's end was or, for that matter, what awaited her there. His only concession to her enquiries had been an enigmatic 'You won't be disappointed.' But now, passing by the concavity, she gave it a fond glance. It was almost as if a giant pebble had been removed, leaving behind it a perfect oval, which, over time, had acquired the softest sward of green she had ever known. Before she went home, she planned to come up here again, on a starry night. There was a matter to attend to – finally.

Catherine had taken a long time to make up her mind to do it. It wasn't something undertaken lightly. And if it hadn't been for Alex's sexual attack, she might never have done so. The status quo suited her conservative nature. But, paradoxically, so too did starting over.

Chris Armstrong also glanced at the hollow. 'Where we met, Catherine; where you were asleep…' He chuckled mischievously. '… like Sleeping Beauty.'

Catherine noted the change of mood. She was relieved to have left local politics behind. 'I was asleep,' she corrected, laughing lightly.

'There be some nice views to be had up yer, especially at night, when all the stars're out.' He engaged her stare, and she saw his eyes twinkling like the stars he described. 'That there be.' He started off along the path again. Then, throwing her a casual glance over his shoulder, he added: 'I'll bring you up here one night, if you want, see how many we can count.'

'I don't think that would be a good idea,' she replied, giving the hollow a final glance, before spritely moving on. She was pretty certain, given the right time, the right place, that he would make a pass at her. Maybe he already had. Certainly there was some sexual innuendo going on. That was natural though. It happened a lot, even in business situations – but she could handle it. Catching up with him, she noted the purposeful stride, the tanned arms swinging as he walked… the dimpled buttocks beneath the summer flannel. She glanced out at the rolling expanse of the sea. Just as well he wasn't her type.

'There she be,' he said, after another half-minute of walking. 'You can see the top of the shaft workings from yer. And that's where we be heading: the old Meva Mine. They be turning it into a heritage site. They got a Lottery grant for part of the cost, and some business folk stumped up the rest. It'll be great when 'tis done. One of me mates is working there, so I can get in whenever I like.' He turned suddenly to her. 'But why wouldn't it be a good idea?'

Surprising herself with the spontaneity of her reaction, she said: 'Didn't you say something about potholes or rough terrain?' Catherine paused, gazing at the stone structure that he had indicated. She couldn't see anything relating to astronomy. She had been to Jodrell Bank, and this was nothing like that. 'Tell me more about the mine,' she said. 'How is it possible to see the stars from there?'

'Oh, you'll see when we get there. I'll be able to explain it better then.' He nodded thoughtfully. 'But you'll be safe with Chris,' he went on. 'I knows me way round potholes… And I'd even let you use me telescope. You'd see more stars that way. Venus is first out, then–'

'Venus is a planet,' she broke in, 'surely you know…' She paused, silenced by his teasing grin. Earlier in the afternoon, he had been ill at ease, self-conscious, and then a little grumpy. Those emotions were past tense. Her gaze took in his stance – feet apart, arms folded across the muscular torso… and the focused stare that again reminded her she was a woman.

'Sure I know,' he said tersely. 'But with the naked eye you wouldn't know the difference.' His features became mischievous once more. ''Tis only when you do a Lord Nelson that you can tell.'

Catherine remained silent. Other than his probable allusion to the use of a telescope, she wasn't sure that she understood Christopher's meaning. Perhaps it had something to do with another side of Nelson's character.

Maintaining his roguish expression, he now led her on to another path which left the coastal route and turned inland.

She followed him through a meander of spreading gorse, and shortly they arrived at the double gates of a fenced compound.

Catherine gazed through the wire mesh. She was not impressed by what she saw. Except for a stone building, which she recognised from pictures as the head of a mine shaft, there was nothing much to see. Just a scattering of single-storey brick buildings populated the area. She thought it looked a bit like a Western ghost town, barren – abandoned. There was still no sign of a telescope.

'It ain't much I agree,' he said, studying her look. 'But when 'tis finished, it's gonna look really great. Anyway, all the interesting stuff be underground. C'mon, I'll show 'e what they've done.'

He opened one of the gates and ushered her through, then carelessly swung the barrier closed behind him – and just then a man came into view, striding across the compound towards them. Dressed in denim jeans, red checked shirt and a hard hat, he was clearly a workman. From the look on his face, Catherine thought they were going to be turned away, but as he drew closer his expression broke into a grin and he shook Christopher's hand warmly.

'Hi there, Chris,' he said. 'Come for another look around, have you? Well, I'm afraid that we haven't made much progress since your last visit.'

Christopher Armstrong introduced Catherine to the man. 'I guessed you wouldn't have done much more, Dave,' he said, 'lazy bugger that thee be.' He turned back to Catherine. 'But thought I'd show young Catherine here how to see the stars in the day time. That'll be all right, will it?'

Dave's face broke into a slow grin, and his stare alternated between his two visitors. 'Yeah, course it is, mate – no problem.' He settled his gaze on Catherine. It was an astute look, concentrated, and she quickly became uncomfortable under its scrutiny. Then, to her surprise, seemingly having made up his mind, he winked at her. 'I don't suppose he's told you how he does it.'

Catherine stared back at him. He had sallow, pockmarked cheeks… shifty eyes that were closely set – an angular physiognomy. She did not like the look of him. 'I assume that it's some kind of telescope,' she replied. Her gaze surveyed the derelict area, looking for clues. She could see none. 'Or a concealed camera obscura… a powerful one,' she added dryly.

Dave shook his head solemnly, then shot a meaningful glance at his friend. 'Oh, no, it's nothing of the sort. It's much simpler than that, there's no technical wizardry involved, no hidden mirrors or magician's sleight of hand.' He sniggered. 'This is how it's done. Big Chris here takes them underground, a long way underground to where it's dark… pitch black mind you. And then…' He paused, grinning inanely. 'And then Chris…' He sniggered again. 'And then Chris cracks them on their nut, and they see stars.' And with that, he started guffawing loudly.

'Don't tell her me secret, Dave,' Christopher Armstrong said, furrowing his brow theatrically, 'or I'll never persuade her to come down into the mine with me.' Then he too dissolved into ribald laughter.

Catherine clenched her fist, her gaze flitting challengingly between the two men. 'I won't be the only one seeing stars. I've got a pretty mean right hook.'

'Then it's a good job that I've got this on then,' Dave said, rapping his knuckles against his headgear.

Chris Armstrong placed his hand on Catherine's shoulder. 'C'mon, Catherine,' he laughed, 'let's leave this joker to it.'

'This will be the visitor centre,' he said, as a short while later they entered the first building. 'It used to be the offices, when the mine were working, but it's roomy and will serve well as that.'

Catherine slipped her sunglasses into her bag. Being the butt of a joke had not bothered her, but the frequent knowing looks that had passed between the two men was a different matter, unsettling. She suspected there was another layer to the jest, and that she was not its first victim – it was plainly well rehearsed. Her earlier cheeriness had taken a knock.

'What do 'e think?' Armstrong said, studying her look. 'Thee has to imagine it finished – when 'tis fitted out and all the information paraphernalia has been brought in.'

Catherine turned her attention to her surroundings. She saw that the interior of the building had been gutted to reduce it to bare brick walls, and the floor was littered with broken plasterboard panels. In the centre of the area, a trestle table was stacked with workmen's tools. There were hammers and chisels, trowels, a power drill, something that may have been a grinder... or sander. And, pushed against a wall, she recognised a concrete mixing machine. 'It looks as if they still have plenty to do,' she observed, glancing around to emphasise her comment.

'There ain't that much, really.' He made a dismissive gesture with his hands. 'This'll be the last bit to be done – won't need it till the visitors come. Early on they concentrated on the mine itself. They shored up the underground workings against flooding, then they put in a modern ventilation system, upgraded the electrics, too. Part of the shaft's been stripped out ready fer the new feature, and there's a workers' lift down to the bottom.'

Catherine picked a cautious way across the floor to an

open window. Outside was a paved area that stretched away to another brick building. She saw that nettles grew from between the cracks of the skewed paving stones, and buddleia bushes had invaded a strip of wasteland, beside a crumbling brick wall. She wondered then if it was safe to go underground with him. She knew that he was not going to "crack her on the nut", that that was merely a part of their horseplay. But nothing here seemed organised, in progress.

She turned back to Christopher Armstrong. 'It's quiet, nothing being worked on. With the exception of your friend, there doesn't appear to be anyone else here.'

'Clearly nonplussed by her lack of enthusiasm, Christopher Armstrong joined her at the window. 'That's right,' he said, peering out at the scene. 'Apart from when they has to employee professionals, most of the work's done at weekends. Dave's unemployed at the mo, so 'e just keeps an eye on it… does a bit here and there. But they be getting there – doing a proper job.' He shrugged. ''Course, it won't be as grand as what they did at the old Geevor Mine, can't expect that, but it'll be pretty good all the same.'

Catherine nodded absently. 'The Geevor Mine?' she inquired.

Christopher Armstrong told her about the other mine, on Bodmin Moor, how it was turned into a heritage centre, following the end of mining. 'Yeah,' he ran on, 'it's got a museum, film shows and underground tours – real educational. And,' he concluded, turning away from the window, 'there's even a place there where you can pan for semi-precious metals.'

He appeared to know his subject, was convincing anyway. She said: 'Can you also see daytime stars at the Geevor centre?'

At the question, a huge grin broke across his face. 'Nah,

that they can't do. And that's gonna be the trump card here, see – it'll fetch in the visitors.' He started for the door. 'C'mon, I'll show 'e how 'tis done.' He halted halfway across the room, looked over his shoulder. 'We've gotta go down in the lift – any problem with that?'

Catherine made her decision. 'None whatsoever,' she said.

'Then off us goes,' he said, jogging theatrically on the spot.

Smiling at his showy enthusiasm, Catherine followed him from the building. Her earlier bonhomie had returned.

Five minutes later they stepped out of the lift at the bottom of the mine. The first thing Catherine noticed was the drop in temperature. At the surface it had been at least twenty-five degrees Celsius; it was a good ten degrees lower here. She shivered in the timbered area by the lift shaft, wrapped her arms round her shoulders. 'If I'd known about this, I would have brought a coat,' she said.

'Sorry – should've warned 'e,' he replied. 'Don't worry though, you'll get used to it soon enough. It's not that cold. It's more down to the contrast between up there and down yer.' He looked her over, nodded a grinning face. 'But don't thee worry you'll be warm enough later, when us gets in the chamber.' He paused to let out a chuckle. 'You might even get too warm... be hot.'

Catherine eyed him suspiciously, his self-confidence... his brazen smile. She thought his behaviour forward, over-familiar. Up on the surface, with his friend David, innuendo had been acceptable, just. But now, alone, and in an isolated place like this, she felt that he should be showing her more consideration, greater respect. He had given her no reason to suggest that he might be planning to take advantage of her, but his remark had highlighted her vulnerability, nonetheless.

She was beginning to regret her decision to come down here with him. She made a show of glancing at her watch. 'I think we should proceed with the business that we came here to conduct,' she said tautly, rubbing her bare upper arms.

His laughter left him and his features took on a quizzical mien. After a moment or two, turning away from her, he said: 'Follow I then.' The tone was flat, offhand, leaving Catherine with the impression that her words had ruffled him. She recalled her earlier assumptions about his character. Clearly he could be prickly, too. Well, so be it, he should learn his manners.

He now led her along a tunnel that she saw was lit by inset electric lighting. Although the illumination was clearly a recent addition, Catherine assumed that the passageway itself was part of the original mine workings. The roof of the tunnel was not very high. At five feet, five inches tall she was okay. But she noted that Christopher Armstrong was forced to bend forwards as he walked. The tunnel was not so very wide either, adequately passable in single-file, but surely too constricted for tin extraction.

'Did miners actually work in here?' she called, as she followed him down the subway. 'I mean, it's not big.'

He let out a good-natured hoot of derision. 'Nah, this was just a service tunnel, nowt to do with the actual tin-bearing workings. There's more room down there, but not a lot when you 'ave to swing a pickaxe. 'Course I'm going back a few years. In modern mines, most of the hard work's done by machines.'

'Did they have machines here?' she asked.

'Nah, it was never mechanised. It were a private affair – small scale. They never produced much.'

With their conversation now turned to the nature of their

surroundings, Catherine began to relax. She did not appreciate sexual suggestiveness, especially from a man she hardly knew.

'It must have been profitable,' she said.

'It were. But when the price of tin fell in the 1980s, that were that.' He glanced over his shoulder. 'And the banks wouldn't help.'

'Some of them are mercenary,' she said.

'They're all the same,' he mumbled, starting off down the tunnel again.

After they had traversed about twenty metres the tunnel merged with a larger passageway, similarly lit to the one they had just exited – and shortly after that they came to a heavy steel door.

Christopher Armstrong swung the door open. 'Mind how thee goes,' he said, leading her through the doorway, 'the seating ain't in yet and there's still rubbish piled about.'

Catherine found herself in a circular chamber of some thirty feet across. From the light that spilled through from the tunnel, she saw there was plenty of room to stand upright. And an updraft of air now moving through the space gave her the impression that the chamber had no ceiling. She could not see a telescope. 'Is this where we can see daytime stars?' she asked.

Ignoring her question, he flicked a switch and the chamber became flooded with light. She could see that all was bare rock. 'Here us be,' he said, grinning and moving into the centre of the area. He spun around, like a circus showman. 'Now, Catherine, if you care to look up…'

She followed his instruction, raising her gaze in no little expectation. She saw that her supposition had been correct: there was no ceiling. They were in fact at the bottom of a mineshaft. A long way above her head she could see the shaft head, and beyond that a patch of clear blue sky. She stared overhead for several moments, squinting into the brightness of the day. At length, puzzled, she said: 'I can't see any stars. I… The sky is too…' Then realisation dawned: she'd read about being able to see the stars in the daytime from the bottom of a well or mineshaft. But it was a fallacy, a myth. In reality, it couldn't be done. He must know that? She turned to Christopher Armstrong, to see his face set in a new kind of grin.

Catherine's heart leapt and she took a step backwards. What a fool. She had allowed herself to be tricked into coming to a deserted place by a… by a stranger. She took another step backwards. Then she saw his grin change to something else, an expression she had seen before.

And in that moment she knew she was going to be raped.

Lying recumbent on his bed, Alex listened to the sound of splashing water. It was coming from the adjoining bathroom. He imagined her in there, in there right now, soaping her body, her skin like silky velvet, the stinging water jets cascading onto her plump breasts, making the nipples turgid and hard, jutting and proud… big, extra big. He flexed his muscles, cradled his head in his hands. But as big as they might be, he would make them bigger. He'd make them stand out like bloody hat pegs. Holy smoke was he up for this, ready to go. He had gone without long enough, too long, but now he was going to get some.

He caught sight of himself in the mirror above the bed. God, he was a big boy tonight, like a tree trunk. She had better get in here quick or she would miss the premiere. If she did miss it, he would make the matinee memorable for her, something she would remember for a very long time to come. He sniggered at a sudden thought. If she missed the premiere, she could call it a premiere ejaculation. But she wouldn't be able to call what followed a matinee idle.

No, she would not. He'd have her calling him the man, the daddy, before this session was over. He reckoned he was good for three turns, at least – and the last one would be a two-hour stint of unbelievable sex. She would feel like she had lived (just) through a bloody tornado, a cyclone. He saw her at the end of it, stretched across the bed, her pussy scarlet, riven and gaping, like an over-ripened pomegranate, turned near inside out by his relentless pounding. In the picture, she turned glazed eyes to his, her lips moved... 'You're the man, Alex. I've been fucked before but... You are the daddy.'

Alex glanced at the doorway to the ensuite. She really was taking her time in there, overdoing her preparations. Perhaps he should go in, gee her up a bit, shag her in the shower... or over the bath tub, duck her head under every now and then, make her gulp and gurgle. He loved to hear a woman do that, swallowing the sap, gulping it down before the sheer volume of the stuff choked her. It was a macho thing – couldn't be avoided. It was the way evolution had shaped us. The selfish gene had ordered the selfish man. But either way would do. Yeah, get in there and... No, he reconsidered his options, let her take her time. He knew she was doing it on purpose, prick-teasing him, dragging out the preliminaries so that he would be chomping at the bit when she eventually showed. And she was right: the longer she kept him waiting, the hornier he would be when the action started. He closed his eyes and tried not to overdo the hornier.

The sweet scent of honeysuckle blossom unclosed his eyes... and there she was, framed in the doorway of the

111

ensuite, Aphrodite… bashful and coy, the virgin bride come to be deflowered. And he had just the instrument with which to do it. He suppressed a smug snicker. Yes, he certainly had. He had a hard-on like a stallion, a hard-on that would take some shifting, a hard-on like a battering ram.

He became fascinated by her tits, two giant teardrops that seemed to sway with the swing of his eyes. Hams… That's what they were: two butchers' hams – jutting and jaunty, jolly and juicy, enough to make your mouth water. And he'd been right about the nipples. You could hang Christmas decorations off those two. By the time he'd finished, you would be able to hang the whole damned tree.

With a jiggle and a juggle and a jingle she crossed the room and stood before him, at the footboard of the bed. He could have sworn she was shaved, earlier, when she had stripped off. But the blonde hair against the pale skin must have fooled him – just a neat little triangle that nestled on the pubic mound. He'd square the hypotenuse of that little beauty before the night was over.

'Where do you want to start, Alex?' She commenced a pirouette, turning herself ballet style until she faced him once more. 'Will it be missionary, doggie, cowgirl… or would you prefer a blowjob?'

He watched her, his dick twitching like the trigger finger of a Western gunfighter facing Wyatt Earp. It was a shame about her arse though. He liked something to get hold of, something to dig his mitts into. On the other hand, to give credit where credit was due, it was a woman's arse: low slung, and with womanly wobbly. But he would have preferred a bit more meat, a bit more…

And it was then that she vanished, a puff of smoke, abracadabra, disappeared… gone. Just like that. Bewildered,

Alex scanned the room. Where was she? Where the heck? His gaze became frantic. Where? He was cheated. She'd fooled him, run off – left him high and dry, stiff as a ramrod. He was back to hand jobs again. The bitch! Then he saw her head appeared above the footboard of the bed, like a charmed snake rising from its basket, complete with the tongue, flicking and licking, and full with the promise of joys yet to come. He breathed a sigh of relief. Holy cow, that was some slick move; she must have dropped to her knees just as he blinked – still prick-teasing him. She would regret doing that. Once inside her, he would do her so bloody hard that friction would set light to her bush.

Over the footboard she came, like an anaconda with tits, lumpy lava, with the stealth of a bitch intent on wringing every last drop of manhood from his manhood. Let her try… Bring it on. Once he got going his gonads could produce it faster than his dick could ejaculate it. He watched her coming, head, shoulders, tits, nipples dragging coarse across his flesh, until… How could she do that?

Alex stared up into the mirror. How could she do that? No one had… She was a bloody sword swallower. He wasn't complaining though. But how could she do it – and that too…? Every nerve end in his body, every neuron in his brain, seemed focused on that part of him that was no longer visible… and the tongue that was (incredulously!) licking his balls. Alex closed his eyes and concentrated. He wasn't complaining.

He was not complaining. Alexander King did not complain about things like that. That would be like having the longest dick in the world then grumbling because it was only a millimetre longer than your nearest rival.

No, he was not complaining.

On the contrary, he was in paradise; he was in heaven. He

had just been awarded the biggest bonus in banking history. He'd been given the keys to the coffers of the Bank of England. He was on cloud *soixante-neuf*...

How could she do that as well? How? She was an acrobat, a trapeze artist... a contortionist. She'd damned well squared the circle – she'd need quantitative easing if she wasn't careful.

Alex watched her, unable to comprehend what he was seeing let alone what he was feeling. He settled down for a long night... the longer the better.

The more protracted the better...

And on and on she went...

It took him long enough to do so, but eventually Alex realised that something was amiss, that not everything was perfect – hunky-dory, to use her favourite phrase. For an awareness came to him then that it wasn't going to happen for him. There was no need to hold back, to save himself for her – he just knew that, when the time came, he would not be able to consummate. There was feeling there... plenty, but it wouldn't go any further. He was held in some kind of pre-orgasmic suspension, his bell-end cryogenically frozen. His view was blocked, but he knew that she was grappling with his gonads. She must have hold of something that was preventing completion. He'd read somewhere...

And now, as if by some magical spell, she was sitting on him, doing her thing – and doing it bloody well. Go for it, girl. He would come now. No worries. He would fill her full of it. He had names for when Catherine did this. *The Western Weave*; *The Polish Plunger*... He might have to come up with a new one for this. But he couldn't think what. There was too much going on... too much of everything. That was the trouble. You couldn't pin it down. It was changing all the time. She was defying the laws of physics. What about *The Helical*

Helicopter? Or… *The Spiral Screwdriver?* Neither was quite on the money.

But it didn't matter. It really did not matter. He would get on top in a minute, then he would show her.

Alex knew he was beaten – gazumped. She had been going at it hell-for-leather, for ever, for all time, and still he was thwarted. He was stretched to his limit. Her pussy was attached to his prick like a limpet, a slippery clam that wouldn't let go. He needed to come, urgently. He kept feeling like he was going to – but he couldn't. Every time he got near, the feeling cut out. She had him trapped on the edge, fixed in an event horizon, suspended on the brink – on the brink of ecstasy, yet a billion light years from it. If she didn't allow him to release soon, he was going to erupt in an explosion of gory oblivion. Oh, come on, please.

Please…

But Alex knew her game, knew what she was up to. He had seen through her scheme, her diabolical scheme. It was obvious. She was paying him back for all the rebuffs he had dealt her, that was it. The bitch had spiked his drink earlier. She had slipped in a spiteful potion, and instead of coming he was going.

He was going to die. He knew it. There was no doubt about it. If he didn't come soon… or get her off him, he was going to be extinguished, snuffed out like a trodden on fag end.

Alex attempted to push her away… but the strength in his arms had already gone. He tried again. But it was futile. She had done a Samson on him. Without cutting his hair, the evil bitch had emasculated him… castrated him. He was at her mercy. His life was in her hands.

And now, with his ending nigh, he could see the

aftermath. Triumphant in her victory, she would fetch Catherine home, show her his effete body: 'There you are, Catherine – *hunky-dory*. That's how you do it, that's how you defeat them, a little feminine wile, turn their animal lusts against them.' Feminist pig! He saw Catherine grinning, laughing, cruelly mocking his shrivelled body, rejoicing in his comeuppance. Tears sprang to his eyes and he started to cry. Oh, Catherine, I love you. Catherine, I'm sorry.

Through his remorseful tears, he stared up into the mirror, and still she was grinding him, pile driving him into oblivion. Grown men don't cry. But he could not stop. He could not staunch the flow of tears, scalding tears that were cascading down his face. And in his ruin he saw that her hips had become as rotund as Catherine's. He saw the cheeks of her arse, a fleshy metronomic duo, counting down the death-knell blows to his demise.

'I don't want to die.' His words emerged from his mouth like a crybaby's blubber – spittle ran down his chin. 'I've always meant well.'

'I love you, Alex.'

His manhood seemed ready to explode, split like a busted banana. 'Oh, please… please… I won't do it again. I'm sorry.

'I'm so sorry…'

And it was then that it happened, at the extremis of his woes, at the point when he thought that nothing worse could happen, absolutely nothing-on-earth worse, when he knew that shortly he would face his Maker, that the transmogrification occurred. It wasn't over, she was still going at it full tilt, and he could still feel the clutch of her female parts, but in that dreadful, awful, dire *moment* her flesh simply melted away, dripped like candle wax from her bones, and he saw that he was being ridden by a skeleton.

Alex shot bolt upright in his bed. 'Annaaaa!' He cried the name of his nocturnal visitor, his succubus. 'Annaaaa…' He shouted it again, and again… And in that brief post-nightmare moment, the clutch of her female parts remained with him… and he knew that he could… in fact, he knew that he was going to…

In a little while, grown cold in the bedtime heat, using his free arm, he scooped himself out of bed and made off for the ensuite. What a dream. What a bloody fabulous dream. He wouldn't need a hand job for a week. He stepped into the shower. If he could find a formula for that, a formula to create dreams like that, he would make a bloody fortune.

Catherine felt her back make contact with the rock face of the chamber, cold, damp, jagged, like a rack of icy spikes. She pressed harder against them. Her knees felt weak, as though they might give way, and she would sink to the ground. She knew that must not happen – her best chance of escape was to stay upright, on her feet. But he looked so menacing, alert, ready to block any move she might make. She tried to speak, but her words would not come, merely a nervy croak – fear had paralysed her vocal cords. And still he came, corralling eyes, inching forward, stalking her, like a cat cornering a mouse.

The atmosphere in the chamber seemed colder, clammier, and from somewhere along the tunnel the sound of dripping water became a physical presence. Her senses were attuned; her adrenalin was up. It was the classic flight or fight syndrome. A thought came to Catherine then that she might be able to dodge round him, get out of the chamber and into the passageway. But… but that would not do, for he would surely overhaul her. She wouldn't make it to the lift. And even if she did get that far, there would not be time to get inside, close the door, operate the controls. And trying to resist him would be futile. He was as strong as Alex… stronger.

This was worse than the time with Alex, for then she had known that he would not physically hurt her. She wasn't sure with Christopher Armstrong. She did not know what he was capable of – she did not know him. Would he simply take what he wanted, not harm her otherwise? She could suffer that. Or would he be rough? She did not want to be beaten… punched. Catherine knew that for many men rape had less to do with obtaining sexual pleasure than it had with intimidation, control, using sexual violence against their victims. She experienced nausea knot her stomach like a cramp. This was her fault: she should not have come down here with him. But he had seemed so kind, so trustworthy. She knew now that he was not.

It was likely that she would not leave here alive. To evade prosecution, a jail sentence, he might decide to kill her. For a criminal, it would make sense to do so – it was logical. And there must be a myriad of places in which to hide a body, where a search party would never find it. He must know that. Catherine was famed for her clear-headedness, her nerve under pressure, but now, as she pressed her spine against the cold rock, she could feel her heart pounding as never before.

Just the other day she had read an article about a woman's body being discovered in a disused mine. The corpse had been concealed under a pile of gravel in a little byway off a side tunnel. The woman had been missing for months, and only chance had solved her disappearance: mining was to be restarted and survey work had revealed her decomposing body. By the time Catherine's body was found, it would be a skeleton.

She didn't want to die. Maybe it would be best, she thought, to offer herself to him, to make as though she wanted him. At least that way she wouldn't die. But he might see through her ploy, kill her anyway... Another thought, desperate, born of a desire to survive, entered her head: she could pretend to enjoy it, imply willingness for more. And she would not actually have to go through with it a second time. Once she was free... out of here...

He caught up with her then, was just an arm's length away, his features shadowy in the low-level light. She determined then that she would not submit, that she would not meekly lie down. Doing so had contributed to her downfall with Alex. This time she would resist, defend herself. And with that thought, Armstrong came into sharper focus, and the sound of dripping water grew louder. Having resolved to fight back, adrenalin was making sure she was ready to do so. She gathered her hands into claws... Then she heard him say:

'Catherine, be thee all right?'

She stared at him, like a rabbit caught in headlights, her heartbeat palpitating, her mind muddled, trying to understand, struggling to relate what she was hearing to the scene, to her circumstance.

'Catherine... be thee all right?' He repeated his question, but with more feeling, added concern.

She continued to stare... trying to believe.

He posed his question again. 'Be thee all right?'

Catherine suddenly felt as though she were about to pee herself. She was. An incipient belief that he did not mean to... Right there, in front of him, she was going to piss her pants. Half-turning, she placed a hand on the rock wall to steady herself. But the sensation continued to well. It was as if she had consumed a vast amount of water, the consequence of which had spontaneously overhauled her. Not now, not here – please. Somehow the thought righted her and, slowly, little by little, the feeling ebbed away.

'Thee looks ill. Catherine, be thee well?'

The effort, the determination to quell the urge to urinate, had further focused her mind – had straightened her thinking. She fixed him with a suspicious eye, alert for any sudden threatening advance; her heart was still going all out. Her voice would still not come.

He took a pace backwards, his eyes examining her face. Catherine saw that his expression had changed: the taut features had relaxed, the bottled lines had dissolved. He no longer appeared threatening. 'You be as white's a sheet, Catherine.'

Catherine trembled as a small sense of relief rose within her breast – he had, expressed a concern. He wasn't going to attack her. But... but she wasn't sure: she thought the change in him might be a cover for something else, a ploy to get her to drop her guard, then she would be easy game – and he would strike.

'Yer, have a go at this,' he went on, taking a hip flask from his trouser pocket. ''Tis summut I always carries with me: a ready tot of rum.' He unscrewed the cap and offered her the flask. 'Go on. 'Twill make 'e feel better.'

She realised then, belatedly, stupidly, that he did not need a ploy to get her off guard. He could overpower her whenever he wanted to. Catherine started to accept the proffered flask... But then she paused, withdrew her hand. For the fear came to her that it might be drugged, that he might have added a sedative in preparation for this moment. 'No... No, thank you.'

'Go on,' he repeated, still holding out the flask. ''Twill perk 'e up no end. And you're still as white's a sheet.'

Catherine continued to stare. She thought that he seemed sincere – and if he had intended to do anything, wouldn't he have done it by now? She gazed into his eyes, saw something there, kindness, anxiety for her wellbeing? Maybe her experience with Alex had affected her judgement, had made her see a threat where none existed. And he had backed off even farther now; he wasn't threatening her personal space anymore. She nodded, accepted the flask from his outstretched hand, her own hand still shaking.

'Thank you. Thank…' Then, abruptly, precipitously, on the heels of her gratitude, the earlier feeling returned. And this time she discovered that it was unstoppable, heedless to endeavour, and, unable to control her bladder, she wet herself, felt the hot bloom as the liquid flowed from her – a great relieving gush that left her weak-kneed and trembling.

Mortified, feeling her femininity undermined, she stared at him, gripped the flask as though she meant to throttle it… and waited for his signal of repulsion, his disgust at what he had witnessed – and the anticipation of the clinging coldness of wet linen to come.

That it had been caused by a nervous reaction, a physical response to a traumatic event, Catherine was aware. She had seen it before, in a friend. Only twelve at the time, she would never forget it. Marilyn suffered from anxiety attacks, and if she did not empty her bladder in a timely manner, a sudden shock or threatening situation could set her off. They had been walking home from the cinema when it happened. A group of teenage boys had followed them outside, were being a nuisance, pestering, taunting – showing off, as adolescent boys are sometimes disposed to do. Catherine had seen that her friend was getting more and more agitated, and had tried to calm her, but a spate of suggestive remarks had finally provided the trigger. Poor Marilyn had wet her knickers, a veritable torrent… like she herself had just done.

She continued to stare… continued to wait…

'Go on,' he encouraged, inclining his head towards the flask in her hands. 'You'll feel better fer it.'

Catherine glanced at the flask. He hadn't noticed. But surely he soon would. He couldn't fail to do so. She waited… and waited… watched his expression as she waited. Then, slowly, little by little, awareness came to her that she hadn't urinated. Pretending to examine the flask, she shot a glance down at herself.

'Go on,' he repeated, following her gaze.

After a moment, she brought the flask to her lips. No, she had not peed. Raising the flask, she took a thoughtful sip.

He watched her swallow the liquid. 'You gave I quite a turn then,' he said. 'I thought fer a moment thee were gonna faint spark out.'

She shivered as an after tremor ran through her body. 'I'm fine,' she said, fighting now the desire to let go in a bout of hysterical laughter. 'Just give me a moment.' She took another sip of the drink, a bigger one this time, then another, a veritable gulp… and coughed as the fiery liquid burnt her throat.

'Yer, leave some fer I,' he joked. His expression became serious. 'Are thee sure thee be all right?'

Catherine handed him the flask. 'I'm okay… I think.' She watched him take a draw from the container. 'I'm okay,' she repeated. His concern was genuine – he wasn't faking it. She was certain of that. She had misread his earlier expression, had attributed something to it that wasn't there – mistaken his intentions. It was not the first time that such a thing had happened – she was famous for it. And alongside this final realisation came a reciprocal feeling. Catherine now wanted to forestall any risk of him thinking he was the cause of her fear. It was part of her psyche, her mental makeup, an overriding desire to assuage others, to place concern for their feelings above her own discomfort – even when she herself had been scared half to death. Glancing down at her hands, she said: 'I just suffer from claustrophobia from time to time, that's all.'

'But thee said, when I asked 'e about going down in the lift, that you were okay with it.'

'Generally, I am,' she said. 'It happens so rarely nowadays.' She then embarked on a rambling story of childhood claustrophobia, involving a supposed episode of being stuck in a lift, before concluding: 'I thought I'd grown out of it.'

'Then I'd best get 'e out of this place, hadn't I?' he said, starting to turn towards the exit from the chamber.

Catherine remained where she was. 'I'm all right now,' she said confidently. 'Give me another minute.'

Christopher Armstrong studied her face. 'You still don't look so perky. Yer colour's returned, but thee still ain't right. I thinks I should get 'e back up to the surface. A bit of fresh air will do 'e well.'

But still she hesitated. With the fear of assault behind her, together with the fillip from the alcohol, her spirit had rebounded. The feeling was little short of euphoric. Her adrenalin was still up, but it had nothing to do. 'I came here to see daytime stars,' she said challengingly, pointing to the patch of blue far above their heads. 'But it can't be done from down here, can it? I've read about the so-called phenomenon. It's fiction. It appears in books. But it is an invention.'

Chris Armstrong also glanced skyward. 'Be it?' he said. 'Be it really?'

She nodded. 'Yes, it is.'

He went across to the wall by the steel door. 'I had planned to give 'e the wow factor,' he said, grinning, 'but because of your little turn just now, I won't switch on the primary lighting without warning 'e first.' He snickered knowingly. ''Tis about to get pretty bright in yer.' He reached up to a panel that was set into the wall. Catherine hadn't previously noticed the panel but now she saw that it contained a row of electrical switches and a numbered dial. As he had indicated, she guessed that he intended to turn on additional lighting. But for what purpose she had no idea. 'Now, be thee ready, Catherine?' he asked. 'Best look down at the ground... till thee gets used to it.'

She directed her gaze to the rock floor. 'I'm ready,' she said, shutting her eyes against the anticipated brightness.

'Here us goes, then... Oh, mustn't forget to warn 'e, don't look directly into the lights. They be halogen and pretty powerful. Here us goes then.'

Catherine tried to close her eyes, only to discover that they were already shut. It felt as if she were on a sunbed: the light and heat were palpable. It was quite pleasant. Already she felt warm... Of a sudden she recalled his earlier remark, suggesting that she might feel hot later. He had made it when they first arrived underground, when she had complained of feeling cold. She had been affronted by it. It appeared she had got that wrong as well. Wondering if it would be wise to put on her sunglasses, she kept her eyes closed. But when she finally opened them, encouraged by Christopher Armstrong to do so, she found the chamber was illuminated as bright as day – brighter, much brighter. Its circular wall had become a scintillating mirror, iridescent, as though lit by the light of a thousand tiny suns, each one seemingly part of the very rock face itself.

Chris Armstrong came and stood by her side. 'Now thee can look up,' he said. 'Look straight up through the shaft.'

Catherine followed his direction. 'Wow. Yes, there they are.' She hopped up and down in her excitement. Her earlier alarm had been soundly acquitted. 'I can see them,' she added gleefully.

'Obviously you can only see a small patch of sky,' he said. 'But different times of the day – and other times of the year – will reveal different stars.' He pointed with his finger. 'But see, there, that bluish one, that's Vega.'

'It's much brighter than the others,' she said.

'It's the fifth brightest star in the sky, not counting the Sun. Furthermore, it is only twenty-five light years away, which makes it one of the closest. It is 2.1 times as massive as the Sun, but its life span is only one tenth that of our star.' He paused and placed a casual hand on her shoulder, indicating with the other hand as if pointing something out to a child. 'It's in the constellation of Lyra.' Catherine thought briefly of asking him to remove his hand from her shoulder, but he seemed so engaged, so taken with his description, that she let his familiarity pass and continued to listen to his enthusiastic commentary on the overhead scene. After a while, seemingly content with his performance, he concluded: 'And although we can't see it at the moment, Proxima Centauri in the constellation of Centaurus is the closest to Earth at just over four light years' distance.'

Catherine gazed at Christopher Armstrong. During his discourse she had noticed the disappearance of his accent, noted too the absence of idiom. She realised now that it had been a strange experience, listening to him – quite a different Chris… Professor Christopher. Catherine was impressed. She said: 'You're quite an authority on the stars. Did you study astronomy at college?'

At her question, he turned abruptly on his heel and made off across the chamber. She observed him, now standing at the door. His expression was perplexed... almost panicked. Her compliment had clearly unnerved him. But why would it do that? she wondered. And she had only added a simple query to it – a valid one at that. He must have acquired his knowledge somewhere. 'Better switch 'em off now,' he said, reaching for the electrical panel. 'Too much of it ain't good fer the eyes.'

She watched him coming back across the chamber. With the dimming of the lighting, the area was returned to an eerie twilight. The brightest thing now was the beam of light coming down the shaft from the patch of clear blue sky above their heads. 'How's it done?' she asked. 'You know, being able to view stars from down here in the daytime?'

'It's me hobby, Catherine. That's how I knows about 'em.' He shot her a furtive glance. 'Mind you, I don't know that much: there's too many of 'em fer that.'

'You know a lot more than I do, Christopher...' She fell silent. That was the first time she had actually addressed him by his name. In a flash, it seemed to have added a new dimension to their association, a familiarity. And, she realised, it had given her an odd feeling, a buzz, almost as if she had agreed to an illicit liaison. She frowned through a smile. There was more to Christopher Armstrong than initial impressions suggested. He was turning out to be an enigma – hard to fathom. 'You didn't answer my question,' she said, gazing almost shyly into his deep-set blue eyes.

'It's quite simply, really, Catherine,' he began. 'See, when 'tis dimpsy down yer, your eyes become accustomed to it and the brightest thing is the sky outside the shaft – and you can't see nothing.' He paused and pointed up. 'Like now. But if you makes it really bright, brighter than the patch of sky overhead, yer eyes get used to that and the sky outside the shaft appears darker than it actually is… And, hey presto, there they all be.'

'Well, I wouldn't describe it as simple,' she observed. 'In fact, I would say that it's extremely clever.' She paused, assessing him. 'Who worked it all out?'

'We'd best be getting back, otherwise the stars a be out and you'll be asking I questions about 'em. Then you'll see just how little I really knows.' He opened the door. 'C'mon then,' he said, grasping her hand. 'This way.'

Catherine thought about freeing her hand from his. But of a sudden his grip seemed pleasantly secure. 'Okay,' she said.

Chapter 8

Catherine returned her mobile to her bag, then continued walking along the quayside. It seemed that nothing much was happening at home. Alex was being a good boy, if a little tetchy at work. Anna appeared to have lost interest in him in favour of a new recruit in Accounts. And Alex's friend Gregory Hitchins was conspicuous by his absence. "Tetchy". Was he having recriminations for what he had done? Or was his tetchiness due to his enforced celibacy? She would like to think that it was the former but had to admit that it was probably the latter. Or could it be that he was ruing his missed opportunity with Anna? She smiled wryly. But of course he had not done that, far from it. Procuring a new boyfriend had never previously deterred her from looking for more. With Anna it was a case of the more the merrier.

The sky was overcast today and an onshore breeze had arrived, bringing with it wispy strands of sea mist. In the distance, through the spray, she could see that the ocean was choppy, with white horses cresting the waves. The change in the weather was ill-timed, as she was going sailing. Well, not exactly sailing, not in the yachting sense anyway. Following the trip to the disused mine workings, and the thrill of daytime stargazing, she had accepted an invitation from Christopher Armstrong to go mackerel fishing.

And there he was. Catherine spotted him, farther along the quay, standing beside his boat. She saw immediately that it was a big one... a large cruiser. She could not recall it being there yesterday. But perhaps his crew had been at sea then. It did not appear to require repairs, as he had indicated. On the contrary, it looked new, as if just delivered. Despite what he had said, fishing must be a lucrative living. She started to wave.

That was odd. He must have seen her waving to him. So why was he darting off across the wharf like that? There was nothing there, just a plain rock face. It was, Catherine thought, almost as if he was trying to avoid her? Maybe he had had second thoughts about the trip today, decided against taking her out.

When she arrived at the point adjacent to his boat, she saw what the attraction was: about halfway up the precipice, balanced precariously on a narrow ledge, was a cat. It was obviously trapped there, seemed unable to move forwards or backwards. Her gaze settled on Chris. From his posture at the base of the wall, it appeared as if he intended to try and rescue it, to climb up and bring it down. She thought it a decent thing to do. But it was awfully steep, sheer. Fearful of an accident, Catherine clasped nervous hands. Nevertheless, she was relieved to discover that he was not trying to give her the slip.

She noted that he was returned to his workaday clothes: dungarees like those he had worn when escorting her down from the cliff top, but a dark blue polo-neck sweater had replaced the shirt. His hair was once more in working duties mode too – at least so were the extremities that protruded from below his nautical cap. He looked every inch the seafarer, every fathom the skipper. She wasn't so sure about the mountaineer though. Those leather boots would not provide much adhesion on the climb. And the rock looked damp, and coated in places by a type of mossy growth. Those things would make it slippery.

Listening to the cat's plaintive meowing, Catherine watched as Christopher Armstrong began to scale the rock wall. She thought it was a long way up: much higher than a house. She could see that it wasn't going to be an easy climb. The only way seemed to be via a series of ledges, where the moss was growing. Those would require scaling one by one. And, other than the ledges themselves, she could not see any obvious handholds. The rock was smooth. And if he made it to the ledge where the cat was trapped, he would have to move sideways until he reached it. That would not be easy. And how would he bring it down? He would have to hold onto it – and that would leave him only one hand for gripping.

Already a group of holidaymakers had gathered nearby. She heard one observe in a Birmingham accent: 'The bugger must be barmy, going up there like that. Those ledges aren't even as wide as his boots.'

'Dead right, mate,' came another voice. 'One slip and he's done for.'

'And all for a stupid cat,' someone else commented.

Catherine held her breath as she watched Christopher Armstrong haul himself up onto another ledge. She estimated that he was at least thirty feet above the ground, and that was solid rock too. If he fell onto that, he would surely break some bones… or worse. She released her breath in a sigh, thinking. If she had arrived earlier, maybe she could have persuaded him against the venture. Nevertheless, he was almost there: the next ledge up was where the cat was trapped. It looked as scared as a mouse. Its whiskers were twitching as if it was thinking of making a leap for freedom. Catherine hoped that it decided against doing so.

Then she realised that she had seen it before – black and

white, with ginger markings, it was Conger, the one that had stolen the mackerel. She could hardly believe the evidence of her eyes. He had seemed such a crafty cat, sharp-witted, not the sort to get himself stuck on a rock ledge. And why would it want to go up there, she asked herself? Perhaps something had frightened it. Maybe a fisherman had caught it stealing a fish and had shouted at it. Poor thing. She crossed her fingers… and waited.

As Christopher now shuffled along the final ledge towards Conger, Catherine noted that the group of holidaymakers had grown into a crowd. People were actually jostling one another to get the best view; and cameras were clicking as though a pack of paparazzi had descended on the town in pursuit of a visiting celebrity.

'He's nearly there,' somebody observed.

'Aye,' came a Scottish response, 'but he still has got ta bring the bairn down.'

A hush descended on the onlookers as Christopher Armstrong made it to the trapped animal. Catherine almost gasped aloud as she watched him bend his knees and reach towards it. The man who had made the comment about the ledges not being as wide as his boots was right. She could clearly see the overhang of the soles. If one foot slipped off, then the other would surely follow.

Then it happened. With Christopher's hand just inches from it, Conger started to back away farther along the ledge. Catherine watched, anxious hands clenched, as it now showed Chris its teeth and hissed threateningly.

'Guessed that would happen,' somebody said smugly. 'How's the moggy supposed to know that his saviour has arrived?'

'Idiot!' Catherine muttered under her breath.

But then in a movement that brought a collective sigh

from the onlookers, Christopher Armstrong hopped forward, collared the animal by the scruff of its neck and stowed it down the front of his dungarees.

Catherine thought he had an excellent sense of balance – like a tightrope walker. But the descent would have to be done backwards, she knew, essentially feeling for blind footholds. That would be harder.

'And now for the easy bit.' An ironic voice rose above the hubbub.

'Oh, shut up,' Catherine murmured unpleasantly.

A camera clicked. 'That may be his last portrait,' the photographer said. 'I should make something from the local rag if it is.'

'Idiot!' Catherine muttered, repeating her earlier expletive.

Clutching her bag to her chest, she watched as Chris now commenced the return journey. It seemed to take for ever as he descended the rock face, hand over hand, ledge by ledge. She could see that coming down was indeed even more precarious than going up. In the tradition of dramatic rescues, her heart was in her mouth, her breath held. But at last, to a chorus of cheers, he stood once more on terra firma – where, to more cheers, he released Conger.

'Well done, mate,' a voice said, as several people now emerged from the crowd to slap him on the back.

'That'll be something to tell them back home,' another voice said.

'Not arf,' came a Cockney accent.

Congratulations arrived from all quarters and more photographs were taken. Catherine noted that even the man who had "predicted" the cat's retreat went over to congratulate the hero.

Then she noticed Conger peering warily from behind the stack of nearby drum barrels. Smiling, she winked at him, wondered how many of his nine lives he had expended today. If they caught any mackerel, she decided he would have one – to make up for his experience.

Eventually the crowd dispersed and Christopher Armstrong came across to where she was standing. She paused for a moment to assess him: the hooded eyes, as blue as hers were green, the square jawline, the determined line of his mouth, the way he held himself – erect, proud... a man defiant of convention. He may not be her type but he was nonetheless continuing to awaken her awareness. Unable to prevent her mind from running on, she imagined being in his arms, his strong arms... Catherine scolded herself: it was too soon for such thoughts. Anyway, even if she and Alex did not get back together, it was not her way to engage in casual sex – and that was all it ever could be between them. She was no longer a teenager, no more the kid seeking silly adventure. Youthful dreams had long since been usurped by mature pragmatism, and professional ambition. It was called growing up. Basking in his metaphorical shadow, she said:

'That was quite a show.'

He shrugged broad shoulders. 'It were nothing.' He looked her up and down, from her "sensible" shoes to her bobble hat. 'I sees you're well dressed up against the elements.' He felt the sleeve of her Barbour jacket. 'Ah, that'll do 'e... keep 'e warm enough out there.'

'No, I mean it,' she said. 'What you did was awfully impressive. It must... it must have taken a lot of courage.'

Ignoring her comment, he took her arm and led her across the walkway. 'Well, what do 'e think of her, *The Lucky Lady*?'

He was clearly a man indifferent to compliments – a complex man, as she had already surmised. She gazed up into his eyes, questioning eyes that were waiting for her opinion.

'Well..?' he repeated, raising his arm.

Catherine followed the sweep of his hand, past the sign that advertised mackerel fishing trips at £15.50 a head, to the pristine cruiser. She decided that it looked even nicer close up – sleek, like a streamline spacecraft. She would enjoy her trip today – a touch of luxury, a taste of... But then, denying her any more time for anticipation, and to her dismay, his gesture swept past the cruiser... to *The Lucky Lady*.

Perhaps fishing wasn't so lucrative after all. She ran an appraising eye over the vessel at which his finger now pointed. At the bow was a small wheelhouse. She saw that paint was peeling from the woodwork and a pane of glass was missing from the storm windows at the front. The door to the wheelhouse was propped open and inside she could see a panel containing knobs and dials. With no little shock, she guessed that it was the boat's radio equipment... Her father had collected old wireless sets. He had had an old Marconi a little like that one.

She moved closer, peered over the side. Single-plank seating encircled the exposed middle and stern of the boat, in the centre of which was a hold. She shot a disparaging glance at the wheelhouse. The whole package appeared basic. And it looked so tiny: not much larger than a family car. She was not impressed. Neither was she convinced by the boat's name. It might be a lady but it did not appear auspicious. Catherine recalled then the amount he had said was required for renovation. She was no authority, but to her eye twenty-five thousand pounds seemed less than adequate – far less. She turned back to its captain. 'Is it safe?' she asked. But then, noting his sudden look of dismay, she added quickly: 'I mean... to go out fishing today. You know... the weather, the choppy conditions.'

His face broke into a grin. 'Ah 'course 'tis. You should see some of the weather we has to go out in sometimes.' His grin widened, and he waved an arm towards the sea. 'Today is as flat's a mill pond.'

Catherine gazed across the quay to the open sea. The harbour looked all right but out there was anything but, and that was where they were going. 'I think I'll give it a miss. Perhaps another time...'

'Ah c'mon, Catherine,' he said, taking her hand. 'Don't be a sissy. Us is only going out in the bay. The land a be always in sight.'

'I don't know.'

'And you'll have a life jacket on – self-inflating. But thee won't need un, I promise. That be just a precaution we has to do nowadays, fer the public. So don't thee worry none; you'll be safe enough.'

'I'm not sure...' Catherine threw a glance at the boat. 'It's just that–'

He gave her arm an encouraging tug. 'Everybody knows I be the safest skipper in the port.' His expression became a broad grin. 'Ah, thee'll be fine. I'll hoist the Jolly Roger, me hearty, an' neither Captain Flint nor Blue Beard a bother us.' He paused, pulled on her sleeve. 'Now, what will 'e say, Jim Lad?'

She made up her mind. Scowling as though she were being pressganged, she said: 'That's the worst imitation of Robert Newton I've ever heard.' Then she allowed him to lead her onto the boat.

'That's me girl.'

Catherine shuffled along the space between the seating and the hold to the prow, stood by the wheelhouse, took her nautical bearings. Actually, she decided, in spite of its limited size, it seemed quite a solid construction. There was no indication that it wasn't seaworthy. On the contrary, it felt quite stable beneath her feet. Perhaps she had worried unnecessarily.

Christopher Armstrong fetched a leather holdall from the wheelhouse. 'Fancy giving us a hand?' he said, offering her the bag. 'All you gotta do is stand over there by the steps and smile whenever a likely-looking holidaymaker comes by.' He squeezed her arm. ''Course, you can wink too, if you want.'

Suddenly taken with the idea of helping out her skipper, Catherine took the holdall from him. 'Ay, ay, captain,' she quipped. If Alex could see her now: the financial guru luring holidaymakers aboard the good ship *The Lucky Lady*. He would never believe it.

'There's a roll of tickets in there, and change… fer the high rollers.' He cast an eye over her figure, finally coming to rest on her face. 'Ah, you'll do well enough, with the young men.'

And he was right. For in no time at all, every available seat was occupied, mostly by lads but with a sprinkling of female faces amongst them. Catherine mentally totted up the takings: fifteen customers at £15.50 each came to two hundred and thirty-two pounds and fifty pence. From his contented expression, she could see that Captain Chris was happy with her stewardship so far. Smiling, she said: 'All ready to cast off, sir.'

Christopher Armstrong now passed around the previously mentioned life jackets, and then read out a standard safety drill. It appeared that, in the unlikely event of the ship capsizing, all they had to do was stay together, floating in the sea, until they were picked up, which would only be a matter of minutes. He would already have sent out a distress call. What could be simpler? And he hadn't mentioned anything about whales or great white sharks. She caught sight of her reflection in the wheelhouse glazing, turned up the collar of her coat. Call me Ahab... Or should that be Quint? She turned down her collar once more. It didn't matter: each man had met the same fate.

Chris started up the motor and, in the wake of a weary chuff, the boat edged away from the quayside. Catherine coughed as diesel fumes from the engine found her nostrils. She hoped they didn't bring on sea sickness. That would spoil the trip... for everyone.

She recalled then a school outing on a pleasure cruiser. They had sailed down the Thames from their school in Twickenham to Greenwich. The plan was to visit the observatory in the afternoon, where a guided tour had been booked for them. The young Catherine had anticipated it for weeks. But even before they reached Battersea Park she had started to feel ill, and by the time they chugged under Tower Bridge she had just wanted to die – and the feeling had lasted long after their landing at Greenwich. She had spent most of the afternoon sitting on a bench in the observatory grounds, trying to keep something down that would have been better jettisoned. That was the problem of course: her determination. If she had given in to the feeling and been sick, she would have felt better. Catherine smiled suddenly. Although, that was the afternoon she had memorised her twenty-four times table. So it hadn't been an entirely wasted day. But it was a pity she hadn't remembered that trip earlier. Too late to back out now though, for already they were heading for the harbour exit... and the open sea beyond.

Outside the protection of the quay wall, the sea was decidedly choppier and Catherine, not a little unnerved, braced herself against the wheelhouse framework. It was a little bit like standing on the Tube. The boat didn't go as fast, but its lurching movements were just as unpredictable. Seeking reassurance she glanced at Chris, but he was occupied at the wheel.

'You the captain's mate, Miss?' The question raised Catherine from her reverie, and she turned her head, to see a boy flashing her a toothy grin. When he came on board with his parents, she had marked him out as trouble – strutting round like a little Napoleon. His mother and father had seemed subordinate, even in awe of his assumed importance.

She eyed the impish smile. 'Oh, yes,' she fibbed, blatantly attempting to give herself some street… sea credibility. She tightened her grip on the wheelhouse upright. 'I often accompany Chris on these trips.'

'Then you should be passing round the rods by now,' came the swift retort. 'Surely you know that.' He glanced at his mother, who nodded a silent accord. 'We come out quite a bit, and all the others have done that.'

Reckoning herself already fully repaid for her hollow boast, Catherine stared at the boy, whose grin had now been replaced by a tight-lipped impatience. "All the others have done that." She wondered how many others there had been. She was clearly not the first. She caught herself. It was none of her business, nothing to do with her. He could invite whomsoever he pleased. Besides some of the others may have been men.

'They're in the locker.' Chris's voice disturbed her thoughts. 'It's beside you… your left.'

Catherine returned her attention to fishing matters. No, she had no claim on him – neither did she want one. She opened the locker door... but only to be halted in her metaphorical tracks. Were these the fishing rods? She had seen fishing rods before but these were tiny things, like toys – no more than a metre long. Nobody was going to catch anything with these. They wouldn't cast far... just over the side into the water. But then common sense came to her rescue. Out here, on a boat, they were sailing amongst the fish, casting was not required – neither were the unwieldy things she had seen anglers using on the beach. Attempting to appear nonchalant, she commenced to distribute the fishing rods.

'There's bait in the hold.' Chris turned round. 'It's already cut up. Give a hand to all those who need it.' He eyed her expression. 'If you can.'

Catherine stared at the bucket. The smell revealed its contents. Surely mackerel didn't eat mackerel? She started to look towards Chris but at that moment the young lad plunged his hand into the bucket and grabbed a piece. 'It's for the hooks,' he said, staring at her as if he thought she were stupid.

'They'll bite at anything, Catherine,' Chris said, grinning at her bewilderment. 'Put a bit of silver paper on yer hook, and they'll even go fer that.'

Then why bother with this smelly stuff? Catherine was beginning to feel out of her depth.

'C'mon lass,' someone cried from the rear of the boat. 'You don't have to touch it. Just walk round. We'll do the rest.'

Proffering the bucket as if she were inviting comment on a profiterole selection, Catherine started to move along the line of anglers. She decided her first fishing trip would also be her last. And then, as if in support of her decision, the boat climbed a sudden wave, teetered momentarily on its crest, before plunging like a roller coaster into the accompanying trough. In her panic, her gaze took in the anglers… who all appeared oblivious to the boat's imminent sinking. Foolhardy, she concluded, all of them – but not her. It was merely a question of knowing one's limits, of being aware of one's capabilities – and fishing was clearly not one of hers. She completed her circumnavigation of the boat, then stowed the bucket ready for the next round. No, she would not come again.

But things got better as the afternoon wore on. The weather improved, the white horses became white ponies, and fish were caught readily. It was as easy to catch them as Chris had said. She learnt how to attach bait to the hooks, how to stow fish in the hold – alive. It was a little upsetting to witness their frenetic flapping, which of course got them nowhere. But it was easy to see where the phrase "Like a fish out of water" came from. And, most important, as Chris had indicated, they did not sail too far out to sea: the shore was always within sight, and gave her something to focus on when *mal de mer* threatened. Everyone had a good time, all caught fish. And as they headed back to harbour, she even felt a little disappointed that the trip was coming to an end.

Chris put his hand on her shoulder. 'You did good, Catherine,' he said, glancing at the boy, then quickly winking at her.

'I'll do better next time,' she said, returning her skipper's gesture. Indeed, she would. And she would buy one of those caps, like the one Chris was wearing. It would make her look the part. Adopting what she believed to be a seafarer's stance, she thought she might even have *The Lucky Lady* printed on the front. She too glanced at the boy. Then there would be no mistaking her status.

Christopher manoeuvred the boat alongside the harbour wall, nudging first one way then the other to ensure a safe mooring. Catherine marvelled at his agility as he secured the craft, leaping between boat and quay, then back again. For a man of his size, he was extremely nimble, an adjunct of working on a fishing boat, she guessed – little wonder then that he was so good at rock climbing. She watched him lay out the gangplank, affixing it between guides on the side of the boat. To her mind, he was clearly an adherent of health and safety, for the device seemed hardly needed. In fact it was only a tiny thing and obviously designed to make stepping from the boat onto the wharf even safer than would otherwise have been the case.

Catherine now stood to one side as the passengers left the boat, each one proudly clutching his catch – one or two even dropped loose change into the hat that Christopher Armstrong had given her to hold – until only she and her skipper were left on board. She observed him, busy now in the wheelhouse, adjusting a lever, moving a handle. The motor was still running and she wondered if there was anything else she could do to help. She had stowed the fishing rods. But she was eager to learn more. Next time…

Then all at once, breaking into her reverie, she heard him instruct her to go on ashore, to wait for him there.

'I just gotta shut down the engine,' he added.

Determined to hide her disappointment at being discharged so summarily, she managed a chirpy: 'Aye, aye, captain.' She wondered if the "others" had been more useful to him, more practical. Well, she had done her best – he couldn't ask for more than that. Catherine placed the hat containing the gratuities on a convenient shelf in the wheelhouse, and turned towards the gangplank. Then she turned back. 'Is there anything else I can assist you with?'

'No, I can manage,' he replied. 'Thee go on. I'll join 'e in a minute.'

'Are you sure? I don't mind—'

'Just do as I say.' He caught her eye, seemed to read her thoughts. 'Just be careful,' he said, less abruptly. 'I don't want 'e falling in.'

A little chagrined at his changed temper, she considered jumping onto the quay, as he had done earlier – show him that she was no slouch, that she had found her sea legs. She could feel him watching her. No, Catherine thought better of it. He had told her to be careful – she would not show off. She placed one foot on the gangplank. Then she remembered Conger's mackerel, glanced over her shoulder, considered fetching him one from the hold. But, following a brief reflection, she decided that it would be best if Chris brought that with him, in a moment, when he finally came ashore. He was obviously busy and wanted her off the boat. She started to transfer her weight onto the foot, leaned forward. Then she felt something move. Maybe the wake of a docking trawler shifted the boat, which in turn dislodged the plank from its guides. She may even have been distracted by a gull swooping for a morsel of fish, and lost her balance. But whatever the cause, as she lifted her other foot, she sensed the boat move a little more.

Obviously, at the first sign of movement, she should have stepped back from the little bridge. Certainly, after the second slippage, she should have done so. But she did not. The quayside was but a step or two away. She thought, if she were quick, that she could make it – and so she stepped completely onto the plank. But no sooner had she done so, than she experienced the boat move again; she lost her footing, and, with a heartfelt shriek, fell between it and the harbour wall into the sea.

In spite of the shock of the cold water, which for a second

robbed her of her breath, she did not panic. That was not in her nature. In any case, she knew that Chris had witnessed the fall – he had been watching her. It wouldn't take him long to pull her out. And her self-inflating life jacket had operated as it was supposed to do: it had righted her. She was safe enough, of course she was. However, contrary to her belief, she soon discovered that she was mistaken; for as she bobbed in the water, it became apparent that the swell of the incoming tide was beginning to buffet the boat against the harbour wall – with increasing force. She was trapped between the two objects and clearly in danger of being crushed. And that's when she started shouting for help.

Alex placed his cup of cocoa on the side table, rose wearily from the sofa and went out to the entry phone. He wondered who was calling on him so late in the evening. It might be Greg. Well, if it was, Alex decided that he wasn't going out for a drink. He'd had a hard day, and an early night he was going to have. All these late nights, and drinking, were affecting his work. He had got into the office late this morning, hung-over, nearly missed an important meeting, for which he had failed to ensure himself fully briefed. And, far more serious, he had made himself look less than competent by not fully addressing the Company's long-term financial exposure to the Heathrow project. Sure it was only a provisional report, but he should have given it more consideration, more of his time. In any case, instead of larking around with Greg like a couple of undergrads, Alex knew that any spare time he had would be better spent trying to find out where Kate was.

But how to do that? he asked himself. The police would not be interested. Catherine was an adult and, moreover, she had left of her own accord, had made it clear that she did not want to be contacted. They would not want to know. They had better things to do than investigate the aftermath of a domestic dispute, for that was all it would be to them. It wasn't for him of course: he loved her and he wanted her back. He missed her. What he wouldn't give to have her here now – to go to bed, make love slowly, tenderly, gazing into each other's eyes. He liked that more than anything else. It drove him near crazy to witness the rhythmic dilations of her pupils, a reflex response to his deeply measured thrusts. Then the heave of her breasts as he brought her to orgasm – the gasps that his lovemaking had brought about... the descending sighs of contentment. And then afterwards to lie together, still fully embraced, to hear her say how much she loved him. Alex swallowed dryly. Fuck! He hoped his visitor was Greg. They didn't have to go clubbing. They could walk round to *The Pen and Wig* – a couple of whiskies would do no harm.

Suffering more from self-pity than from anger, he jabbed a finger at the entry phone's response button, waited impatiently as the picture took life. Three whiskies wouldn't hurt... really, and he needed to talk. If it came to that, they could break open a bottle here. He had plenty of...

Alex came down to earth like a dropped tomato – squashed. The caller was not Gregory Hitchins. 'What do you want, Anna?'

'Oh, Alex,' came the hurried reply, 'you've got to help me. It's Michael. He's given me a pile of notes to type up.' Alex listened as she explained how incredibly technical the notes were, so esoteric that only the Firm's "top brain" could decipher them; how Michael needed the report first thing tomorrow morning. 'Please, Alex,' he heard her conclude breathlessly. 'He is my *boyfriend*.'

Boyfriend! He shook an incredulous head. Tarquin had gone the day before yesterday, usurped by Michael. And he too would find himself written out of the soap before long – that was a given. Boyfriend... She didn't keep them long enough to call them that.

He stared at the woman on the screen before him. It was Anna but not the one he knew. She was wearing an old blouse... with frayed cuffs, even older jeans... and trainers. He had never seen her looking so scruffy. And her hair was a mess, frizzled, bedraggled, as though she had attempted to pull it out by the handful. Maybe the story was genuine. But Michael Mills, Anna's latest conquest, was new in the Company, on the apprenticeship scheme. Alex thought it unlikely that he would be working on anything urgent, let alone important. On the other hand, Mills might be trying to make an early impression, appear keen. And she did look desperate, he could see that. And she was clutching what he thought might be a sheaf of papers. Anyone less panicked would have put them in a briefcase. He decided he would take a quick look, see if there was anything he could do, and then get rid of her. Reluctantly, he pressed the enter button.

Two minutes later, the apartment doorbell rang.

Alex opened the door, then stood aside to allow her to come into the hallway. He thought she looked even more dishevelled in the flesh than she had on the screen. The entry–phone system had masked much of her disarray. But he was still not sure of her motive. He would give short odds that her reason for coming over here tonight had nothing to do with work. It would be interesting to find out if he was right. If he was, she was going straight back out of that door quicker than she came through it – even more dishevelled. 'Look, Anna,' he said warily, 'this had better be urgent, otherwise I'm not going to be amused.'

'Oh, it is urgent, Alex.' She brushed past him, carried on down the corridor to the living room. He followed in her whirlwind wake, watched her take a seat on the sofa. She looked up at him, presented a perplexed face. 'It's so complex... depreciation... liquidity ratio... Huh!' Then, sighing as though her very life was ebbing away, she held the papers towards him. 'Please see what you can make of it.'

Alex took the bundle of A4 papers from her. He saw that the Company logo was genuine – and the report format looked okay. But he still didn't trust her. The reference to her boyfriend had partially reassured him. But she may have mentioned his name for that very reason. He would do well to remember that he was dealing with a particularly resourceful woman – a wily one. Alex sneaked a surreptitious glance over his shoulder. Well, he could be wily too. And he had been – he had prepared his defence before any crime had been committed. Putting aside his concerns, he went to his armchair, then shuffled the papers until they were tidy.

'If you don't mind, Alex,' Anna said, watching him begin the task, 'while you're working your magic, I'll just pop into the bathroom.' And with that, she scuttled from the room.

Alex nodded his head absently and started to read the opening page. Twenty seconds later, less, he looked up. It was gobbledygook, infantile rubbish, the work of a kid. He scanned more pages. If possible, it got worse; even the figures didn't add up. It had to be a trick to get in here. But why write so much of it? A page would have sufficed for her purpose.

And why stage such a charade anyway. She could have simply come by, asked to see Kate – he wouldn't have turned her away. He would not have welcomed her but he wouldn't have refused to let her in. The woman was deranged.

'Hi there, Alex.'

He looked up... and his jaw dropped. Framed in the doorway was Anna. Her blouse was ripped open; her jeans had been removed, as too had her brassiere. In her hand was a pair of torn knickers. He stared at her, shell-shocked. He had suspected trickery, a pass, a proposition, but not this. Not this shit.

'Look what you've done, Alex.' She held the knickers aloft. 'You didn't have to go this far; you didn't have to rip off my clothes.' Alex continued to stare, bemused, unsure of what to do, temporary thrown out of kilter by the action unfolding before him. After a while, reclaiming some lost mental ground, he decided that he liked the way untrammelled tits jiggled when women talked... and it worked best on agitated women. She shook a sorry head. 'But I suppose you men will stop at nothing to get your way.'

He knew he should not have believed her — bloody obvious now. He should have guessed earlier. All that spiel about writing up a report after work — in her own time; in her own *fucking* time. He must have been nuts to have been taken in by it. 'Put your clothes back on, Anna,' he said wearily. 'If you think you can blackmail me, you're going to be disappointed.'

'There's no call to use language like that, Alex, especially when I'm trying to keep you out of prison.' She took several paces towards him. Alex took in the jingle-jangle of her tits, the sway, the swing... the fiery nipples, teats and aureoles that were glossed a florescent red... probably lipstick. Despite himself, his determination not to fall for her routine, he wondered if it was flavoured. 'All I want is a fuck, Alex. Just one and we go our separate ways.'

'Put your clothes on, Anna,' Alex repeated, holding her

stare – a look that now struck him as being a little crazed, askance, as if she was on something... possibly hash. She didn't use the hard stuff, but he knew she smoked now and then. Sighing tiredly, he added: 'Put it back on... like a good girl.'

Ignoring his comment, she came closer. 'You know what I think, Alex,' she said lazily, showing him the tip of a pink tongue. 'I think Catherine has left you.' She threw a desultory glance round the room. 'She's not here, is she? She's gone. And I think I know why.' She paused and her stare narrowed. 'Let's say... let's say that she's gone because you were aggressive with–' She stepped back as Alex started to rise from his chair. But then, seeing him sit down again, she went on cockily: 'If that were the case, maybe I *would* be believed.'

She couldn't know, Alex told himself. No way could she know anything about what had happened after the party. She wasn't here. And Kate would not have told her – neither would Brenda. 'Catherine hasn't left me, Anna. As I told you before, she's visiting a client.' He added focus to his stare. 'And I do not get *aggressive* with anyone, male or female, and certainly not with the woman I love.' He leaned forward in his chair, brought himself nearer. 'You got any idea what the sentence is for defamation of character?'

'You wouldn't come out of a court case too well either, Alex dear,' she said – 'bad publicity. Whatever else happened, some shit would stick. That Mr Squeaky Clean image would take a knock. And the plum job in America...' She inched her hips towards him, aggrandising the peaks and trough of her enticement. 'Just one little fuck... one that you will never forget.'

His warning hadn't fazed her – and he had to admit, it had sounded juvenile, like a playground riposte. He mentally reproached himself. Anna was outwitting him. She had

148

obviously thought all this through, planned it well. She could cause trouble, if she carried out her threat, accused him of molesting her. Sure he'd covered himself. But a good lawyer… Alex considered his options. He really only had one: get her out of here. But how? Not easy, he concluded… without physically throwing her out. And he didn't want to touch her, be drawn into a scuffle, possibly leave a bruise… For the moment he was stymied.

He assessed her, her brazen deportment. She was waiting for his response. "One little fuck, one that you will never forget." Alex wondered what she would be like in bed. From what he'd heard, she was a bloody nympho, insatiable – the more she got, the more she wanted. Once her pussy was turned on, it was all but impossible to turn it off. If Catherine hadn't taken that dildo with her, he would plug her with it, see how long she lasted. No contest. She would probably fuse the lights in the whole bloody building. Anyway, it was an academic question. No way was he going to shag it. He continued to stare, working on his next move.

Clearly taking his silence as a positive, she repeated her entreaty. 'Just one little fuck, Alex…'

His gaze settled on her shaven mons pubis, her front botty, seemingly a hair's breadth from his face. With her having such a small arse, a blind man would find it hard going working out which way round she was. Smiling knowingly, he said: 'But it wouldn't be just one, would it, Anna? Once I'd taken the bait, you would be threatening to tell Catherine. You might even–'

'No I wouldn't Alex,' she interrupted, her face alight with cheery hope. 'I'm a girl of my word.' She gazed around the room, almost as though she were selecting a site for copulation. 'We get it together… once, and that's that.'

'You might even,' he repeated, ignoring her reassurance, '*ensure* that she found out, so that you had an exclusive deal.'

'Think a lot of yourself, don't you?' Her bonhomie vanished and the words came out like a dagger thrust.

There was only one answer to give, and he gave it. 'You seem to, Anna,' he said, bouncing a brief glance to her sex.

'I love you, Alex,' she declared, embarking on a new approach. 'You know I do.' She rolled her eyes theatrically. 'I love you, Alexander, and your snubs are breaking my heart.'

'We've been through all this before,' he said tiredly. He placed his hands on his knees and started to get up. 'Now, if you don't mind—'

Alex's manner of rising from his chair was to prove his undoing; for, noting both of his hands occupied, Anna seized her chance and launched herself at him. His reactions were quick, but not quick enough. He was of course the stronger of the two, and it didn't take him long to push her away. But not before she had raked her fingernails down the side of his face.

Chapter 9

Catherine contemplated her drink, cradled the glass in nervous hands. The crisis was over and she was returned to her hotel. A shower, a change of clothes, and she was feeling fine – recuperating from an ordeal that had seen Christopher Armstrong jump into the water to save her.

She sipped her gin and tonic, swallowed the liquid, then frowned. It was not particularly pleasant, had a metallic taste… faintly petrol? She swirled the drink round the glass, then raised it to her lips, thinking. Maybe the seawater had affected her palate. She recalled the surface being discoloured by fuel from the boats. Possibly she had imbibed some of that, when she fell from his boat, when she fell… when she… Dreamlike, she saw herself, observed as if by a bystander, toppling from the boat, plunging towards the cold sea. Catherine was both the player and the audience. She heard the life jacket fire with a percussive burst, felt the tightness round her chest as it filled with gas, saw herself bobbing like a cork in the churning current, then the shock-wave impact of the gangplank as it landed beside her – and, finally, Chris swooping from above.

Catherine turned to him. 'You saved my life,' she said. She trembled, then took another sip of her drink, pulled a face. 'However much you protest, you can't deny it. I am sitting here unscathed because of you.'

Christopher Armstrong placed the glass that he had been nursing on the table. 'If it hadn't been I, it would've been

151

somebody else,' he said casually. 'Anyway, it were Gyke and his cronies who actually pulled 'e out.' He laughed hoarsely. 'Then they fished I out straight afterwards.'

Catherine gazed at him, relaxed in the chair opposite hers. In his pink shirt and grey trousers, and with his hair slicked back, he looked quite the dandy. The hotel management had loaned him the clothes, when he brought her back here, the pair of them soaked to the skin, cold, shivering. 'Agreed,' she said. 'But your prompt action gained time; it kept the boat from squashing me until help arrived. A lifebuoy would have done – but you actually jumped in.'

'I told 'e to be careful, but it were still my boat that thee fell from. Thee were my responsibility. But I suppose I just reacted to yer cries.' He shrugged his shoulders, threw her a cockeyed grin. 'Anyhow, I couldn't let me first mate drown, could I? Thee did good. That were the first time all summer that I've had a full boatload of paying passengers.'

Catherine was pleased to hear him acknowledge her usefulness, although she suspected that he was merely being kind – she had made several gaffs... and then to fall into the sea, like a novice... like a landlubber. And if the boat had trapped her... trapped her against the harbour wall, she could have... She dropped an absorbed glance to her glass, then returned her gaze to Chris. 'I could easily have drowned,' she said meekly, staring into his craggy features, which she saw were now wreathed in concern. 'I could... I could have di...' Her voice broke suddenly, trailed off to a maudlin pang. Tears clouded her eyes. Crossly, she brushed them aside. How she hated such emotional responses. It always embarrassed her when someone choked up while describing a traumatic episode. Sentimental weakness was on the increase: you saw it on television all the time. Now it was happening to her. She tried again, but could not finish her sentence. 'Shit!' she said angrily.

She drained her glass and placed it back on the table. The drink tasted better now. Her taste buds had obviously recovered. 'I feel tired,' she said. 'I don't feel…'

'Do thee want I to leave 'e to it? You've had a bad experience and I don't want to make that worse by hanging around.'

She tried to laugh. 'You've been extremely kind,' she said, touching his arm. 'But, yes, I am feeling tired.' She guided a fingertip to the corner of her eye, shrugged apologetically.

''Tis all right,' he said. 'I understand.' He gazed deeply into her eyes. 'I'll be pushing off, then.'

'Sorry… I…'

'It's all right, Catherine,' Christopher Armstrong said, drawing his chair closer to hers. 'Don't thee worry.' He took her into his arms, drew her head to his chest. 'Let it all out. You'll be better fer it.'

'Shit,' Catherine repeated into his shirt, although this time with less vehemence.

'It be a delayed reaction, me beauty.' He stroked her hair. 'You be suffering a bit of shock, that's all.'

'Shit,' Catherine said for the third time. She started to extricate herself from his embrace. 'I'm fine now,' she said between sniffs. She blinked away a stray tear. 'But I'm feeling really tired. Sorry but I think I'm going to have to go to bed.'

He held onto her upper arms, and she experienced him staring into her eyes, questioning, seeking… surely now gauging whether she was fit to be left alone. She hoped that he didn't suggest staying the night. He was kind, fun to be with but it was a big step to take, to commit herself after Alex, so soon after the breakup. She returned his gaze. Apart from feeling sleepy, not quite with it, she thought that she was okay now, her normal self. Her mawkish moment had passed. She smiled into his anxiety. He really was a very kindly man.

'I'll be going then,' he said, still staring into her eyes.

Catherine smiled, nodded weakly. She decided that she would see him to the door and then go straight to bed. With an effort she freed herself from his hold and started to get up. But in doing so, she overbalanced, tottered drunkenly, and sank back onto the chair again. She felt suddenly strange, listless, her energy dissipating, draining like sand through an hourglass. It was different from simply feeling fatigued: it was almost as if someone had doped her muscles. She was not going to be able to right herself. So instead she sat there, gazing at him through eyes that now seemed unable to focus properly.

'*I'll be going… I'll be going… I'll be…*' His words came at her in a sing-song chant.

Catherine raised a loose stare. The trauma of falling into the sea had exhausted her, she knew… And it was as Chris had said: she was suffering from shock. He was right: the after-effects, the realisation of what might have happened, were coming out like that. But they would be temporary. She would be all right in the morning. After a good night's sleep, she would be… Catherine's thought process faltered. Then, as if in a dream, she felt him turn her head and place his mouth on hers.

Surreal lips, tasting of whisky, moving on hers, kissing… leaden hands on his shoulders, attempting to push him away… but her arms having no strength; feeling lethargic… a dopey apathy. And there was now a creeping feeling of wellbeing, a desire to yield, a desire to dissolve into the illusion… comforting… soothing. She relaxed into the kiss… slid into the dream…

She liked being kissed...

Now being lifted... carried... being laid... on the bed.

A presence stooping over her, hands on her body, touching, undoing, caressing... coming up under her skirt, moving inexorably upwards, unstoppable, her thighs being parted with the irresistibility of the movement.

And now a rising instinct, an inherent impulse, endeavouring to close her legs, to draw them together... But the neural instruction falling on indifferent synapses – and an absence of motive power.

Time passing in uncoordinated sequences...

The rucking up of her skirt – her underwear already gone... and a moment of lucidity... swimming upward through the murky liquescence... head breaking the surface... and trying to push the phantom away... But her hands seeming to merge with it, to pass through it... and her eyelids that would not unclose... so that she was captive within the dream... no escape from unreality.

A sepia psychedelic trip... *Once upon a time and a very good time it was...*

Then from a long way away, like a distant brook, a burbling intake of breath... unseen spectral eyes taking in the look of her, of her supine body. Echo words: 'Ah, thee be a woman, Catherine. Thee ain't like most females who comes down yer looking fer a thrill.' Her legs being set open... one... then the other... then the other again, until her nether was spread-eagled. 'No, thee ain't like t'others.'

Being numbly cupped... feeling a distanced nothingness... being squeezed, being squashed... being manipulated as if under anaesthesia.

'It's all right, Catherine,' the crooning voice, coming again, soothing softly... and her body controlled more tightly... sinewy, insistent fingers working her flesh. ''Tis a natural thing...'

Time passing in uncoordinated sequences...

Confined within a surreal quiescence... unknowing of whether it was a dream... or a waking figment. Why sentience... why cognizance of what was going on... want to stop what was happening? But how to order a dream from which there was no awakening?

Lifted limbs drawn up... then being unclosed... being unfolded... being held open... spread like the pages of a book, then the reptilian thing... lapping... feeling so real, as though it were actually occurring.

Time passing in uncoordinated sequences... And then...

From the depths of a befuddled mind... something... some kindling quality, striving to salvage a power of will, a determination to gather resolve, to demystify perception – to force her mind awake... And, for a moment, lucidity swimming on the far edge of consciousness... but floating away again... to sink... and the return of the shadowy presence... but then to rise once more... to rise up into...

Disappearing feelings... A fading incubus...

She opened heavy-lidded eyes, to see him standing before her, waveringly, as if held in a mirage... And now a materialising genie... and she could see that he was ready for her.

With an effort, for the stupor still gripped her, she shinnied onto her elbows. 'I don't want to.' The words not her own... The speech not hers... The hands pulling down the hem of her skirt not hers. 'I don't want to.' The sound seeming to come from far away, as though whispered in a gallery. Then abstract embodiment... to a gathering realism... to a vague awareness. For Alex's sake she had to avoid him making love

156

to her – but how to refuse him, to stop him? She glanced up, and with a focused effort, she heard a voice: 'We don't know one another well enough.' A giddy gaze, a whirling ceiling. 'I'm not ready for that kind of commitment… yet.'

He approached her. 'Oh, me beauty…'

A mind made up. Alex always referred to them as hand jobs. And it wouldn't be betraying him – not like the other thing… It would be done for him. She shouldn't be able to think, to reason in a dream… Perhaps this was part of the dream… Maybe she was dreaming she was awake.

Maybe she was awake and dreaming she was asleep…

'Oh, me beauty.' The hoarse sigh as she grasped him. Heavy hands resting on her shoulders, gripping… 'Oh, me little beauty…'

In a little while, Catherine knew what she had to do. She knew how Alex liked this done… all the way… all the way and beyond… manipulation until he was done. She had to do that now. Following this, he had to be incapable of making love to her. He had to be copiously depleted.

After a few moments, through a returning miasma, she felt his fingers dig into the flesh of her shoulders. He was taut, straining, twitching… She heard the gasp, sensed the sag of his knees. Then: 'Oh, me little angel…'

She continued to work him, through his asyndesis, until he had no more to give, until all his seed was spilled – to the collapse of his tumescence.

Then she looked up… to see Alex standing in the open doorway of the room. She opened her eyes and fell asleep.

Alex placed the disk in the CD player. He had never actually had to do this before and had no idea if the quality of the recording would meet his needs. He reckoned it would be okay. The salesman's demonstration had been convincing: '2M pixels will give you all the optical resolution you'll ever need, sir.' And it had cost enough. The equipment was programmed to activate when an intruder entered the apartment. But of course she hadn't been an intruder, and so he had had to switch to manual mode, pretty darn quick – in the time it had taken her to enter the building and take the lift to the fourth floor.

He returned to his armchair and picked up the remote control. It took him a little while to locate the sequence he wanted, but eventually the screen showed a familiar image. Excellent! You could see the majority of the room. Most important, the view of the door that led through to the bathroom was unimpeded.

Alex pressed the "Play" button, watched himself open the door, smirked as Anna came in. Did she look scruffy, or did she look scruffy? Dishevelled wasn't quite on the money. He wondered if it was called method acting or getting engrossed in the part. Whatever it was it had fooled him.

The "Fast-forward" button took him to where he wanted to be, and Alex watched Anna emerge from the bathroom corridor, face stricken and torn knickers in hand, as if they had actually been ripped off. She'd done a good job there: it looked as if the gusset had been snatched away by a sex maniac... Well, so it had. He studied her stance, her posed posture, pussy pushed forward, presented for inspection. It was neither method acting nor getting engrossed in the part: she was a natural, a Bafta winner, an Oscar winner.

'Look what you've done, Alex.' Reliving the event, he listened to the words again, watched the knickers being held aloft... like some bloody hunting trophy. 'You didn't need to go this far, Alex.' Well, he hadn't gone this far. He had not –

full stop. She'd gone in there fully clothed, and come out like this. He gazed at the ripped blouse, the garishly painted teats, the jiggling tits… and the smug look as she came across the room towards him. She thought she had outsmarted him, that she was going to get her way.

Fat chance of that. Well…

Alex watched the recording to the moment when she had gone for him. He wanted to be sure that he had not done anything or said anything that could be construed as provoking her or, more precisely, that could be misconstrued by some smartass barrister as provoking her. He played it twice; then, convinced of his innocence, he pressed the "Pause" button.

Whatever capital she tried to make out of the episode would be bankrupt stock. He didn't think she would take it further, let alone go to the police, but if she did, this video, especially the ending, would ensure that she dropped her case. Played in court, it would scupper her good and proper.

He aligned his stare on the feline readied to pounce, shook his head. What a sad, sad woman – pathetic. Even in still-frame you could see the glint in her eye, the warp of her mouth, the cunning look that told you she had planned it all, that she had set him up.

Alex imagined her at home, preparing her routine, writing out her script, page after page of the crap, rehearsing her lines, gathering her props… Or should that be destroying her props? He was surprised that she owned any worn clothes. Maybe she was a hoarder – yeah, something like that.

She lived relatively close by – had an apartment in Kensington, a garden flat that Granddad Jack had bought for her. She would never have been able to afford it on her salary. He and Kate went there once, for Jack's seventieth birthday celebrations. Nearly all her stuff was art deco: ornaments, mirrors, pictures, furniture... She had a fantastic credenza sideboard, even a1930s Bakelite telephone that had been adapted to work on the modern system – all told it must have cost a bomb. She was really into it. In that respect, she had good taste. Alex grinned. Of course she had: she fancied him, didn't she?

He steeled himself, then pressed the "Play" button. Whoops! Watch out. There she goes – like a hungry hyena going for the jugular. Alex winced and touched a reflexive cheek as he relived Anna's launch at his face... and the fingernails, raking like talons.

The scratches weren't actually that bad, he recalled, at least not after he had concealed them with some makeup that Catherine had left behind. All the same, they had been noticed today in the office. But that hadn't been the worst of it. Anna had not turned up for work. Sure he had some sort of legal defence, if it came to that, but the office was another matter. People there would draw their own conclusions, would make two and two equal five. They were bound to link the two things: his scratched face and Anna's absence. Add to that Catherine being away all week, and two plus two equalled six.

And there was history between them. Everybody knew how she chased him. He had always acted properly, turned her down courteously, never encouraged her, but people liked a bit of gossip, enjoyed a bit of titillation. It would be a guilty verdict. And with the new job offer, his promotion, it was hassle he could do without.

Suddenly, with his eyes glued proverbially to the screen, Alex started laughing. This next bit was a classic. You could watch a thousand blue movies and not see better. He wasn't particularly proud of it, of his reaction. But he had been bloody angry. A combination of factors had triggered it: Anna's deception, his annoyance at falling for it, the realisation that the fingernail scratches would be seen at work, would invite speculation, those things, acting together, had made him lose his temper – had made him lose his cool. Now he watched himself, having pushed Anna away, scoop her up and upend her across his knees.

Not a little unaffected, he watched the rising and falling of his hand, listened to the slap, slap, slap as his vengeful palm repetitively visited her naked backside… and Anna's cries of protest as she wriggled to free herself from her antagonist. Not a hope – left hand holding her down, right hand doing the business. Small wonder she hadn't been at work today. Just look at his rhythm, slap, slap, slappity slap, over and over, spank, spank, spank – and the further reddening of her arse with every smack. She would have needed a bloody rubber ring to sit on. Smack, smack, smack, on and on, like a perpetual motion machine – no let up.

But why had he gone on for so long, tanning her arse? Alex asked himself. There had been no need: by this juncture, he'd had more than enough recompense. Taken together with the ending, she would see it as a victory – even that he had enjoyed himself. He grimaced as a particularly enthusiastic slap whiplashed Anna's torso, as her arse performed an involuntary upward jerk… only to encounter his hand on its way down to the next smack. And if he hadn't continued for so long, it might not have happened. In all his experience he had never witnessed anything quite like it before, nothing so spontaneous.

A lot of women enjoyed it, got pleasure from pain… from the rat-a-tat-tat tattoo of spanking. There was undoubtedly a psychological element at work – domination, submission. But the real catalyst was surely a physiological one: for anything of that nature was certain to create vibrations that carried through to the genitals – heat, too. Those were the simple mechanics of it. That was how sexual arousal occurred, how some women became turned on. He focused his attention on the screen. Turned on, yes – but not actually to…

Spellbound, he listened as Anna's cries of protest now changed to shrieks of delight, watched as her pummelling fists opened into hallelujah hands. She was climaxing – with him spanking her, she was coming off. She had skipped foreplay and gone straight to payoff. It was incredible, mind-blowing stuff – unbelievable. Shaking an incredulous head, he listened as the ecstatic shrieks ebbed into contented sighs. She was done. Ironically, she'd got what she came looking for.

He hit the "Eject" button. He had no desire to watch any more of her antics. A wry smile spread across his face. But she hadn't finished with her surprises: she had saved the best till last. For as she was climbing back into her clothes, she had told him that if he ever fancied doing it again to give her a call. His smile faded. You had to feel sorry for women like that.

In a little while, Alex loaded another disk into the player, settled comfortably into his chair. Now this was a different ball game altogether, a different woman altogether, a woman of intelligence and charm; the woman he loved – the woman he wanted to spend the rest of his life with.

He set the disk going. *Clovelly, Devon* the title read. Yes, a weekend away break last year. The summer had been awful, rain, wind, cold – the usual stuff. But then, early September, the sun had remembered what season it was; and so off they had gone. Most of the early scenes were of the village, the quaint shops and thatched cottages but, now and then, there were the special ones. These were his favourites: Catherine buying a souvenir, a postcard, Catherine laughing, skipping ahead to view something that had caught her interest. Alex swallowed the lump in his throat, as he saw her emerging from a shop, grinning impishly, clutching two iced lollies. His gaze took in her red T-shirt and denim shorts.

'Oh, my God,' he muttered aloud, his gaze focusing exclusively on her T-shirt. Alex had watched the disk before but he exclaimed anew as for the thousandth time he saw that she wasn't wearing a bra, and she had the most erectile nipples, ultra-responsive. A single tweak would have them standing to attention, like a couple of squaddies on parade – and if it rained and her T-shirt got wet... He replayed the sequence, held the disk in freeze-frame mode, ogled the screen. What he wouldn't give to lollypop those – now.

The scene switched to the harbour and the curl of pebble beach that formed a crescent round the bay. Ah, there was the hotel – nice place, spectacular views... comfortable bed. And Catherine was now operating the camera, for he saw himself sitting on the harbour wall with a drink in his hand. That beer had tasted good, one of the best pints he'd ever had; a full nutty flavour, strong with a nice frothy head. Catherine had had one too. That was the measure of the woman: clever, sophisticated, but down to earth with it. No wishy-washy lemonade or fruit juice for her on a hot day. If her man was going to have a proper drink, then so too was she, and in a real pint glass, like his – with a handle.

Alex particularly liked this next sequence. They had walked way out along the beach, found a secluded cove, nobody else there – excellent for sunbathing. He watched as Catherine climbed onto an outcrop of rock – smooth as a table top. Determined not to blink in case he missed anything, he saw her take off her shorts and T-shirt. No, that's too much. Don't do it Catherine, not this time. Every time he played the disk she did it. She was teasing him, teasing him by tugging at her panties, as though she intended to take those off as well. It was all right on the day, they were going back to the hotel then. But not now… please. God, these trousers were tight.

He watched her sit down, loop her arms round her drawn up knees, her bare breasts squashed against her thighs. He saw her smiling at him, affectionately, lovingly. She looked like she didn't want to be anywhere else in the whole world, or with anyone else. She looked utterly content, a woman at one with her lot, and her man, Alexander King – the luckiest man on the planet, in the universe. At least, he had been, then.

Alex was glad that he hadn't videoed what happened next. He had switched off the camera and joined Catherine up on the rock. What a perfect day: sky higher than a mile, waves rippling against the shoreline, the gentle hiss of shingle rolling in the current, seabirds calling, distant voices drifting from the main beach – so different from the hustle and bustle of the city; and Catherine, serene, happy, revelling in their quality time together. No, he was glad he hadn't videoed it. In his present mood, it would have been unbearable to witness such bliss.

How, he asked himself, had their relationship gone so awry – and just when so much was within their grasp? Why had she run off like that, without a word of warning? If he'd been having an affair, he would have understood. But a bit of an argument, a misunderstanding… and the ill-advised playing of a game – that was all. Of course, Anna had played her part – but that was nothing. Kate had just gone, made off, hadn't even given him an opportunity to talk to her, to dissuade her. He'd thought a lot about it since last Friday, had thought of little else in fact. Once or twice his reasoning had turned maudlin and he had felt sorry for himself. At a particularly low point, it had occurred to him that, prior to the party, there might have been somebody else in her life. Maybe she had been thinking of leaving, making up her mind, and the row had provided the motivation – had decided her. She had been awkward that night, refused to accept the obvious, was dead set against making up. Was that because she was seeking an excuse, a reason to leave him? But as stealthily as the thought had come, he had dismissed it. That wasn't Kate. No way would she go with another man – not while they were together.

After a little while, Alex returned his attention to the screen, to see Catherine scaling the shingle bar beside the harbour, two strides forward and one back on the shifting shingle – good exercise though. Not that either of them needed any more of that. They'd had plenty back there on that rock. They hadn't been able to wait until they got back to the hotel.

Then later they'd sat on their balcony and watched the sun set over the ocean, fiery reds and tawny ambers, intermingled in leaping flames, as though the sky were on fire. If you hadn't known otherwise, you would have thought that it was. Alex sighed. Sitting there lapping it up, he had become fiery as well, had asked Kate to stand holding onto the balustrade while he stood behind her. Of course she had been up for it... up onto the bottom rail to save his knees, to help things along. He made another sigh. And then, at the final going down of the sun, she had teased him by calling for a break in proceedings so that she could "listen for the hiss" as it dipped into the sea. No chance.

Alex set the CD rolling again. This was his all-time favourite piece. It was the next day and they were climbing up the cobbled street. He had let Catherine go ahead a little way… so that he could film her. Were these trousers shrinking? She was wearing those white shorts (Oh, God) and that silk top. He watched her moving up the incline away from him, uncertain steps on the cobbled surface, steps that seemed to exaggerate her movements. Then she turned back towards him, to see where he was. 'Come on, old man,' he heard her cry. What a disarming smile. And now he could see that, like the day before, she wasn't wearing a brassiere. Reaching down, he released the tautness of his trousers, freed himself from purgatory.

Good God, just look at that lout ogling Catherine's rear end, no shame, blatantly staring… enjoying it. Alex hadn't noticed that on his previous viewings of the CD – obviously too busy doing his own ogling. What a nerve. Good thing he hadn't seen him doing it on the day. He would have… Still, you could hardly blame the bloke, could you? Just look…

Up and down, sway, side to side, swirly flow, up and down, sway, side to side, swirly flow… Purr… fect… Like nothing so much as a lava-spewing volcano, Alex's whole world erupted in Devonshire's finest.

Chapter 10

Following her fall from the boat, Catherine was unable to remember a great deal about last night. She could recall being taken back to the hotel, changing into dry clothes, Christopher being loaned some clothes. She remembered him being kind, being reassuring – the usual Chris, attentive, making her a drink. After which the evening had starting to get nebulous, and she'd begun to feel drowsy – and then nothing until this morning, when she'd woken up with a monster headache, fully clothed on the bed. She could not even recollect having a dream, which was odd in itself – there was usually something.

She gazed round the public house. It was basic, shabby, an advertisement for staying at home. Several mushroom tables and chairs, upholstered in a cheap plastic material, and a few barstools similarly padded made up the majority. She guessed that it was an old-fashioned working men's pub, used predominantly by men off the boats. It was situated in a street of terraced houses at the far end of the harbour. A group of men were sipping desultory beers at the bar. There was a dartboard in one corner, but no one was playing on it. In another corner a pinball machine was similarly unused. When they came in, she had been surprised not to see sawdust on the floor. However, he had told her that he would show her a "real" pub.

'Yer us be, me Catherine.' Christopher Armstrong set

their drinks on the table. 'Red wine fer thee and a pint a cider fer I.' He sat down, nodded an eager head. 'Well, I said I'd take 'e to me local… What do 'e think of un?'

'It's different,' she replied, wondering if she could get away with wiping the rim of her glass with a tissue. But Chris was clearly delighted with the setting; he was in his domain, at home. She decided against the idea. 'It's *certainly* different,' she said, smiling weakly.

'Ah, I expect 'tis that… fer a city woman.'

Catherine studied him, her eyes holding his as she searched for clues. In view of her amnesia, she had intended to question him about last night – that went without saying. But something else had occurred since then that had made her questions now even more pressing.

Following lunch she had driven to Newquay. She was sitting on Fistral Beach, watching the surfers and pondering yesterday's events, when all at once a picture of herself had flashed into her mind. It was only a snapshot vision, subliminal, vanishing as soon as it appeared, but lasting long enough nonetheless for it to register in her memory. Catherine had seen herself lying on her bed in the hotel room. She was fully clothed but there was a male figure bending over her, stooping low over her body, stealthy, as if up to no good. It hadn't been possible to see who the man was but it could only have been one person: Christopher Armstrong. There was no reason to believe that the image depicted an actual event. On the other hand, there was no reason to doubt it either: she had no recollection of last night – and such images do not spring naturally to mind. Something must have inspired it.

Catherine continued to study him, her eyes still searching his for clues. She thought he appeared at ease, relaxed, confident. He did not look like a man with a secret to hide. But that meant nothing. People had a knack of disguising their real motives, of hiding their past deeds. 'When you phoned this morning to invite me here,' she began thoughtfully, scrutinising his reaction, 'I was happy to accept. But… but I have some questions concerning last night.' Was that a miniscule frown, a marginal narrowing of his eyes? She decided to come straight to the point. 'I can't remember anything… after you brought me back to my hotel.'

His face remained impassive, hard to read. 'That ain't surprising. After the bad experience you 'ad, yer brain's just blanked it out.' He shrugged his shoulders, took a pull of his drink. 'They say that be a common reaction.'

'I believe it's the actual traumatic event that is erased,' she said, 'not something following deliverance from it.'

'Dunno about that.'

She nodded, still holding his stare. 'But you were there. Did I… did I simply fall asleep, pass out… faint?'

He pursed his lips in a thoughtful aspect. 'Well, I were speaking with 'e and you seemed all right. You know, talking and all that, aware of I. Then I noticed you was having trouble keeping yer eyes open, staying awake. Thee were obviously tired out, exhausted. Shock can do that. Thee had been through a nasty time. Anyhow, then you fell asleep, right there in the chair; I couldn't rouse 'e so I laid 'e on the bed and left 'e to it.' He stopped abruptly, as if remembering something. ''Course, afore I left,' he went on, holding her gaze, 'I made sure you were all right. You know, that you were breathing okay. But it were obvious that you were just asleep. So, as I said, I left 'e there. I knew thee'd be all right in the morning.'

Catherine nodded, thinking. His account tallied with how she had woken up this morning, even with the mental picture – for what it was worth. He had answered all her questions... honestly, as far as she could tell. Nevertheless, she had a feeling that he was holding something back. She decided to test him, to put a proposal to him and see how he reacted. 'You didn't think to undress me, before putting me on the bed?' She paused. He seemed embarrassed, fidgeting with his glass, the beginning of a flush on his neck. Was there more to his story than he had told her? 'That didn't occur to you?' she asked.

He shook his head, appeared affronted. 'Undress thee? That were the last thing on me mind.' His discomfiture increased. 'Fer all I knew thee might've woken up when I were doing it, thought I were up to summut. Besides, I didn't know thee weren't gonna remember nought, did I? So if I'd done anything like that, I might be up at the police station now, instead of being down yer.' He took a long draught of his cider, smacked his lips appreciatively afterwards. 'And I prefer it yer.'

She relaxed her gaze. No... no, she decided, she was pretty certain that he hadn't done anything. He sounded truthful and, as he had said, he wasn't to know if she would suddenly awaken. And there was no way that he could have anticipated her loss of memory. 'I had to ask the question, Chris,' she said.

He moved his glass on the table thoughtfully. 'Seeing 'tis a night fer questions, I has one of me own.' He looked her in the eye. 'I don't wanna offend ye, but do 'e usually drink that much?'

'What do you mean?' she asked.

'I know 'tis none of my business but with 'e not being able to remember anything, I think 'tis summut thee should consider.'

'I had one gin and tonic,' Catherine said defensively. 'I can remember that – you mixed it for me.'

'Ah, and I mixed 'e another four after that.' He raised surprised eyebrows. 'I couldn't keep up with 'e meself.'

Knocked a little off kilter by his accusation, she examined his expression from beneath thoughtful lashes. His embarrassment had gone. He looked altogether more confident now, more sure of himself. His mouth was set straight, thin-lipped. Was that mirth, a grimace, annoyance? Catherine wasn't sure. She could recall having a drink, one – and it had tasted unpleasant, because of the seawater that she had swallowed. But if what he said was true, it might explain the headache, and her loss of memory. She made up her mind. 'I'm sorry, Chris,' she said. 'But the question had to be asked. I mean, I was alone in a hotel room, with a man. I fell asleep…' She shrugged, left her implication hanging.

'And as you *indicated* just now, you woke up with yer clothes on.' He finished his drink. 'Perhaps thee shouldn't judge us country folk by the standards of yer city gents.'

Catherine apologised again.

He rose to his feet. 'I'll get us more drinks.' He pointed to her glass. 'Will it be the same again?'

Catherine shook her head. 'No thanks, not just now.' She smiled. 'Perhaps I'll have another later on.'

He stared down at her. It was a mocking stare. 'I ain't out to get 'e tipsy so as I can take advantage of 'e, if that's what thee thinks,' he said brusquely, before turning on his heel and heading for the bar.

Her questions had clearly hit a nerve. She studied him at the counter, apparently sharing a joke with the barmaid. His back was turned to her, and Catherine couldn't see his face, but the barmaid was certainly giving him the glad eye, the welcoming look. When they had been out together on previous occasions, she had noticed other females doing the same thing. He was obviously popular with women, not lacking their company. So would he really resort to molesting her, when she was asleep? She did not think so... He certainly deserved the benefit of the doubt.

Just then the door opened and two men entered the public house. Catherine observed them as they passed her table. She was glad that Chris was with her. At the bar, one of the men threw an arm round Chris's shoulder. Then she heard him say: 'What's the matter, Conger? Where's your lady friend tonight, then?' He laughed heartily. It was a coarse-sounding laugh, a guffaw. 'Stood you up for a cruise ship captain, has she?'

Conger? Catherine recalled the rescued cat, and the man in the skiff who had told her how it had acquired its name. She wondered how Chris had gained his nickname. Surely not for... Perhaps it was for his rescue of the animal.

She watched as the three men jostled one another in matey animation. They were obviously friends – although, she noted, Chris did not seem particularly pleased to see them. His participation in the bonhomie appeared muted, less genuine than that of his friends. Then she saw him turn in her direction, heard him say: 'Nope, she be over there.'

Catherine frowned. So she was his *lady friend*, now. The man had clearly used the term in a derogatory manner, as though a certain kind of speculation had taken place concerning their friendship. And Chris had acknowledged it as fact, albeit perhaps not in the crude sense that the man had implied. She wondered if anything had indeed been discussed. Raising her glass to her lips, she sipped her red wine, studied the three men over the rim of the glass. Something told her that Chris would bring his friends over to their table. She still had a slight headache and the last thing she wanted was to spend the rest of the evening with three boisterous drinking men. Well, if need be, she would leave early.

'Catherine,' Chris said, a moment later, 'these be me mates Tom and Will.' He turned to them. 'Tom, Will, this be Catherine.'

'Hello.' She smiled up at them. Tom looked reasonably okay, if a little portly, a feature exaggerated by the tightness of his unbuttoned leather jacket. Will, on the other hand, wasn't so okay. Taller than Chris, he was probably less than half the other man's weight. Despite the warmth of the evening, Catherine noted that he was wearing a heavy fisherman's pullover. His head was shaved and he sported dragon tattoos on either side of his neck… or were they sea serpents? She noticed that he had a squint in one eye. Catherine did not like the look of him.

Tom shook her hand, was pleased to meet her. Will, the man who had made the lady-friend remark, grasped her extended hand in both of his, then bent and kissed it. '*Enchanté, Mademoiselle*,' he said, clicking his heels together.

Catherine did not respond: she was too busy trying not to giggle.

'Well, might as well sit down lads… now thee be here,' Chris invited, less than enthusiastically. 'What will 'e say, Catherine?'

Catherine nodded and shuffled her chair nearer to the door to make room for the two guests. She would definitely be leaving early; she could feel her headache getting worse. And she had just noticed that Will's squint meant that only one eye was ever looking at her at any one time. Furthermore, whichever one it happened to be, it always appeared to be fixed on her breasts. Just as well that she had chosen to wear a loose-fitting blouse tonight.

After several minutes of listening to male banter, Catherine was about to make an excuse and ask Christopher to walk her back to the hotel, when she noticed Will do a strange thing. Taking a swig of his drink, he swilled the liquid round his mouth, retained it there for several seconds, then, winking at her and nodding towards Chris, swallowed it in a series of exaggerated glugging sounds. At the same time, Tom tried but failed to suppress a snigger. Puzzled, she turned inquisitive eyes to Christopher Armstrong. But he now seemed preoccupied, his stare fixed on the flashing lights of the pinball machine, and appeared not to have noticed the incident. But she knew that he had seen it. What was going on?

Catherine switched her attention to Chris's two friends, whom she saw were now exchanging knowing glances. She tilted her head enquiringly, inviting an explanation – but neither man appeared ready to offer one. She shrugged. It was clearly an in-joke and she wasn't in.

And then, with Catherine still attempting to decipher the private joke, Chris came out of his reverie, to embark on the telling of a story about Tom and Will. He told in frenetic, runaway prose how they worked on an Atlantic trawler, often fishing as far north as Icelandic waters, where, on winter nights, they regularly witnessed the aurora borealis, or northern lights. Tom was a helmsman and Will worked below decks preparing the catch for transport to the fish merchants when the ship docked. It really was a feverish telling of a tale, a transparent attempt, Catherine concluded, to divert her thoughts from the bizarre behaviour of his friends. They had clearly embarrassed him. Nevertheless, the story prompted both men to take the mickey, claiming that they were real fishermen, whereas he was just an inshore boy, who relied on tourists for his bread and butter.

'Thee can laugh all thee likes,' he said, staring them down, 'but at least I've got me own boat.'

'Call that a boat,' Tom retorted, rocking on his chair. 'Why it's barely fit for river fishing. Anybody daft enough to put to sea in that old tug is asking to be delivered straight to Davy Jones's locker.'

Catherine shivered as an image of herself falling from the boat into the harbour leaped into her mind. Thankfully, the accident hadn't happened when they had been out at sea. If it had…

And then, as she hauled herself from a metaphorical ocean, the curious incident happened again. Will took another swig of his drink, gargled noisily, and, winking at her and nodding towards Chris, swallowed the liquid in energetic guzzles, and all to the accompaniment of Tom's half-suppressed snigger. And as before, Chris looked uncomfortable and pretended not to notice. Catherine stared at Will, trying to decide if his actions were caused by an unfortunate affliction or habit. But, she concluded, they appeared too complex, too planned for that.

In a little while, with the repeated incident some minutes distant, Will turned to Chris. 'They say you've joined the RSPCA, Conger.' He paused to allow a snigger from Tom to subside, before continuing: 'There's talk abroad that you risked life and limb to save a moggie from the cliff behind the outer harbour.'

'Ain't nothing,' Chris said, clearly annoyed. 'Cat got stuck on a ledge and I went up and brought un down. Ain't nothing to brag about.'

Tom nudged Will and winked shrewdly. 'Oh, our Chris is always resuscitating pussies.' He glanced at Catherine. 'He gives the kiss of life to half a dozen every summer. Isn't that right, Conger?'

Christopher Armstrong silently finished his drink. His

look turned thunderous. 'Don't know how to behave in front of a lady, do 'e both,' he said angrily, glancing from one man to the other. He rose to his feet. 'C'mon, Catherine, let's go back to yer hotel.'

The last thing Catherine heard from Tom and Will as she and Chris left the public house were their hoots of derision.

Catherine lay on a beach, a curvature of golden sand that unfolded quilt-like until it merged into flush horizons. The ocean, aloofly separate, though a lunar warp pulled it a little closer with every breaking wave, was an admixture of green and blue – marine turquoise. A single puff of cotton wool cloud wandered high and lonely across an otherwise untroubled sky. The sound of an airplane, much like that of a single-engine propeller was barely discernible in a faraway vista, a soporific drone. It was a good place to be.

Other folk, mostly families, also occupied the beach, children playing games, splashing in the sea, exuberant, whooping, shouting to one another, calling to their parents. A beach ball, colourful as a lap of knitting and carried along by a wayward toss, rolled fitfully towards the sea. Two teenagers pursued it, sprinting to overtake before the ocean tightened its tidal grip.

A queue of people was gathered by the bar selling soft drinks, and beside it a plump woman was sitting on a bench eating an ice cream. Her husband, for that was surely his role, was drinking iced soda water through a straw. He was a thin man… *Jack Sprat could eat no fat, his wife could eat no lean, and so between them both they licked the platter clean*. A dog of indeterminate breed was tethered to the bench, its nose attuned and a-twitching to the aroma of a nearby diner.

In behind the bar an avenue of palms paraded along the

highway, their fronds like green pleated sunshades cast vague shapes on the shiny asphalt. Colourful chromed cars, blues, reds, greens, cruised by, a Cadillac, a Pontiac, and a '65 Chevy sporting white-wall tires. The drivers looked like college kids come down to the resort for the summer vacation. *We always take my car coz it's never been beat. And we've never missed yet with the girls we meet.* The swish of the passing cars seemed an extension, a fusion of the airplane's purr.

Not far off was a collection of rocks that had once been part of a cliff, long ago, before tide and time razed them to the beach – probably before the dinosaurs became extinct... or older. The rocks were of all shapes and sizes, haphazard, and made up of a series of sedimentary layers – shifting shades shimmering in the sun.

In the shallows there were rock pools and, in one, Alex was showing Nathan how to catch fish that had become trapped there after the last tide. Here and there kelp lay on sea-rounded boulders, like chintz curtains, drying in the salt-stung air. She saw Nathan jump up and down, giggling in his high-pitched excitement, as Alex scooped something into the net and tipped it into their bucket.

Close by, Eleanor was building a sandcastle. She watched the child run down to the sea and scoop up a bucketful of water, turn and run back again, hardly spilling a drop, for it was needed to dampen the dry sand. Then off she went again, across the beach to fetch a pail of water. *Jack and Jill went up the hill to fetch a pail of water, Jack fell down and...* In no time at all, Eleanor had wetted her chosen patch of beach – and sandcastle making recommenced.

Little Nathan just ten and already so like his father, strong-limbed, the same dark hair, wide piercing eyes, someday some girl would... just like she had with Alex, all those years ago. *A long long time ago on graduation day you handed me your book I signed this way...* Where had the time gone? Yes, Nathan would wow the girls all right. You could see it there now. And Eleanor, quiet – even shy – studious in third grade, with her mother's aptitude for figures, and blonde as a clutch of corn... *On the good ship lollipop it's a sweet trip to the candy shop...* and already the star of a soap ad – how strange it was that genes could skip a generation. Her grandmother would have adored her.

She adjusted her sun lounger and closed her eyes. Soon the children's voices and Alex's husky tone merged into the background sounds of the seaside idyll. A radio was tuned in to the local station and, in between the songs – mostly country and western – an announcer told of the traffic out on the interstate, and waxed not far off lyrical about the weather. The airplane purred contentedly, remote, faraway, wooing the cloud – a stanch suitor.

Once upon a time in a far-off land there lived a prince and a princess. He was extraordinarily handsome and went on crusades and slew dragons, and any other fabulous beasts that came his way. He was very brave. He had never been defeated in battle... nor would he ever be. The prince and the princess had two children, a son who was as handsome as his father, and a daughter who was even more beautiful than her mother. One day...

They were lucky, their lives charmed. Running the branch out here was hard work, but balanced by the opulent lifestyle. They owned a colonial-style house just outside Jacksonville, an apartment in lower Manhattan. They were partners in the business, shareholders, living the American Dream. Success bred success, as the saying had it, in the land of plenty.

With the business established there was now more time

for leisure. Skiing in The Rockies, Beaver Creek, was on the agenda and driving along Route 66 – diners and motels, adventures along the way. *Good evening, Norman. We'd like a family room, please. I have the very thing, madam. Thank you. Oh, and by the way, has it got a bathroom? Why, no. I am sorry... But it's got a lovely shower, madam.* They visited the UK every six months, saw old friends, colleagues. Anna's wedding had required an extra trip. Quite a do, it was. Her old rival had finally found true love in the arms of an Iraqi businessman, a dapper little man with a bushy beard. She had thereafter converted to Islam and embraced the burka. It was not known which, if any, other Islamic rituals she had adopted. She had honeymooned over there... Catherine sighed contentedly. They still owned the Chelsea flat, rented it out to business people, mostly bankers. It was their bonus. And Brenda was due to visit next week. Yes, life was good... Drifting now on the airplane's drone, she let herself doze.

Sometime later she comes out of her nap and uncloses her eyes. The ocean is closer now, a rapid-running tide rising between the rocks, but Alex and Nathan are still clambering there, searching for unplumbed pools. And Eleanor's sandcastle is becoming a sculpture.

And the airplane is heading inland, seeming to approach on a wing and a prayer. The pitch of its engine is changed, a deeper tone, throbbing, more powerful, as though it is climbing, gaining height, going up through the troposphere and... *Somewhere over the rainbow bluebirds fly high...*

Something disturbs the sand by her sun lounger. Catherine turns a languid head... to see that Alex is kneeling beside her. The black hair of his chest is sand-matted, his frame muscled and tanned, toned like that of a mythological god.

He bends forward and, as their lips meet, she places her arms round his neck, moaning as his kiss moves her to passion.

Then she hears Nathan's voice. 'They're doing it again, Eleanor. They're being soppy again.'

Eleanor's giggle, as the child turns from building her sandcastle to see what her brother says is soppy.

Alex's voice: 'You look delectable.' Then his lips reconnecting with hers, moving on hers… his tongue… and the half-imagined hand… here on the beach, in front of the children, in public view, bringing dalliance to the everyday scene.

Shifting sand as a gathering gathers about them, an amphitheatre of spectators – but who cares who is watching. The children, bored by their parents' soppiness, are returned to more exciting occupations. She closes her eyes against the crowd… and the airplane.

The wonderful airplane, climbing higher and higher, into the thinness of the air, hanging on an apex, teetering on an apogee… teasing… tantalising as a thrill… *Somewhere over the rainbow way up high…*

And now it comes, dipping from the sky, an accelerating momentum, coming out of the blue like a hunting hawk, the hum of its engine already drumming in her ears, hurrying like a kamikaze… plunging down… *Somewhere over the rainbow…*

The agitation of its approach, urgent physical atmospheres, firstly tremulous, like a sea flux but borne on a different dimension. Then, increasing, convulsing – the air a maelstrom of upward current.

The crowd scatters in pandemonium, in panicked pandemonium, like a handful of scattered thoughts. No one wants to die in paradise.

'I love you, Alex—'

'I love you, Catherine…'

'Kiss me… one last time…'

The explosion is louder, more percussive than she expects, and, despite herself, she gasps in protest as the tsunami washes over her, an amniotic ocean fluid seizing her body in a seismic shift… the wicked wave, rolling, roaring, swooping, soaring like a lark, riding its crest in a crescendo of crashing surf… The perfect prelude… Then the thing, the deep whooshing vortex, bearing her away into oblivion.

I'm picking up good vibrations… good, good, good vibrations… It's giving me great excitations… good, good…

Christopher Armstrong brought his drink to the table, took up a belligerent stance. His stare flashed between his two cronies. 'I suppose thee thought that were funny.' He raised his glass high into the air. 'You be lucky that I don't tip this over yer two gormless heads.'

'Aw, c'mon, Conger,' Will said, trying to disguise a smirk, 'we were only joshing. No harm's been down.'

'No harm,' Armstrong said, red-faced. 'Is that what thee thinks? Well, she just refused to 'ave I up in her room.'

'No long-term harm then. She still loves you, Conger – you could see that in her eyes. Why, she's smitten with you, man.' Snickering, Will turned to Tom. 'You know what I think, Tom?' His friend shook a solemn head. 'I think our Chris here hasn't had his end away with her yet. That's why he's so pissed off. If he had, he wouldn't give two hoots. Ain't that so, Conger?'

''Course I 'ave,' Armstrong shot back angrily. 'They can't say no to Chris. I 'ad her first bloody night.'

Will studied Armstrong for some time, his eyes taking in

the sullen expression, the shifty look, the discontented grimace. Eventually, his expression broke out into a knowing grin. 'No you haven't,' he mocked. 'No you haven't, Conger. You haven't harpooned her.' He turned to Tom. 'He's been lying to us, Tom.' He guffawed loudly. 'He hasn't dipped his wick.'

'What if I ain't,' Armstrong said sullenly; ''Tis only a matter of time afore I do.' He took a long pull on his cider, then smacked his lips together. 'Ah, 'tis that. Thee wait and see,' he added, belching noisily.

'I'll tell you something else too, Tom,' Will went on, winking at his friend. 'I reckon she didn't do the other thing that he told us about either. You could see she didn't have a clue what we were talking about.' He turned and grinned at Armstrong. 'She didn't, did she, Conger. She didn't give head. She didn't draw on the straw, let alone anything else.'

'Think thee be smart, don't 'e? But I ain't bullshiting. And, what's more, when she'd finished, I were fit fer nought.'

Will and Tom both broke out into peals of laughter. 'I can believe that,' Will said. 'A wank would do that.'

'You're past it, Conger,' Tom joined in.

'No I ain't,' he said flatly. He finished his drink, hurried his mates to finish theirs, then went off to the bar to refill their glasses.

In a moment he returned and placed the glasses on the table. 'I'll tell 'e summut else,' he went on. 'I'll have her, you mark me words. I knows her… I knows…' He stammered to a halt, shot his grinning mates a placatory glance, then added: 'I knows of her, anyway. She's got history. She be hot, she be.'

'More bullshit.' Will scoffed. 'You know nothing, Conger. Why don't you admit it? She's too upmarket for the likes of you.'

'Ah, and they be the types who like it… sex… and plenty of it – at least, this one does.'

'And how would you know, Conger?' Will taunted. 'She's in a different league to your usual *clientele*.'

Armstrong tapped his nose. 'I knows.'

'C'mon then, Chris,' Tom wheedled, sending Will a sly glance. 'Tell us your secret. Spill the beans for the boys.'

Armstrong supped his cider, then wiped the back of his hand across his mouth. 'All right, I'll tell 'e, smartasses.' He took another pull on his drink, before slowly setting the glass back on the table. 'Thee remember young Chris Ford.'

Tom and Will exchanged glances. Both men nodded. Then Tom said: 'Him whose father owned… What was the boat called?'

'*Serendipity*,' Armstrong said, grinning at their sudden seriousness. He swigged his cider energetically. 'Well, she be the one who he was knocking around with… Or should I say shagging?'

'So?' Will asked, reaching for his drink.

'So, he says,' Armstrong mimicked. 'So… so, they were shagging like rabbits. She couldn't get enough of un… going at it every night, so they say.'

'Who says?' Will asked, plonking his drink down heavily on the table.

'Old Gyke. He recognised her when she turned up last week. He told I all about the first time she were yer – about ten year ago he said… when she an' young Chris got it together. He told I how he were going home one night along the east cliff when he heard summut going on in the bracken just off the path. It were a bit of a racket so he said, moaning and groaning, like somebody was mortally hurt… Scared un, 'e said.' Armstrong paused and wetted his whistle. 'Anyway, thinking somebody might need help, he went closer. The noise was louder, so he edged a bit nearer... and 'twas then that he saw this white thing going up and down–'

'Chris's arse,' Will broke out, laughing uproariously and banging his fists on the table. 'That's what he saw. Chris's arse.'

Armstrong smirked. 'Ah, that's what 'e saw. But thee be interested now. Believes I now, don't 'e both?' He paused and his expression became conspiratorial. 'Anyhow, he circled round a bit and recognised Chris Ford... and she were under 'im. He said that he never saw that look on any woman's face afore. He said it were like she were in Heaven... like she'd died and woke up and found herself in the arms of the Virgin. And she were whispering sweet nothings in his ear: "My darling, love me. Oh, my precious, I love you. Oh, I love you, my Christopher".' He scoffed, then took an agitated draw from his glass. 'And she'll be saying all that lovey-dovey stuff again soon... to I this time.'

'What did Gyke do?' Will asked.

'What do 'e mean? What did he do? He went on home... after a bit.'

Tom sniggered. 'He didn't think to join in, then? From what you say, it sounds like she wouldn't have minded.'

Armstrong belched noisily. 'Anyway, he went home that way most nights after that, and they were always there, shagging as if it were going out of fashion.'

'So she likes a bit of the other,' Will said. 'That don't mean to say she's going to do it with you.'

Armstrong tapped his nose. 'I ain't daft: I've done me homework. The first time I came across her was up there. Just off the footpath, there's a bit of a hollow... where they used to shag; and that's where I found her – fast asleep. That place obviously means summut to her... I'm working on how I

184

can use that to me advantage. And Gyke said she's interested in the stars... astrology–'

'Astronomy,' Tom corrected.

'Yeah, that's what I said,' Armstrong replied testily. 'I've boned up on that; and when I took her out to the old Meva Mine, I impressed her with me knowledge about it. That's put I in good stead.' He paused, thinking. 'I rescued the cat for her... And I yanked her out of the harbour. She thinks I'm the bee's knees.' He buttoned his lip as Will pointed out that he had only done so after pushing her in there in the first place. Then, staring his friends down, he added: 'Ah, I'll have her. Despite your darned meddling, I'll have her... one way or t'other.'

Catherine switched off the device and the sound of the airplane cut out. She saw that Alex and their two children were no longer on the beach. And then, as she came all the way back, that too faded and she was returned to the hotel.

In a little while she stepped from the bath, slipped on her dressing gown and went out into the bedroom. She cast a glance round the room – almost a surreptitious one, the mien of a schoolgirl wondering if Mum has discovered her secret. Then, pulling her suitcase from the storage cupboard, she placed the device inside.

It seemed her fantasies were becoming more mature of late. It hadn't always been that way. Before Alex, she had mostly imagined her teenage love, passionate events on the cliff, with discovery an ever-present danger. After the distress of the public house, that had been her intention this evening. But, despite the fracture with Alex, it had just happened this way, spontaneous, unchoreographed – Alexander and their two children, with their new life in the States thrown in. It was almost a family saga. Whatever subconscious desire, or Freudian slip, had ordered the fantasy, Catherine decided she could live with it. Nathan and Daddy fishing in rock pools, and little Eleanor building sandcastles. Yes, she was happy with that, as long as it remained a fantasy… and the end result was the same.

Her headache was gone. In truth it had never been that bad – certainly not as acute as she had implied when Christopher Armstrong had tried to talk his way up here earlier. He hadn't been best pleased with her refusal, had gone away in a real huff, striding off down the street, the rejected suitor – presumably to re-join his friends in the public house. But what else could she do? Catherine asked herself. His story about last night had seemed genuine. She had believed it. But then along came his pals to, if not destroy it, then certainly to undermine it. He might be innocent, he probably was, but she'd had no intention of inviting him up here to find out. Naïve she might be, but not stupid.

The evening had been a strange one for Catherine, especially the conduct of Will. All that gargling and noisy swallowing, his winks at her and nods at Chris – only later did she recognise that as being sexual innuendo. And of course Tom's accompanying sniggers also pointed to the same thing, an act staged to suggest that she had engaged with Chris in fellatio. But of course she had not. And Christopher would not tell his friends otherwise. Tom and Will had surely acted alone. Catherine became aware that she was blushing, ashamed that two men had played such a trick on her, in a public place. She decided then that she needed to discuss it with someone. Sleeping wouldn't be easy with it playing on her mind.

She glanced at her watch, saw that it was almost eleven-thirty. It was late and Brenda had to work tomorrow. Catherine hesitated. But her friend would not mind, Brenda would be happy to talk this through.

'Hello, Brenda,' Catherine greeted tentatively, when her friend answered her call. 'I apologise for calling so late but–'

'You can call me anytime, Kate,' Brenda broke in, 'you know that.' There was a pause, as if Brenda had suddenly realised the hour. Then her voice came again: 'Are you all right, Catherine?'

'I'm fine... I'm fine but... how is Alex? I mean, how is his injury healing?' She glanced at her mobile, irritated by her stumbling prevarication. She couldn't care less about Alex's injury.

'Alex is okay. But you didn't phone me at this hour specifically to inquire about him, did you? Is anything wrong, Catherine?'

'No... No, not really,' Catherine began again. 'It's just that there's something I need to discuss, something...' She fell silent. Despite her fresh start, she still didn't know how to proceed or, for that matter, where to begin her story. There was no requirement to mention everything... her experience in the tin mine... the fishing trip... 'I have a problem,' she said at length. 'Something has happened this evening, and I would appreciate your opinion.'

'What is it, dear? Whatever it is, you can tell me, and we'll sort it out – between us.'

Catherine took a deep breath. 'I've met someone here...' She paused anticipating an interruption, but when none came, she continued: 'It's nothing serious, of course it isn't. He has been kind and we have done some stuff together. Anyhow, I accepted an invitation to go out for a drink with him tonight. He said that he would take me to his local... which turned out to be the most dreadful place imaginable.' She then went on to inform Brenda of her experience at the public house, concluding: 'His friends were such coarse characters, so unlike Christopher. But... but even so he didn't attempt to refute any of their sly accusations.'

Following a short silence, Catherine heard Brenda say: 'He didn't do so because, in my opinion, they are true. If they hadn't been, then he would obviously have called his friends out.' Brenda paused, before adding: 'And I think the mockery you describe reflects the man's attitude to women.'

'There's more,' Catherine said, ignoring her friend's comments. In spite of her decision to be parsimonious with her account, she now felt that she should give Christopher Armstrong some credit − balance the books so to speak. 'When I fell from his boat into the harbour, Christopher jumped in and prevented the boat from crushing me, until I was pulled out.'

'You fell into the harbour?' Brenda asked incredulously. 'You mean actually into the sea?'

'Yes.' Catherine described the fishing trip, including her fall from the boat. 'If he hadn't jumped in to rescue me,' she added, 'I might have drowned or have been caught between the boat and the harbour wall. He could have stayed on the quayside and pushed the boat away from there. There was no need for him to actually jump in. But he did. He came straight to my assistance.'

'It seems to me that to remain on dry land would have been the sensible thing to do, the surest way of alleviating the danger you were in. He would have had stable leverage there. With him in the water, too, he didn't have that, and you were both in danger.' Brenda paused, clearly gathering her thoughts. After a few moments, on a deep breath, she concluded: 'But obviously he did it that way to impress you – as the hero, the gallant rescuer.'

Catherine did not reply. She was aware that Brenda had once been a claims adjuster for an insurance company, and knew her subject. Her friend had also done similar work for their company. She was up to speed on people's ruses. Catherine remained silent.

'And his name is Christopher?' Brenda asked over Catherine's silence.

'Yes, that's right.'

'And you say that he is a fisherman too?'

Catherine coughed nervously. 'A coincidence, isn't it?'

'I think you should come home,' Brenda responded. 'You have only just met these people. You know nothing about them, their lives, or their motives. My advice is to leave them well alone.' She paused, before adding: 'Kate, I think it's time that you came home from Mevagissey.'

'I am going to,' Catherine replied, wordlessly acknowledging her friend's insight. 'I'm coming home on Saturday.'

'Why not come back tomorrow?'

'It's only an extra day and there's something I have to do first. It… it's important to me.'

Following a short pause, Catherine heard her friend say: 'Would you like me to be with you, dear? I could catch an overnight train, sleep… Or Joe could drive me down.'

Catherine caught her breath, remembering. She said: 'I'll be okay. Besides, it's really not that big a thing.' She paused. How could she say that? She glanced at her mobile. 'Not so big now,' she added swiftly.

'All right, Kate.'

Catherine ended the call, then made herself a cup of

cocoa. She felt a lot better now. Even though her friend had told her what she didn't want to hear, Brenda had also confirmed her own secret fears. Reluctantly Catherine had to accept that, at best, Christopher Armstrong was a sexual opportunist, at worst, a cunning predator. At the moment she was leaning towards the former – but only just.

She took her drink to the window, sat in the casement seat. The town was closing down for the night, the pubs and bars disgorging the last of their late-night revellers. Among them, she spotted Chris and his two friends. Catherine observed them, their swagger: jostling one another, each playing the fool, boys on a night out – all of them. They seemed in good humour, buddies again, the earlier ribbing forgotten. She saw Christopher Armstrong turn to a group of passing girls, say something, then make an obscene gesture. The girls looked startled, offended, and hurried off up the street. One glanced over her shoulder, presumably, Catherine guessed, to ensure they were not being followed.

Shaking her head in disgust, she carried her cocoa back to the table. Far from being different, better mannered than his friends, it appeared to her that Christopher Armstrong was of the same ilk. Catherine studied her reflection in the mirror on the opposite wall. Her opinion of Mr Armstrong and his morals had just moved to the far end of the scale.

Chapter 11

Alex replaced a thoughtful phone, wondered why Brenda Willis had asked if she could come and see him. He knew that it was unlikely to be work related: she wasn't involved in his side of the business. His heartbeat shifted up a gear. Maybe she had news of Catherine. Maybe she knew where Kate was and was going to tell him. But why would she do that? His pulse went up another notch. Not unless Catherine had given her permission to do so, which was a whole new ball game for it might indicate that she was coming home. Don't raise your hopes, Alexander, he told himself. It's probably got nothing to do with Kate.

Perhaps it concerned Anna. Maybe she had opened her mouth about the other night and Brenda was coming to warn him... about gossip. No. He didn't think that was it. Anna may be dumb but she wasn't that stupid – she wouldn't blab. Not after the way it ended... And then, with him desperately trying to erase a picture from his mind, a knock came to the door and Brenda Willis entered his office.

Alex searched for clues in her expression, in her deportment. She appeared stern, gloomy. It was not good news. 'How can I help you, Brenda?' he said, trying to hide his disappointment.

'May I sit down? It may take some time.'

It may take some time. Alex sucked some air into his lungs. Maybe it was good tidings after all. 'Of course,' he said eagerly, indicating the chair across the desk from his. 'Sorry – should have offered before.'

Brenda settled herself into the leather-bound chair, clasped her hands in her lap, fell to examining her fingernails. Following several thoughtful moments, during which Alex maintained an impatient silence, she looked up. 'Alexander, I have heard from Catherine.' Alex experienced a mental orgasm. Perhaps Kate really was coming home. And with that thought, he advanced a measureable way towards having a physical one. 'I'm not interested in what occurred after the party,' Brenda continued. 'That is none–'

'I don't know what you've been told,' he interrupted, 'but whatever it was please remember that it is only one side of the story.' He was not a little put out that Brenda knew about their private life, let alone felt able to mention it. But that was in her nature, assuming that being a generation older somehow granted her special status to intervene. And Kate had obviously gone running to her, telling tales of woe. That would have given her more confidence to speak out. Biting back his irritation, he added: 'Sometimes she gets things wrong.'

'That's between you and Catherine,' Brenda continued, ignoring his comments. 'My concern is Catherine. Now, Alexander, I know where she is, but first there is a little more to tell you.'

He was going to find out where Catherine was. He savoured the thought, gazed inanely across the desk. He liked the way older women held the backs of their skirts against their legs when sitting down, to avoid creasing the material. Brenda had just done that. Younger women didn't seem to bother nowadays. Kate did. But she was an exception. Alex made a cautious grin. 'How is she?' he asked.

'She's fine... Under the circumstances she...' Brenda paused to remove a hair from the sleeve of her jacket. 'That is she's all right. But I think that she may be in danger—'

'What kind of danger,' Alex interrupted, his temper changing instantly. He gripped the top of his desk and his eyes took on a steely glint, together with a hint of desperation. Why hadn't Brenda come to him earlier? he asked himself. 'Tell me where she is and I'll go and sort it out.' And he would too. She could be on the other side of the world, but he would go there. He would go to wherever she was, to wherever *he* was needed.

'I'll tell you everything I know, Alexander, but some of it might remain unclear, might be difficult to understand, unless I start from the beginning.'

'You said she was in danger.'

'I said that she might be... if we don't act. But it's not immediate: presently she is fine.' Brenda paused, and Alex accepted her thoughtful gaze. 'But, as I indicated, it's necessary to know the past in order to understand the present... and... and also to decide how best to proceed.'

Alex relaxed. 'Go on,' he said.

'I've known Catherine all her life, ever since she was a baby. Her mother and I were at school together... and university – we were always friends. Joe and I have no children of our own, and so I... I suppose that I became something of an aunt to Kate. And, as you know, I am also her godmother. Then after her parents' unfortunate passing, she was taken in by a relative who happened to live near us – and so we have never lost contact.' She fell silent, reflective. 'I'm... I am telling you this so that you will understand why Kate has chosen to confide in me.'

Why was she waffling on? Alex was getting impatient

again. He just wanted to know where Catherine was. Then he could get moving, go there, bring her home. 'I know all that,' he said. He paused. He hadn't meant to sound brusque. 'I know that you are a family friend, also that you have been good to Catherine,' he added contritely.

As if his remark had not registered, Brenda went on wistfully: 'She was only fifteen when Rose and John died… shy… reserved really – but bright as a button, doing well at school. Even then it was plain that she would achieve…' Her words petered out as she suddenly caught Alex's expression. After a moment, she sighed. 'All right, Alexander, I'll cut to the chase.'

Alex reached across his desk and squeezed Brenda's hand. In which TV series had she picked up that Americanism? He said: 'Tell me everything you think I need to know… that's relevant.'

'I don't know how much Catherine has told you of her life before she met you,' Brenda began. 'Knowing Catherine as I do, I expect that she told you everything…' Brenda glanced down at her hands, before returning her gaze to Alex '… everything that she felt able to.' She paused, and Alex could see that she was finding the subject difficult to put into words. He said:

'We don't have secrets… usually. And if this is about what I think it is, I know there was someone, once… a long time ago. She was never really happy to discuss him, and I never pressed her. The matter was history – it didn't concern me. I know she didn't have another relationship, until we met.'

Brenda nodded sagely, as though in acknowledgement of his candour. 'Before Catherine went up to Oxford, after sitting her A levels, she spent the summer down in Cornwall. You know… chilling out – as you young people say – paying her way by taking summer jobs.

'Anyway, while she was there, she met a young fellow – a really nice lad by all accounts, about her own age… eighteen or nineteen. He was called Christopher and worked on a fishing boat, his father's I believe. They became close… fell in love.' Brenda paused. 'She thought the world of him. She used to phone me all the time, excited, telling me all her news, what they had been doing, their plans… their plans for the future. I'm sure if everything had worked out, we… we wouldn't be having this conversation now.'

Alex's gaze narrowed, but he remained silent.

'As I indicated, they were in love,' Brenda went on. 'Except for when he was working, they went everywhere together… the whole summer. She used to wave him off when the boat set sail and then go down to the harbour to meet him when he came home. They… they were inseparable.'

Studying Brenda's expression, which had grown progressively unsettled, Alex sensed that she was building up to something… to revealing something. He couldn't guess what it was, but he supposed that it must have some purpose, otherwise why put herself under pressure to tell him? Then he heard her say:

'They used to go to a place on the cliff – Catherine called it their secret place. She loved it there, especially on clear nights. I remember one card from her mentioning the stars.' Brenda forced a smile onto her face. 'Her words: "They were sparkling like coloured jewels; they looked so close you felt you could reach up and pluck them from the sky".'

Despite his best effort not to allow it to happen, a scene insinuated itself in Alex's mind. He saw a cliff top, a starry night, and Catherine gazing to the heavens… on her back. 'What happened?' he asked.

Brenda held his gaze. 'Christopher was lost at sea, an

accident, a freak accident. Fishing is a dangerous occupation, storms can blow up suddenly; lives are frequently lost. But it was a beautiful day, summer, a calm sea with light winds – nobody could account for the loss… which made it worse for her. If an answer could have been found, an explanation for what went wrong, then maybe it would have helped her. If there had been a fogbank or a sudden storm where they were fishing, then…' Brenda sighed. 'And the boat was never recovered, not even a scrap of wreckage – neither was there any sign ever found of the crew. Everybody agreed that whatever it was that overtook them must have been sudden – catastrophic. They didn't even have time to send out a distress call.' Brenda paused, perhaps to gather her composure, but more likely, Alex thought, to allow him time to absorb the full consequence of her story. After a little while, she went on: 'There was a theory that the boat's fishing nets might have become caught on something, which caused it to capsize. There was even a rumour in the papers that it may have been a submarine that snagged them. The MoD refused to confirm if one was operating in the area, and that added to the speculation.' She shook her head. 'But they were all lost, every man and boy of them… Christopher.'

So that was it. Sure, he'd known about a relationship, the seven years alone – until she had met him. But all this was news. He could see how it could affect a teenage girl, losing her first love like that. Alex noted his computer switch to standby mode. Obviously the feeling had become entrenched. Yeah, some girls had taken religious vows over less, had confined themselves to a convent, or embraced a self-pitying spinsterhood. Lucky he'd come along when he had.

'Catherine had gone down to the quayside,' Brenda was saying, 'to wait for the boat to come in, as she always did. But it never came back... It broke her heart... and so soon after her poor mum and dad, down there waiting, alone, far from her home. She waited all night... and the next day, gazing out to sea, waiting and watching – waiting for news. She wouldn't give up.

'People tried to dissuade her from... from her vigil, but she refused them.' Brenda shook her head. 'You know Catherine: she doesn't give up on anything easily – she's tenacious that way.' Alex nodded. 'She was determined to remain there until... until Christopher came home.' She frowned, sighed. 'Can you imagine what it was like... an eighteen-years-old girl?'

'There must have been other women there too – and relatives, friends – waiting for their menfolk,' Alex said, feeling ashamedly ambivalent about the episode. He felt sadness, real regret, for the effect that it obviously had had on Catherine but, at the same time, he found that he could not wholeheartedly condemn something that had ultimately preserved her for him. That others would consider it a selfish response, he was well aware. But he would prefer to see it as a measure of his love for her – a love that had subjugated all his altruistic feelings. Grimacing in chagrin, he added: 'Having other people there, must have been a comfort to her. You know, talking, supporting one another.'

'There were others there with her,' Brenda said, 'family members – Christopher's mother. So, yes, in that respect, consolation, mutual support, was there, at first. But one by one they dropped away, until only Catherine was left. They're a tough lot, the fishing community – and that was more upset for her, seeing families, even Christopher's own mother, who had also lost her husband, apparently accepting what had happened as just being part and parcel of their lives. She couldn't understand their attitude and even less could she accept it.

'I went down to fetch her home,' Brenda continued. 'At first she wouldn't come. She was bereft. So I stayed with her… for quite a while it was. Most of the time she just moped around, went on long walks by herself. I did what I could to console her; tried to pique her interest in university – she'd already won a place at Balliol. It was difficult going though. She just wasn't with it… You know… apathetic – it was almost as if the tragedy had anesthetised her. I was starting to get really concerned. But then, one day, she said she was ready to come home, but that there was something she had to do first – and it had to be done in the night-time. She didn't want me to come with her… but… but I had to. I couldn't let her go off alone like that… in the dark… I feared…' Brenda wiped a tear from her eye. 'She took me up to the cliff, to the top, to their secret place.' She paused again, then, smiling through her tears, she went on: 'To me it looked like nothing, just a small grassy hollow in the earth a little way off the path, behind the cliff face. But I could see that to her it meant everything.

'She asked me to wait for her, assured me she would be all right. So I left her and went back a little way along the path. I could hear her crying… I wanted to go to her, to comfort her, but I knew that it was best to leave her alone, that she would come along when she was ready.

'And after a while she did, I saw her coming towards me out of the darkness…' Brenda paused. 'Alexander, you… you will never know how relieved I was. I really thought… And she wasn't crying anymore.' Brenda dabbed her cheek with a tissue, smiled sheepishly. 'Unlike me. All she said, when she got to me, was "Brenda, I have said goodbye and I shall never come this way again". She had barely gotten over losing her mum and dad, and then this.' Brenda fell briefly thoughtful. 'But… but I think the experience, even more so than the first and tragic as that was, made her tougher, more resilient. Yet… yet somehow I don't think that she has ever truly gotten over it.' She paused, before adding: 'No, not truly…

'And the next day we came home.'

I shall never come this way again. Catherine's words to Brenda ran through Alex's mind. But she had. Wherever it was, he knew that that was where she had gone. He had hurt her, and she had returned to the place of her first love. But she would be coming home soon, he told himself, coming back to him – then he would make amends. He gazed across the desk at Brenda's tearful expression. 'Would you like me to fetch us some coffee?' he asked.

She stared at him. 'We're not allowed to… in the offices.'

'Yes we are,' Alex said, nodding his reassurance. 'You just hang on – I won't be a moment.'

A minute later he returned and set two polystyrene cups on his desk. He could see that her emotional moment was past. 'So that's the history,' he said, retaking his chair. 'Where's she at now?'

Brenda removed the plastic lid from her coffee cup. 'Please don't be alarmed,' she said, 'but I think… I fear she has become mixed up with some very unsavoury characters.'

Alex was alarmed. Being asked not to be had ensured that he was. 'What do you mean by unsavoury?'

'Catherine is so clever.' Brenda expanded her narrative, as though she had not heard his question.

'I know,' Alex replied.

'But it's always been so difficult to get through to her. Perhaps her cleverness has set her apart in some way… She seems to interpret the world differently to the rest of us, especially where people are concerned.'

'I know,' Alex repeated.

'And she is so very naïve, innocently innocent…' Brenda smiled apologetically, 'if that makes sense. I have often said to Joe that she needs guarding against herself, against her trusting nature.'

'I know that too,' Alex said.

'That's why I was so pleased when you two got together,' Brenda ran on. 'I knew you would look out for her…'

'Tell me what's happened to her.'

'… that you would protect her from herself, so to speak…' Brenda paused, her eyes lightening as she suddenly became aware of Alex's latest interjection. After a moment of thought, she said: 'She phoned me late last night… and… and I guessed straightaway that something was wrong. As I say—'

'I assume that she has another mobile number now,' Alex broke in. 'Do you have it?'

'I do, yes.' Brenda's expression became absorbed, and she took a long sip of her coffee. Alex waited – patiently. After a short while, Brenda went on: 'I would gladly give it to you, Alexander but… Please don't misunderstand me, but I feel that that would be unwise. Catherine is upset, her trust has been undermined… again, and I fear that any unexpected call might cause her to… to… Oh, I don't know, but I had the feeling last night that it wouldn't take much to make her move to somewhere else, and then where would we be?' She glanced up at him. 'She's been through a lot of late and I would rather that you didn't ask.'

Alex was not sure that Brenda's reason for not wanting to give him the number was genuine. It seemed more likely that Catherine had asked her not to – had made her promise not to. He suppressed a give-away grimace. Stubborn to the end, that was Kate. But he didn't need to phone. She was only in Cornwall and once he found out where, he would go there, sort things out – even if she didn't want him to. 'All right,' he said. 'Please go on.'

'As I say, she's fallen in with some awful people, despicable characters. One person in particular has gained her confidence and, I fear, now plans to exploit her.' Brenda then recounted the things that Catherine had told her the previous evening, the behaviour of Will and Tom, her involvement with Christopher Armstrong, her fall from the boat, everything. 'Can you imagine that,' she added, 'our dear Catherine falling into the sea and almost being drowned?' She gazed at Alex, her watery eyes forlorn. 'I've talked to her, tried to persuade her to come home – and she now says that she will, tomorrow. But I'm not sure. I'm really not sure they will allow her to do so... not until they get what they want. They're after something... money... I don't know.'

Alex was already on his feet; he had been for some minutes. 'Tell me where she is,' he said.

'There's a little bit more, Alexander. The fellow who seems to have ensnared her is also a fisherman, as of course was Catherine's lost love. And he is also called Christopher. I fear that the coincidences have struck a chord with her and... and have made her more vulnerable.'

'Okay, Brenda,' Alex said impatiently. 'Now tell me where she is.'

'Mevagissey,' Brenda replied. 'She is in Mevagissey.'

'A hotel, a guest house... or what?'

Brenda bit a tremulous lip. 'A hotel. It's called The Globe Hotel. It's... it's right by the quayside.' She shook her head. 'I hope she will be all right. I do hope…' She fell silent, staring down at her hands. After a moment, a loud noise caused her to look up. The sound was Alex barging his way through the office doorway.

Chapter 12

Catherine pulled aside a corner of the net curtains and peeked out of her hotel room window. Light was fading over the harbour, and away to the southwest the planet Venus had made her debut. Soon she would be swallowed up by the stars, billions of them making up the great swath of the Milky Way. But when it climbed above the eastern horizon, the tiny moon would dwarf them all, and provide enough light for tonight's enterprise.

Even now, so many years on, it still featured in her thoughts, if only in unguarded sentimental moments. But Catherine had always found that sentiment was the most difficult thing to shake off. She had hidden it well down the years. Being open with people, confiding in them, was not always wise. How often had sympathy turned to scorn? She stepped away from the window. This evening would be for the last time. Tonight she would leave the teenager behind, up there on the cliff.

She slipped on a cardigan, fastened the buttons, and took a final look round the room. Her eyes alighted on her two suitcases, by the door, already packed, awaiting her departure. She would take them down to her car in a moment, and then move the vehicle to a public car park – there would then be no requirement to return to the hotel afterwards. Later this evening, she was moving farther down the coast. Following a call from Brenda, confessing her visit to Alex's office,

Catherine had booked herself into The Anchor Hotel at Mousehole. And she had given the management here strict instructions not to disclose her new address to anybody. When her knight in blighted armour arrived, he would find his journey had been a wasted one.

That he would trouble himself to pursue her down here, Catherine found hard to believe. His email and previous behaviour would suggest otherwise. But according to Brenda he had been concerned. She frowned as a thought came to her. Depending on his level of concern, when he arrived he might go looking for Christopher Armstrong – cause trouble. Her frown suddenly became a smile. Let him. It would serve him right if Armstrong gave him a good hiding.

In a short while she had completed her arrangements and was walking briskly along the wharf on route for her destination. This was where Armstrong had rescued the cat. She recalled how, after spotting her coming along the quay, he had darted across to the rock face. Since then, she had worked out the sequence of events. Certainly, the cat was trapped on the ledge, but he would not have climbed up and fetched it down if he had not seen her coming. He would have left the poor thing to somebody else. It was a case of opportunism. He calculated that if she witnessed him rescuing an animal, risking his own safety, he would impress her with his charity – and so off he had gone. She allowed her gaze to drift up to the ledge. Having got to know his character better since then, she would not be surprised to learn that he had placed the cat up there himself.

Just then a sound drew her attention, and she turned to the nearby stack of oil drums. Catherine smiled in recognition. It was the rescued cat. Black and white with ginger markings, it was Conger. She assumed it was waiting for a late boat to return, hoping for a tasty mackerel.

She started towards it, called its name. But at her approach it backed away, into the space between the rock face and the barrels, its eyes filled with feline suspicion. She recalled how it had hissed at Christopher Armstrong, showed him its claws. Wise cat, she thought. Crouching down, she held out her hand, called its name. But Conger was having none of it, and backed farther behind the barrels. Catherine kept trying, coaxing him with a friendly gesture and small talk, apologised for the mackerel forfeited due to her fall into the harbour. But still Conger refused to leave his hiding place. 'Come on, Conger,' she encouraged. 'There's nothing to be frightened of. That nasty man isn't here now. Come on… Good boy…' And eventually, to her delight, Conger extended a watchful head from his lair.

Moving cautiously she edged closer. 'This will be the last time we meet,' she said, as he fixed her with a suspicious eye. 'I'm going back tomorrow. I'm going home to see my friend Brenda. That will be nice, won't it?' She offered her hand again, paused… waited as Conger placed a wary paw forward. 'I doubt that I'll ever come this way again.' She clicked her fingers… went on coaxing. It took some time but, little by little, Conger left his hiding place. Catherine stroked his head, wondered fancifully if he understood the word mackerel. She had said it just now – and she did so once more, whereupon Conger began to nuzzle against her hand. Indeed, she decided, there was a connection there.

Then she had an idea… if it wasn't too late. Rising to her feet, she went hastily back along the quay.

In a little while, she returned to the stack of barrels, where she found Conger still awaited his supper. 'You were lucky, Conger,' she said, placing a mackerel on the ground in front of him, 'the shop was still open.'

She smiled as Conger tucked into his meal. Perhaps, she thought, it was the first step in making him legit, in turning him away from his life of crime. She doubted it though. Anyway, the fishermen didn't mind.

In a little while, she gave Conger's head a final stroke. 'Yes,' she said, sighing, 'I'm going back tomorrow. After tonight I'll have done with it.' She stood up, and was just about to turn and leave, when a familiar voice rang out.

'Well I'll be darned,' it said. 'I've never seen that before.'

Feeling not a little embarrassed that she had been caught talking to a cat, she slowly turned round. The speaker was the man Catherine had previously spoken to, the man in the skiff, the one who had told her about Conger. She supposed that it might be considered odd, talking to an animal. 'I'm leaving tomorrow,' she said, as if offering an explanation for her behaviour.

'I've never seen him let anyone near him before. He's feral; always steers clear of humans – hasn't been treated well by them, I suppose. He prefers his own kind.' Catherine's face broke out into a grin. The man smiled too. 'Didn't mean to suggest anything, Miss,' he said, laughing good-naturedly.

'I'll take it as a compliment,' Catherine said, casting him a lopsided smile. She thought that she must be improving. Several people (men) had suggested that she had a closer affinity to the inanimate than to the sentient. Even Alex had once or twice accused her of being mechanical. Bidding the man farewell, she started off along the quay. Perhaps she should ask him to sign an affidavit to say that he had witnessed her fraternising with a warm-blooded creature.

Soon she was starting the climb up the cliff path. In spite of her plan to avoid him, in the gathering gloom, on the lonely trek, she acknowledged how much more self-assured, more confident, she would feel if Alex was here, by her side. She imagined his hand holding hers, the firm reassuring pressure – the security of male presence… But any man could provide that.

Toughening her resolve Catherine paused, then glanced over her shoulder at the harbour. On the masts of moored yachts, navigation lights were twinkling, moving rhythmically to the turn of the tide. Her gaze widened to take in the whole night-time vista. On the road leading into the town, car headlights winked intermittently as a cavalcade of vehicles descended the tree-lined valley. She wondered whimsically if Alex was among them.

Catherine was okay with being alone. Obviously there were things she missed since her split from Alex. Things like… his companionship… his care… his being there for her… his effect on her social life… his ability to make her laugh… his cooking. She paused, pulled a pained face. The list was getting too long for her liking, and she chided herself for starting on it. But, yes, she had always been all right by herself. Indeed, her single years had been fine, and they would be again. Anyhow she still had her career, her work.

And that had kept her busy down here, at least six hours a day. She had spent more time on the Berryman account, reduced capital exposure, revisited some tax efficiency issues… tidied up a few loose ends; she had helped George Finley transfer components of the McDermitt contract, consolidated the investment foundation. And she had negotiated a great deal on some South American mining stock. Mr Armstrong had put her on to that one.

She accepted that next week would be awkward, back in the office, in the same building as Alex… if she went home, that was. At the moment her timetable was open. She had avoided him today, outsmarted him, but Catherine would have to see him at work, eventually. There would be meetings which both had to attend, chair occasionally. But they were both professional, it would work fine – she had no qualms about that. Besides, they had to talk. There were her personal things at the flat. She would have to collect those at some point.

Of course their jobs in the States would not now be taken up – at least she would not accept hers. Jack would have to find somebody else to be Alex's partner over there. Maybe Anna would be the one. Recalling Alex's words at the party, Catherine paraphrased them. What a team we'll make: Alex and Anna; King and Symonds. Watch out Coney Island!

There it was – Catherine emerged from her satirical interlude – the little scooped hollow, nondescript – one could easily walk by without knowing that it was here. And quite a few had. How many times had they lain there, hushed, hardly daring to move a muscle, as discarnate voices had passed by in the night? Once, when a couple paused nearby to kiss, they had stayed locked together for so long that they thought they had invented Tantric sex. Catherine gazed at the moulded overlap that lidded its edges, an admixture of peat, mulch, and other ancient organics. She had always wondered what geological accident had given rise to that, a feature of its evolution that had afforded them shelter on blowy nights – the wind whistling overhead, adding to the allure, to the romance.

Her Christopher had been romantic – not in the soppy sense. He had been more rudimentary, earthier, sensual, the Mellors type. He had revelled in the use of coarse language. And even though he had never read the novel, he had still come up with the idea of dressing her pubic hair with flowers

– maybe not the allegorical forget-me-nots that Oliver Mellors had used to adorn Lady Chatterley, but his daisy chain had been just as meaningful. Catherine shot a wistful glance at the hollow. But oh how he could fuck – all night long if he had to. She had often wondered how he managed to stay awake the next day... out on the boat. Sometimes he must have been too fatigued to see straight.

Of course Alex could be romantic, thoughtful, buying flowers, chocolates. He was not shy to impromptu lovemaking either – the al fresco kind. Like the time at Clovelly when he had followed her up on to that rock. Golly what a dare. People passing nearby on the cliff path, the main beach just round the headland – anybody could have come by. Catherine had thought that she would die of shame. But, she concluded, it was mostly her fault – she had inflamed him, taking off her T-shirt like that. It didn't do to provoke Alex.

She chuckled in the warm evening air. Then back at the hotel, he had teased her about her bottom, reddened by pat-a-cake contact with the hard rock... until she had pointed out his own buttocks, similarly reddened by prolonged exposure to the sun. That had silenced him.

The moon had risen in the southeast. The stars were out too. She searched for the constellations. *Taurus, The Bull...* That was beginning to show, would become more prominent as the season wore on. *The Plough*, part of *Ursa Major...* But you needed to use your imagination to see that as a plough shear. It had always seemed more like an upended saucepan to her.

Catherine reached into her bag, withdrew the silver locket and chain, laid it in the palm of her hand. She had kept it, treasured it down the years, even after meeting Alex. But now a fresh beginning was to be made – a starting over; her past would be history.

A sudden tear rolled down her cheek as she unfastened the clasp and gazed at the lock of hair, a twist of blond gold – a link to that time... and to this place. She saw him then on that final morning, standing in the prow of his father's boat, tall, broad-shouldered, handsome. He looked so steadfast, so invincible... so young. Their whole lives lay before them... She would give up her place at university, move down here and... The boat reached the harbour exit; he turned and waved, once, twice, and he was gone... for ever. *They shall grow not old, as we that are left grow old...* Just for a moment, she thought of changing her mind. But it was better left here. This was its rightful place, where it belonged. Catherine turned towards the sea. He was out there... somewhere. This was all there was.

Then a noise of someone coming along the path disturbed her solitude, and she turned round.

'Hello, me beauty,' he said. 'Thought I might find 'e up yer.'

Alex turned in to the car park of The Globe Hotel, glanced at the dashboard clock: half past bloody eight. The last fifty miles had been murder. It seemed like everybody was heading south for the weekend, to Mevagissey. Still, at least he was here. Often during the last two tortuous hours, he had seriously doubted that he would make it. But he had. He was in the same town as Kate.

He could not see her car. Perhaps she had driven somewhere for the evening. There would not be much night-time entertainment in a place like this – not the type she went in for, anyway. Maybe she had gone somewhere bigger, more sophisticated: St Austell wasn't far, or Truro.

He got out of his car, stretched, walked round the vehicle.

The hotel didn't look too auspicious. For what he had paid, he was expecting more – and he might not even sleep in the room. Don't build up your hopes, Alexander, he told himself. Catherine wasn't likely to come round that quickly. Her birthday party had been a disaster and she had taken a few knocks down here. Sure, but in a few minutes' time he would see his Kate again. He wondered which room she was in, if she was watching him now, relieved at her deliverance. Picking up his suitcase, he trotted round to the front of the building and jogged up the hotel steps.

Twenty minutes later, he descended them again. Catherine wasn't in the hotel. Where was she? The girl at the reception desk had looked at him as if he had asked her a question on particle physics. So he had asked again, only for her to become vague, not a little confused. She hadn't worked here long; didn't really know the procedures, had only just started her shift. Charming girl but wouldn't last five minutes in a city hotel.

Alex considered his options, surveyed the area. The street leading to the harbour was a parade of summer people – chatter and laughter came at him in equal measure. He could see bars and cafes and restaurants, patrons eating outside. Maybe she had gone out for a meal, if she was still in town, or a walk. Except for the quayside, there didn't appear to be much life anywhere else. He decided to take a look around – he did not intend to do any more driving tonight.

In a little while, he had explored both sides of the harbour and was back outside the hotel again. He had looked in at all the bars and eating places, described her to several people, but had had no luck. No one remembered seeing her. Maybe she had returned to the hotel, while he'd been looking for her.

A check with the receptionist told him that wasn't so. The

girl was just as scatter-brained as before; couldn't even operate the computer properly – nice pair of tits though.

Back on the quayside he positioned himself on one of the many bench seats that overlooked the harbour. He reckoned if he stayed here for a while, kept his eyes peeled, he might strike lucky. But what if she came along with that Armstrong creep? Yeah, but that wasn't likely, not after her talk with Brenda. But Armstrong might have insinuated himself on her, coerced her into some kind of liaison. He gazed at the water, flat, high-tided against the ancient stone – perfect for a drowning accident. No, a sailor was bound to be able to swim. He tried but failed to suppress a grin. Not if the bastard was unconscious he couldn't.

After ten minutes Alex was getting impatient. He was not used to waiting, to hanging around. It was an impotent occupation. His line was doing, forcing the pace, not mooching around like a loser. He rose to his feet and marched across to some railings, by a small jetty, thinking.

The place up on the cliff that Brenda had mentioned had crossed his mind earlier. But who would go up there after dark? he asked himself. Nobody with any sense, that was for sure – and Catherine had plenty of that. Brenda said that Catherine used to go there on starry nights with… with… What was his name? But she wouldn't go there alone. Anyway, it was overcast tonight. The moon was out though. Maybe he would give it a try – he had nothing to lose. Then, focusing his gaze more intently, he noted several stars become faintly visible.

During his walk round the harbour, he had seen a street leading up towards the base of the cliffs. The coastal path would be in that direction. Then he finally realised something. The reason the stars were difficult to see from the town was because of the brightness of the street lighting. He knew that it was still a longshot that Catherine was up there, but he had searched just about everywhere else. And he had nothing to lose.

Chapter 13

Catherine snapped the locket shut, looped the chain round her neck. 'What do you want?' she asked.

'I thought as it were a good evening, that I'd do a bit of stargazing.' He nodded towards her. 'Looks like thee 'ad the same idea. I reckons us should make ourselves comfy yer on the grass and see what comes up?' He made a leer. 'It shouldn't be long before Uranus rises… with its silvery moons.'

How could she have been duped by such a man? Catherine rebuked herself. He was nothing short of villainous – vulgar. She took a half-step down the path. 'I was just going back,' she said bluntly.

'Thee don't seem so friendly tonight, Catherine. I hope I've done nought to upset 'e.' He ran avaricious eyes over her body. 'If I 'ave, I apologise to 'e.'

Catherine stood her ground. 'I'm expecting a visitor tonight, so if you don't mind, I'll have to return.' She made as if to move past him.

But Armstrong refused to move aside – standing now barrel-chested on the path, preventing her from going by. 'I'm sure yer friend won't mind waiting a bit,' he said, grinning brazenly, 'when thee tells un what thee's been doing.'

Experiencing an unwelcome dryness in her mouth, Catherine shot a nervous glance over Armstrong's shoulder, in the direction of the town. 'I must go back,' she said. 'I must…' She fell silent. Her voice wasn't hers – sounded squeaky, an octave higher. Attempting to control her fear, she took several deep breaths, then completed her declaration, licked nervous lips.

His eyes followed her gesture. 'Us've got some unfinished business, Catherine.' He too licked his lips. 'I've put a lot of time and effort into you, and I reckon 'tis time I saw summut in return.'

The pretence of politeness, of him being up here by chance, was over. Catherine recognised that the critical moment was reached. She inched aside, on to the narrow grassy area between the path and the cliff edge. 'I've put a lot of time and effort into you.' His words rang clear in her mind, chimed with everything she had learned about him. Brenda had summed him up as a womaniser. She was right. From the start, from their very first meeting, here in this spot, sex had been his goal. Catherine could see that now. Well, despite his time and effort, she determined that he would get nothing in return from her. She glared at him, took another calming breath. 'Get out of my way,' she said defiantly, tensing her body as though about to walk on. 'I am going back to my hotel.'

'Of course thee be, me beauty. Ah, of course thee be… later. But first thee be gonna do Chris a little favour, a little service, nowt thee ain't done afore… nowt thee ain't *enjoyed* afore.' His stare held hers. 'Maybe it would help 'e, if thee imagined I were somebody else called Christopher.' He nodded his head once, knowingly. 'If thee follows me drift.'

So he did know. Catherine tugged nervously at the strap of her shoulder bag, thinking. He knew about her Christopher, her time here, her story. But she had guessed as much – and it did not matter. All it did was confirm what she already knew. How infantile, she thought, to assume that he could profit from something that had occurred years ago. But that was the sum of the man: a simpleton – but cunning all the same... and determined. Moving her weight onto the ball of her left foot, she repeated her earlier assertion: 'Get out of my way. I am going back to my hotel.'

He grinned, and his eyes adopted an eager cast. 'Ah, and I'll take 'e there meself, Catherine, after we've finished, I promise 'e that. I'll make sure thee gets back safe and sound.' He rubbed a hand against his crotch. 'Now, what will 'e say?'

Catherine returned his avid stare, took in his attitude. From his unsteady stance, she thought that he might have had a drink. He looked as if part of his mind was consciously occupied in maintaining his balance. If he had indeed been drinking, that might have affected his reactions, slowed his responses. If she could edge round him, put herself on the town side, then...

But as if reading her mind, he moved swiftly to obstruct both the path and the narrow strip of ground between it and the cliff edge, cutting off all possible avenues of escape. He leered knowingly, and a dribble of spittle ran down his chin. 'You'll enjoy it, me beauty, thee knows you will. Thee be a sexual thing. I knows that.' He wiped the back of his hand across his mouth, and his eyes took in more of her body. 'And you've got the arse for it.'

That he did not intend to let her go, Catherine was sure. He did not mean to be denied; he meant to have his way. She swallowed dryly, and tried to force herself to think clearly. Her best chance, she decided, was to remain calm, engage him in talk, and dissuade him by conversation, if she could. And there was always the chance that somebody might come along, might intervene. It was a public footpath. 'The courts take a dim view of people–'

'Oh, me sweet, innocent Catherine,' he broke in, 'do 'e think I be that daft?' He came closer, and the smell of cider

216

came with him. She was right: he had been drinking. But he was still alert, agile, ready to grab her if she attempted to run away. And even if she did manage to slip by, she would not outrun him: he knew the terrain; he would quickly overhaul her. Then she heard him say: 'I've people who'll swear they saw us both heading off up yer, hand in hand.'

'Then they are liars.' Catherine all but spat the words at him.

Armstrong bared his teeth. 'That they be; that they be, me beauty. But they'll be believed. And more than that, thee and I 'ave been seen out together... at the mine... on me boat...' A twisted grin warped his expression. 'And who would doubt the word of a man who saved 'e from drowning?'

Catherine stepped nearer to the cliff edge, her mind engaged in a desperate bid to outwit him. She decided that she would try to frighten him, scare him into leaving her alone. She started to turn towards the void.

'Thee won't jump, Catherine,' Armstrong said, grinning as he watched her now teetering on the brink of the drop. 'Thee ain't the type. You be used to the good life. Nah, thee won't jump, not over summut as paltry as the repayment of a debt. That ain't worth dying fer... not when all thee gotta do is open yer legs fer half an hour.' He nodded slyly towards the scooped hollow. 'I reckons that be a good place fer it. What'll 'e say?'

The man was insane. Catherine turned back from the edge of the cliff, stared at the hollow, their secret place, shadow-lit now by Virgo. She saw the two teenagers, holding hands, embracing, eyes only for one another, in love. Her first love... She shook her head, and tears sprang to her eyes. 'No... Not there.'

'That be more like it, Catherine.' He looked around, his

eyes shiftily victorious, clearly anticipating the successful culmination of his plan. 'Don't 'ave to be there. My place ain't far.' He held out his hand. 'C'mon, me beauty, thee knows 'tis going to happen... one way or t'other.'

Catherine felt sickness welling up inside her, experienced the bitter taste of bile rising in her throat. She would rather die than go to bed with him. He was repulsive. Fidgeting with the locket, she turned to face the cliff edge, near enough now to feel the updraught of the onshore breeze. And from a long way below came the sound of waves breaking on rocks. Christopher was out there...

Alex vaulted the stile onto the dirt path, balanced himself, then took his bearings. He could just make out the direction the trail took, straight ahead for about twenty metres then curling upward and round to the left to bring it to the cliff top. He hadn't thought to fetch the torch from his car, and reproached himself for his oversight. But the moon was climbing higher in the sky; it was getting lighter by the minute. He reckoned he could manage – just had to watch his footing.

After a little while, breathing hard, he paused from his climb, peered over his shoulder. The path was steeper than he had first assumed, rougher underfoot too; and it was hard to imagine Catherine slogging all the way up here, particularly at night. But according to Brenda, it meant a lot to her. Yeah, but that was years ago. Besides, if it wasn't for that stupid misunderstanding, she wouldn't be here at all – so it couldn't mean that much, now.

Ironically, he had once suggested a holiday down here. He knew she liked the coast, walking on the cliffs, and so he had made some enquiries. Mevagissey had come out top;

besides the walks, it had all the other ingredients Kate would go for: wildlife, great scenery, nearby moors, olde-worlde inns, boat trips, gardens – and the Eden Project wasn't far away. But she hadn't been interested – had been persuasively against the idea in fact. No, it couldn't mean that much to her.

He decided against going far along the path, just up to the top, have a quick look around. It would be just as well to return to the hotel, wait for her there, over a beer… or two. She was bound to come back sometime. Then they would have their reunion. He had to admit, now that it was near to happening, that he was ambivalent about it. On the one hand, he couldn't wait to see her again. But, on the other, what sort of reception would he receive?

He didn't know the answer to that one. It was possible that his arrival would be a surprise, that Brenda hadn't informed Catherine he was coming down. His gut feeling though was that Brenda would have done so. She wouldn't want him turning up unannounced; and she would want Kate to know the part she herself had played. Brenda was an honest old bird. But gently, gently would be his approach – play it by ear. He was mostly innocent, anyway. Catherine had overreacted. She had… And it was then that he heard the sound of voices.

He stood stock-still and listened. Or was it the breeze? That was stiffer up here than back in the town. The area was scattered with gorse bushes and several of those stunted trees that you saw along the coast. It could be the wind rustling the branches of those. He listened some more, concentrating his ears on the evening sounds. No, he concluded, he could definitely hear a male voice farther along the path. He could not make out the words. He listened a little longer, then moved forward again, one step at a time. It might be Armstrong; it certainly wasn't Catherine.

After covering a dozen or so paces, Alex drew to a halt, peering into the dusk. He could see two figures. They were standing just off the path, facing one another, about a hundred metres ahead. The nearer of the two figures was a man. His back was turned this way. The other figure, a woman, was standing by the cliff edge… right next to it. The man was gesticulating at the woman, who seemed cowed, cringing from his presence. They were obviously having some kind of an argument. Alex thought the woman might be Kate. But it was difficult to be sure. From this angle she was partly obscured by the man, but the hair looked wrong. She also looked too short, squat, foreshortened against the male figure. It might be them – but it might not. The last thing Alex wanted to do was bust in on another couple's quarrel. He edged a little closer, incrementally, one lithe foot over the other, little by little… Then he froze; for he saw that the woman was Catherine.

The scene before him did not appear good. It looked as if she was preparing to jump – it really did. He swallowed the sudden lump in his throat, started to move forward, faster than before – urgently. Then he checked himself. He realised he had to be careful, he had to go forward slowly. If he went charging in, he might spook the guy, or even Catherine, who was on the cliff edge. He must not do anything to make matters worse. It was high up here, a long way down. Before he acted, he had to ensure Catherine was safe.

He noted then that the breeze was blowing towards him. Which was good, for it would tend to take any sound he made away from them. If the guy didn't turn round, Alex thought he could get pretty close without attracting his attention.

Moving silently, he stole along the path. Catherine was

in profile, but he could see that her stare was focused on the man, concentrated, as if watching for his first move. Alex nodded, still inching forward. Yeah, that was Armstrong, had to be – fucking creep… Big bastard though.

But why was she up here with him? he asked himself. Surely she had not come willingly, not after everything that had occurred? Maybe he had forced her. But why bring her up here? There was no logical reason that Alex could see. Maybe he had followed her, if she had come up here by herself. Yeah, that was more likely. For his type, that would be par for the course – fucking creep.

With any luck, Alex calculated, Catherine would see him before Armstrong did and, even more hopefully, she would not register that she had done so. It happened that way in films, in books. Yeah, but this wasn't fiction. This was real, and that was Catherine. That was his Kate. He had to ensure she saw him before Armstrong did, and hope to God she didn't give the game away. If that scenario panned out, he would tackle Armstrong hard and fast, and Catherine could get to safety.

He crept a little nearer. He could see now how bad the circumstances actually were. The merest step backwards and Catherine would be over the edge of the cliff. Whatever the bastard was proposing, it was damned obvious she wasn't buying into it. He made another step, then another…

He was nearly upon them, just a few metres away. He couldn't understand why Catherine hadn't seen him. It was damned near as light as day now. Her concentration on Armstrong's face must be absolute.

Armstrong was speaking… saying something about his place not being far. That could mean only one thing: the bastard was trying to force her to go there. Alex could see that Catherine was crying, that she was turning towards the cliff edge… as if she meant to jump. Oh, Kate don't… I'm here. He was, but he wasn't near enough to prevent Armstrong from getting to her before he did. If Alex shouted or went for it, he feared it would spark Armstrong into going for her, grappling with her… pushing her. He hesitated, momentarily stalled by the scene being played out before him… Catherine, for Christ's sake look this way. Then he thought that she did. But at the same time, Armstrong started to turn in his direction.

Tom set his glass back on the table. 'He's going to get himself into a lot of bother, if he goes through with it.'

'He won't do anything. You know Conger, all talk and no action.' Will scoffed. 'He ain't got the balls for it.'

'I dunno about that. Look at him just now. He saw her heading up there and off he went, straight away – didn't even finish his drink.' Tom threw a nervous glance towards the door. 'Maybe we should go after him. You know, see that he doesn't do anything daft.'

Will grinned. 'That's not a bad idea, going after him. It'd be a good laugh to see him give her one, stuck-up bitch.' He swigged his pint. 'And I haven't seen a good live sex act for ages – not since we docked in Rotterdam, and that was last year.' He grinned slyly. 'And who knows, Tom? If he fires her up good and proper, both of us might get a turn. He said she's a goer.'

Tom stared at his mate. 'I'm serious, Will. He could end up in jail.'

'Get on,' Will said dismissively. 'He ain't going to do anything. He's too pissed to get it up.'

'He ain't had that much.' Tom reached for his pint. 'He

didn't score with her the other night. That really riled him...
and he's a hot-headed cuss; he doesn't like to be outdone.' He
gulped at his drink. 'And he's done it before, when he couldn't
get his way legit: that nice-looking piece... blonde hair... last
year. Remember? He doped her. You saw that for yourself, in
here. He was popping something in her drinks all night.' He
took a considered draw from his glass. 'He raped her – and
boasted about it afterwards, too.'

'She never reported it.'

'This one will. A lot of women don't... But she will. You
wait and see.'

Will drained his glass, then belched. 'Maybe you're right.
Can't say that I've ever really liked the bloke but I wouldn't
want to see him in trouble with the law all the same.' He
shoved his empty glass towards the other man. 'But there's
plenty of time. We'll have another one first. It's your shout.'

'Will...'

'Just get them in. Or are you trying to dodge your
round... again?'

Sighing, Tom scooped up their glasses, turned from the
table, and headed off to replenish their drinks.

'Bloody old woman,' Will muttered under his breath, as
he watched his mate elbow his way to the bar.

In a moment Tom returned with their beers. He plonked
the glasses down on the table, spilling some of Will's drink.
'Let's make it quick,' he said. 'Then we'd best get on up there.'

Will silently shuffled their glasses round, so that his was
the fuller of the two. 'I told you, man: he's not going to do
anything. He ain't capable. If she took her pussy out and it
winked at him, he wouldn't be able to do anything.' He
guffawed. 'He'd still have brewer's droop.'

'Conger can hold his liquor – I'll say that for him. And

even if he can't, it's not going to stop him trying – and that's just as bad. And what if she puts up a fight and he clouts her one?' Tom pulled a mobile phone from his jacket pocket. 'I think we should do something,' he said, starting to key in a number.

Will eyed his mate, suspiciously. 'What're you up to?'

Ignoring Will's question, Tom carried on entering the number.

Will snatched the phone from the other man's hand, stared at the screen. 'You bastard,' he said angrily. 'That's the Rozzer's number.'

Tom tried to get his phone back but Will held it away from him. 'I was only going to tip them off,' he said, still trying to retrieve his mobile. 'Maybe they could get there before he did anything.'

'And what if they don't. Suppose they get there and find him hard at it.' Will put Tom's phone in his own pocket. 'What then? Do you wanna see him get ten years? Because that's what he'd get – all the rest would come out as well: how he tipped her in the harbour, how he drugged her… You idiot.'

'Didn't think of that, Will.'

Will regarded his mate ruefully. 'I've known you a long time, Tom, but I never had you marked down as a grass.'

'I was only thinking of her,' Tom said apologetically. 'She may be a bit slow on the uptake but she doesn't deserve to be raped.'

Will punched his mate playfully on the arm. 'Listen to the new man, Mr PC.' He finished his drink. 'But you're right. We'll have one more round and then we'll go up there and rescue the damsel in distress… if she wants to be rescued.'

Armstrong's abrupt shift of attention brought a familiar figure into Catherine's eye-line. She stared at him, goggle-eyed, not comprehending. At first she thought that he must be a hallucination, a desperate illusion inspired by fear, but a blink and a second take of the scene reassured her that Alex was actually here, here in the flesh. Relief surged through her like a warming wave. She was safe; she did not have to jump; she wasn't going to die. 'Alex,' she cried, unable to stop herself. 'Alex.' Then she heard Armstrong say scornfully:

'So you're the little city boy.' She watched him turn fully towards Alex. 'Ah, I thought there'd be one somewhere. Well, if thee 'as come down yer looking for a hiding, then you've come to the right place.' He smacked a clenched fist into his palm. 'And if I ain't knocked yer lights out by the time that I've finished with 'e, you can watch I fuck yer woman too.'

'If anyone's going to be fucked, punk, it's going to be you.'

'I bet thee'd like that, wouldn't 'e?' Armstrong went on, ignoring Alex's remark. 'Seeing I show yer bitch how to come?' On a grin, he reached down and unzipped his fly. Then taking himself out, he said: 'I reckons this'll do the job. What will 'e say, boy? I bet she ain't 'ad nought like this from thee.'

Catherine stared, dumbfounded, trying, albeit without much success, to relate what she was seeing to what she knew the actual situation to be. She had another go. Alex had arrived, apprehended Armstrong, who was threatening her, the two men had clearly been about to have an argument, when Armstrong had... Then she heard Alex say:

'No, she hasn't.' She turned towards him... and her eyes... and her eyes deceived her, for they were trying to tell her that Alex had also exposed himself. And then she heard him continue: 'This is her usual fare.'

Catherine's gaze took in the sight, the bizarre, the

ridiculous… the impossible scene of two men, Armstrong in dungarees and pullover, Alex in slacks, polo shirt and jacket, on the cliff top, in the moonlight, facing one another… with their penises out. It was surreal. They were like two fighting cocks, each attempting to overawe the other bird.

She wondered then if it was some kind of masculine ritual. Catherine had seen wildlife documentaries in which male animals fought mock battles – the theory being that the practice had evolved to limit the kind of injuries sustained in real combat. Would they then, she speculated, now become erect and engage one another in a pseudo sword fight, their penises standing in as surrogate weapons? They might. For the end result of both types of battle, real and pretend, was said to be the same: the winner taking the spoils – usually the chance to mate…

And then, with Catherine's mind going the wrong way, in harmony, as if both men had mutually realised the ridiculousness of the situation, each man put himself in order. She stared at them. The contest was obviously over, with no blows having been exchanged. For all the world, it looked as if Alex had just come onto the scene and caught Armstrong bullying her.

But who had won their contest? she asked herself. Who had outflanked the other? From the continuing belligerent stares of the two men, their puffed-up stances, it was impossible to tell. On the evidence of the TV documentaries, she thought that it must be a stalemate.

She wondered then what would happen next. Would they shake hands, go their separate ways… and she with Alex? For he had…

Then, bringing an end to her confused speculation, she saw him flick a glance in her direction, his eyes indicating that she should move away from the cliff edge. She tried – but her limbs seemed suddenly numbed, her body paralysed. Whether it was due to the bizarre behaviour she had witnessed or the reminder of her peril she did not know but she could not move. And then she saw Alex step off the path and start to circle round behind Armstrong. Something told her that he was seeking the advantage of higher ground. Surely they were not going to attack each other, engage in a fistfight – not after their ridiculous display?

She gazed anew at the two men, and her heart sank at what she saw. She had thought they were about the same height. Catherine now realised that she'd been wrong. Armstrong was a good two inches taller. Not only that, but he also looked bigger, heavier, more muscular. Alex appeared diminutive beside him. 'This has gone far enough,' she yelled fiercely. 'You're not two schoolboys in the playground...' Of a sudden, the fear of an impending fight and its likely outcome unlocked her frozen body and she moved away from the precipice. She stamped her foot on the ground. 'Please stop this nonsense.'

But neither man responded to her plea, and she watched in dismay as the two would-be combatants squared up to one another, each clearly seeking an opening in the other's defence. To her fear-laden eyes, Armstrong looked cunning, sly, a man not to be trusted of conducting a fair fight. Alex, on the other hand, seemed focused, his stare fixed on his adversary's eyes.

Catherine did not want to see either man hurt, even Christopher Armstrong, who had so wickedly deceived her. But it would be worse if Alex was hurt, for then she would be left at Armstrong's mercy – and she knew that he would show her none. Perhaps, she thought, it would be wise, when the fracas got going, to make a run for it, to save herself. She glanced at Alex, saw his face set in stony concentration, his eyes alert, watchful. No, she could not do that. Whatever his faults, whatever he had done to her, she knew that she could not run off and leave him. It would not be right. But what could she do if she stayed?

She remembered once seeing a film where a woman in her position had used a rock to disable the aggressor. But then the adversaries had been rolling on the ground, wrestling. Alex and Armstrong were standing upright: she probably wouldn't be able to reach. And what if she hit the wrong man? she asked herself. She studied the two men – each looked set to kill the other. Deciding it might be worth a try, she glanced around the cliff top arena. She could not see any rocks, at least ones big enough to knock somebody unconscious. There were some pebbles in the path. But how large did they need to be? In the film–

Then it started. A curse made her look up, a grunt focused her attention and she saw, as if in slow motion, a gnarled fist sweeping through the air towards Alex's jaw. And in that moment, she knew he was going to lose.

Catherine saw the ambulance coming out of the night – emergency lamp flashing, siren wailing, headlights bouncing as it negotiated the humps and troughs of the green topography. She saw that it was approaching from the direction of the old tin mine. When Armstrong had taken her there, she hadn't seen any access route to the cliff top – obviously there must be one, otherwise how would vehicles get in and out? But in his condition, she knew that it would be a bumpy ride back. A helicopter would have been better?

She had read of the so-called critical hour, during which

medical treatment should ideally be administered – exceed that time and the victim's chances of survival were severely reduced. The ambulance had taken nearly three quarters of an hour to get here. That meant there were only fifteen minutes left. It was unacceptable to be so delayed. It was not good enough. It was… Catherine's temper subsided a little as she realised there would be paramedics on board, with all the latest equipment. First aid would be given, and he would receive treatment on the way to the hospital – all within the crucial period.

Hearing a sudden movement in the undergrowth behind her, she glanced round. Immediately after his fist had landed and Alex had crashed to the ground, Armstrong had gone running off back towards the town, loping off like the cowardly bully he was. But Catherine wasn't sure how far he had retreated. She couldn't see anything but she had a feeling that he was hiding nearby, waiting to see if he could catch her alone. But she determined that he would not. She was going in the ambulance, with Alex to the hospital. His injury had been sustained while defending her – she couldn't just leave him. And it would be nice for him to see a familiar face when he regained consciousness.

Catherine tried not to look but she could not stop herself. She saw that the entire front of his face, his once-handsome face, was caved in. Armstrong's fist had caught him flush, had gone a long way in, taking all before it – flesh, bone, sinew. Alex had been advancing, had walked straight into the punch, doubling its force… or more – there was bound to be irreparable damage. Blood was everywhere, in his eye sockets, trickling from his ears, from the corners of his mouth, his nose… what remained of it. Even the grass in the hollow, where he had landed, had changed colour – a grotesque bloodshot smudge, coagulated in the moonlight.

The outcome of the fight had been a foregone conclusion. She had known that from the moment the two men had faced one another. It was like putting a little boxer in the same ring as a big one – a mismatch. The bigger man was bound to win. She had briefly hoped that Alex's lighter stature might make him more nimble, enable him to avoid Armstrong's blows while delivering thumps of his own. But it hadn't worked out that way. It had been all too predictable.

Another sound made her turn and peer again, into the darkness, towards the town. Her heart leapt. Somebody was hiding there, beside the path, crouching low behind a clump of gorse bushes. Catherine stared at the spot. Or was it a shadow? She wasn't sure. It was an indistinct shape, unmoving, patient – yet seeming to have substance, a body. Was it Armstrong… waiting for her?

The ambulance swung round in a tight circle, braked, then backed up beside her. Two paramedics emerged from the cab, came round the vehicle and opened its rear doors. Catherine ran to them. 'He's hurt.' She pointed to Alex. 'Look. He is badly hurt. He needs help… He's dying.'

But the men took no notice of her, seemed almost oblivious to her presence. How typical of such people, she thought angrily. Give someone a uniform and he became self-important, officious – a tyrant. She watched them saunter across the turf to where Alex was lying, glance at one another, then exchange a few words. How could they be so casual? They knew what had happened. She had made the telephone call herself, had described his condition – in minute detail. She pulled at a sleeve. 'Hurry!' But the man ignored her, brushed off her petition. 'Please hurry,' she repeated, tugging more urgently at his sleeve. It was as if she were of no consequence – a nuisance, an accidental bystander getting in the way.

Catherine turned aside, paced up and down, impatient, desperately wanting action – wishing they would do something… anything. Alex wasn't breathing – so why were they just standing there, talking, shaking their heads, discussing him as if he were a training dummy? Why hadn't they used a defibrillator, or given him oxygen? Or done any of the other things they were supposed to do? They had taken his pulse, but the activity had looked cursory – more like going through the motions than a genuine medical procedure. Were they just going to let him die?

And why were they talking so quietly, whispering to one another, as if they didn't want her to hear their conversation? They were cutting her out, excluding her from knowing anything. She may not be medically trained, but it was obvious she knew as much about first aid as they did. Paramedics – what a misnomer. They used to be called ambulance drivers. Meat wagon drivers would be nearer the truth for these two… Catherine's thought process paused as she saw that at last they were doing something.

She watched as the two stony-faced medics now fetched a stretcher from the ambulance, rolled Alex onto it… as if he were a lump of clay. 'Be careful with him.' Catherine's words came out in an explosion of indignation. 'He is a human being, you know.' She stomped her foot on the ground. 'Don't treat him like a corpse.' They were so infuriating. Why, she asked herself once more, hadn't they examined him, tried to resuscitate him, or put him on life support? Their incompetence was beginning to make her angry.

Catherine decided she would make a complaint. She read the logo on the side of the vehicle: *Cornwall Emergency Service*. There was a telephone number there, and she memorised it. First thing in the morning, if not sooner, she would register her grievance. They were too lackadaisical – there was no urgency with them.

But at last they were putting the stretcher into the ambulance, securing it to a platform. She watched the medics stepping down from the vehicle. Surely one should have stayed behind, in the back, to attend to him, to look after him on the journey to the hospital – in the critical hour? She saw the trolley ramp being swung back into its storage position, the doors being shut. 'Don't let him die.' Why were they ignoring her? It was as if she didn't exist for them.

She ran forward. 'I want to go with him.' She reached for the door handle, but it was locked. Catherine grasped the medic's shoulder, repeated her appeal, louder, more demanding. But the man shrugged her off, turned away and walked round to the front of the ambulance, climbed into the cab. 'You can't stop me.' She followed the man to the cab. The window was open. 'I want to come too.' Then the motor fired, and the window closed.

The ambulance started to move away, lurched into and out of a rut. 'Where are you taking him?' She made several steps after the retreating vehicle, thinking. They hadn't even put on the blue emergency light. 'Where…' Neither had they turned on the siren.

Standing forlorn on the bleak down, Catherine watched the vehicle disappear over the crest of a slope, until only the reflection of its head lamps was visible against the darkened horizon. Then that too was gone.

Why, she asked herself, hadn't they allowed her to go with him, to the hospital? There was no harm in doing that – and it was her right. Why had they disregarded her requests? It was no way to treat anybody. There was no excuse. Even if she was not permitted to ride in the ambulance, they should have informed her of his condition, said where they were taking him.

Catherine kicked angrily at a tuft of grass, stomped her foot on the ground, shook a frustrated head. Imbeciles… idiots! They…

Coming back to herself in the stellar night, she stared at the arena, saw the two men… the two combatants… and the gnarled fist cutting through the air towards Alex's jaw.

Alex saw the punch coming, a haymaker, a wild swing that told him all he needed to know about his adversary. The man looked strong, fit enough, but he clearly lacked any discipline in the science of hand-to-hand combat. He ducked beneath the punch, then, with Armstrong off balance, brought his left foot down in one seamless movement onto the other man's right knee. It was a classic self-defence move; for no matter how powerful, how agile your opponent might be, with his mobility disabled he was no longer a threat. The resulting cracking sound convinced Alex that the cartilage was gone, even that the kneecap was split.

He knew about these things. In his youth he had done a bit of kickboxing, and in one bout an undisciplined kick had resulted in that very injury. The injured guy had spent four hours in surgery, and the surgeon had done a good job, but the poor bugger had never walked freely afterwards.

Armstrong yelped and fell forward onto the turf but, to Alex's surprise, almost immediately regained his fighting posture. 'So the city boy likes to kick, do 'e? Well, I can kick, too.' And with that he lashed out with his boot.

As before, Alex saw the blow coming. But instead of letting it go harmlessly by, as he had with the haymaker, he caught hold of Armstrong's ankle and, using the momentum

233

of the kick, upended him onto the seat of his pants.

Armstrong struggled to his feet, cursing Alex for being a sissy, afraid to mix it man to man. 'All right, nancy boy,' he said, squaring up with raised fists. 'I sees that now's the time to get rough with 'e. I be gonna beat 'e to a pulp.'

Despite the tough words, Alex saw doubt in Armstrong's eyes, acceptance that he had been floored twice, recognition that he might even lose the fight. Clearly, he had not expected much opposition. How wrong he was. He set himself up to deliver a trouble-free knockout, parried several amateurish slaps, focused… But then, with Armstrong's solar plexus in his sights, a thought came suddenly to him. If he wanted to ensure himself of Catherine's wholehearted sympathy, her compassion, his victory should not be seen as a pushover. Something a little more cunning was required. And he knew what. If it went wrong – and it might – he reckoned he could still outmanoeuvre his man. But if it went right – and he had every reason to believe that it would – he could very soon find himself engaged in something a little more physically demanding than this brawl. Offering an inviting chin, he advanced on his opponent.

Alex saw the punch unleashed, the uppercut that his stance had tempted. But this time, instead of avoiding the blow completely, he merely jinked slightly to his right and allowed the clenched fist to graze his jaw. The annoyance in Armstrong's eyes that his blow had only partially hit its target was palpable. But it fitted into Alex's plan perfectly, for, taking several faltering steps backwards, with a gasp of surprise he collapsed onto his back.

Through narrowed eyes he now watched Armstrong turn a triumphant profile to Catherine, whom he could see was edging away. Just touch her mate, he thought. No, just think about it and I'll show you what it's like when the gloves are off. He tensed his limbs, prepared himself for action... and waited. But there was no need for concern, for he heard Armstrong say:

'That's how we deal with city boys down yer.' He dusted his hands together. 'Look at un... Just look at un. I only caught un a glancing blow, and he's out fer the count. Bloody sissy!'

'Leave him alone,' Catherine shouted. She stamped her foot. 'Leave *us* alone, you big bully.'

Almost as if he was aware that Alex was watching him, Armstrong backed away from Catherine. 'Ah, I'll leave 'e alone,' he said vehemently. He looked her up and down. 'I can fuck better than thee any night of the week.' And with that, he turned and made off along the cliff path towards the town.

Alex suppressed a contented smile, relaxed. It couldn't have worked out better. He had fooled Armstrong, conned the conman. And the prick had departed, had run off like the coward he was. Not only that, but he had put himself in the best possible light – Catherine would be grateful, relieved at her deliverance... ready to discuss their rift. Had he knocked Armstrong down, that may not have been the case. Alex thought that he was halfway to achieving his goal... halfway to paradise. *Put your sweet lips close to my lips...*

'Sometimes I wonder why I listen to you.' Will drew to a surly halt on the dirt path, brushed a teasel from his trouser leg. 'I can't believe I let you persuade me to come up here. It's a wild goose chase, man. He won't have done anything.'

Staring back at the harbour below, Tom took several rasping breaths. 'Given half a chance he will. If he finds her, he'll do her all right.' He took several more intakes of the night air. 'And he's our mate. We can't let him go to jail.'

'Yeah, but look at you, you fat oaf, you ain't fit enough to climb up here.' Will prodded Tom's gut. 'He's not worth risking a heart attack for.'

Tom batted aside his mate's hand. 'I'm as fit as you, you… you beanpole.'

'You're as fit as Conger: fit for nothing.' Will too stared at the distant harbour. 'I'm going back to the pub.'

'We're at the top now,' Tom encouraged. 'We might as well go a bit further.' His eyes took on a crafty cast. 'Like you said… we might get a turn as well.'

'I was taking the piss. You know Conger; he don't share anything with anybody.' Will scoffed. 'Besides, I don't fancy her – thinks too much of herself.' He turned back to Tom. 'How far is it along here, anyhow? I don't want to miss last orders.'

'I dunno. But Conger lives out at the inlet – and that's only a mile or so. So it can't be far.'

Will stared down at his mate. 'Are you trying to tell me you don't even know where it is? You drag me all the way up here, and you don't even–'

'Shush, Will. There's somebody coming.'

'Where? I can't hear…' Will fell silent, gazing along the coastal path… before, a moment later, bursting into sudden ribald laughter. 'What's the matter, Conger?' he said, stifling his mirth. 'Kicked you in the bollocks, did she?'

Armstrong limped up to his mates. 'What be thee two idiots doing up yer? Think I couldn't handle her by meself, be that it?'

Will nodded at Armstrong's leg. 'Looks like we were right.'

'We were worried about you, that's all,' Tom put in. 'We didn't want to see you land yourself in trouble.' He shot Will a mollifying glance. 'We thought a couple of witnesses might come in handy.'

'I don't need no witnesses – no need fer they. I told 'e afore: she's hot. And I were right.' He nodded purposefully. 'She were up fer it... and I did the job on her.' He rubbed his crotch. 'Ah, that I did.'

'Where is she?' Tom asked, glancing down the path.

'She's all right, if that's what thee means.' He thumbed towards the inlet. 'She's gone back t'other way... by taxi.'

'What happened to your leg?' Will asked, grinning.

'Fuck me leg,' Armstrong spat angrily. 'That's nowt.'

'Your knee looks pretty swollen,' Will persisted. 'It's nearly busting through your dungarees. You'd best get it seen to, man.'

'C'mon, Conger,' Tom said, reaching for Armstrong's sleeve. 'We'll get you to the hospital.'

Armstrong pushed the hand away. 'I told 'e, 'tis nowt – nowt that a pint a cider won't cure, anyway.'

'Will's right: it don't look so pretty.' Tom said. 'How did it happen, Conger?'

A slow sneer materialised on Armstrong's face. After a while he hawked noisily, then spat on the ground. ''Twas an accident. When... when I went down on her, I whacked un on a rock.' He felt his knee, winced. 'I should've been more careful, but the horny bitch was begging me for it.'

'Yeah, yeah, yeah,' Will mocked. 'Now tell us how it really happened – how a kick in the balls laid you low.'

'Go on, Conger,' Tom coaxed. 'We won't laugh.' He turned to his friend. 'We won't will we?'

Suppressing a snigger, Will shook a solemn head.

Armstrong let out a sigh. ''Twas like I said. She were pulling I, yanking at me zip, begging I to fuck her. I'd never known a woman like it – couldn't pissing wait. It were all "fuck mes" and "do it nows". So I gave her what she wanted; I went down on her… and me knee hit a rock… and… and…' His account petered out and, glancing between his two mates, he said: 'Well, if thee must know, her boyfriend turned up and we had ourselves a bit of a scuffle.'

Will hooted. 'Not when you were on the job,' he said, guffawing. 'Don't tell me he caught you on the job.'

'Naw!' Armstrong said brusquely. ''Twer afore that. She were getting all lovey-dovey with I and he–' He paused as Will let out a contemptuous scoff. Then, staring threateningly at the other man, he went on: 'And he came along, saw how his woman was coming on to another man. Obviously 'e didn't like it. Jealous bastard started to get uppity, squared up to I. "C'mon, my fellow. Put them up. Let's see who's the best man. I'll…" Anyway, I put the bugger down, knocked un cold.'

'Is he all right?' Tom asked. 'Maybe we should–'

'Ah 'course he is,' Armstrong snapped. 'Little punk. I didn't hit un that hard, just enough to keep un quiet fer a while… while I fucked his bitch.'

'All the same,' Tom said, 'I think we should–'

'I tell 'e, he's all right. Bloody pansy. I hardly hit un, just a glancing blow. But down 'e went all the same.' Armstrong paused, seemingly thoughtful. 'I ain't even sure he was really right out. He knew that I could lick un and he just didn't fancy it anymore.'

'And you did her?' Will said, winking at Tom.

'Yeah, 'course I did. Afore we started fighting, I told un he could watch I fuck her.' Armstrong smirked. 'I told un I'd show her how to come.' He swung a nasty head towards Will, who had just jeered loudly. 'Don't believe I, do 'e both?' he added challengingly.

'Oh, we believe you, Conger,' Will said nudging Tom in the ribs. 'When have you ever lied to us?'

'That's right,' Armstrong said, nodding. 'I ain't. And I ain't now. I fucked her right there and then, in front of the punk.'

'What did he do?' Tom said. 'You said you didn't think he was unconscious.' He shot a sly look towards Will. 'No man would just lie there and watch another bloke do his bird.'

'He did, I tell 'e. He was too shit-scared to move. Ah, that he was.' Armstrong thought for a moment. 'And I'll tell 'e summut else. When she came, he started snivelling… like a little kid… Yeah, he did… just like a snooty nose little kid… when he seen her come.' He eyed his mates, who were grinning at one another. 'I doubt the little punk 'ad ever heard her make that sort of noise afore.'

'C'mon, Tom,' Will said, turning towards the town, 'I've heard enough of this bullshit. I'm going back to the pub.'

Armstrong stood his ground. 'Naw, thee don't believe I. But I'm telling 'e, that's what happened.'

Tom scoffed. 'Hang on, Will,' he said. 'I'm coming, too.'

Armstrong hobbled after his mates, who had started off down the path. 'I ain't no liar.' He caught Will by the shoulder, spinning him round. 'Why don't we *all* go back there?' he said. A shrewd look came to his face, and he added: 'Then you can see fer yerselves.'

Will grinned smugly. 'I thought you said they went back the other way, by taxi.'

For a second Armstrong appeared nonplussed, outfoxed, at a loss for an answer. But then, following a brief hiatus, with a dawning look, he said: 'I meant they were gonna go. They won't have gone yet. When I left, she were seeing to un… wiping his eyes.'

'Bullshit.'

'Prove I wrong, then,' Armstrong said defiantly. 'If thee don't believe I, prove I wrong.' He pulled Will's arm. 'Let's go back.'

Will turned to Tom, grinned knowingly... then shrugged.

Chapter 14

Catherine ran to where Alex had fallen. That he must be badly hurt was obvious. She hadn't actually seen the blow hit him but from where she was standing it appeared to have been delivered with vicious intent. She expected to find a broken jaw, black eyes, blood, missing teeth, a fissured skull – her fear-inspired vision brought to life. She was therefore somewhat surprised to find Alex's face almost unscathed... just a little graze on his cheek. She decided his injuries must be hidden, possibly internal bruising, even a brain haemorrhage.

She scrambled around on the grass, searching for her shoulder bag. It couldn't be far... Oh, where was it? Then she found it. Fumbling in her haste, she extracted her mobile phone, then started to key in the emergency number.

Alex groaned. 'Don't phone for an ambulance,' he said shakily, rolling his eyes. 'I'm... I'm really not too badly hurt.'

Catherine dropped her phone, cradled Alex's head in her arms. 'Oh, my darling, I saw him hit you. I thought you were badly hurt.' Impulsively she kissed his forehead, then again, and again. 'I thought you were dead.'

Alex moaned and attempted to raise himself onto his elbows. With relief, she saw him smile. It was a brave smile, a gesture surely made to allay her concern. She all but cried with joy. He wasn't as badly hurt as she had supposed. Her fears were unfounded. He would recover, hospital, convalescence; and she would help; she would look after him – Catherine's runaway thoughts planned the future. In no way had she intended to return with him, but this was different. Alex required nursing… from someone who cared. Then she heard him say: 'Is the big bad bully gone now, mommy?'

Catherine stopped kissing him. He was concussed, delirious… His mind had regressed. He didn't know what he was saying – where he was. He was a schoolboy again, in the playground, struck down by the school bully. She gazed down at him, her heart melting. If he had sustained brain damage, he might never… Oh, Alex… She glanced at her mobile, reached out… Then she heard him repeat his question. 'Is the big bad bully gone now, mommy?' She realised then that his condition was even more serious than she had initially thought… He might even slip into a coma… or worse. Then she noticed the flickering eyelid. She stared at him. He was going; he was slipping away… And then she observed another flickering eyelid. She continued to stare at… at an imperceptible twitch of his lips… as if… almost as if… Something clicked in Catherine's mind. He wasn't, she asked herself… he wasn't acting, pretending to be hurt? That would be beyond belief. And now a further twitch of his lips, another flickering eyelid… No, he wouldn't… No… Of course he would. And what was she doing kissing him like this? She dropped his head onto the turf. 'You idiot – that's not funny. With you lying here like this, he could have turned on me. He could have—'

'No he couldn't,' Alex interrupted. 'I was watching him. Believe me, if he as much as moved a muscle in your direction, he was in trouble.' His face brightened. 'But don't stop kissing me. I was enjoying that.'

Catherine remained kneeling on the grass, beside him. 'I

don't want to kiss *you*,' she said. She could not believe it – his mindlessness. Five minutes ago she was preparing to jump off the cliff, to kill herself, and all he could think about was playing the fool. She fixed him with an angry stare. 'You don't care about me. You're treating this as a... as a Boy's Own adventure.'

Alex's smile evaporated. 'Kate, that's not true.' His expression became suddenly perplexed. 'I apologise for what I did... for my stupid faking. But I was so relieved that you were all right that... that I just didn't think.' His eyes searched hers. 'Sorry.'

Catherine did not answer – she was too angry for that.

'And I do care,' he went on over her silence. 'I care about you a lot. When I came across you two just now and saw the situation, you on the cliff edge, him threatening you, I froze up; I didn't know what to do...' He shook a troubled head. 'I was afraid, really afraid. Yes, really. Not of him, that jackass, but because of what I might do to him.' He paused to shake an even more troubled head. 'For the first time in my life I realised I was capable of murder. If he had hurt you, he was a dead man. I might have spent the rest of my life behind bars, but his life was over. That's... that's how much I care.'

Catherine's anger subsided, a little. 'I'm glad that you aren't hurt,' she said coldly. 'But there was no need to pretend that he had knocked you down. I didn't know that he hadn't.' She shivered. 'I was scared stiff.'

'I'm sorry, Catherine,' he said, pushing himself into a sitting position. 'But it was the only way. Once I saw you were safe, I started thinking clearly again. I realised that if I won the fight, injured him, there might be repercussions? Even with Armstrong being the aggressor, if he found out that I've studied martial arts, I could have found myself in trouble, legally culpable. This way, he's walked away thinking himself the winner – with his pride intact.' Despite her obvious reluctance, he took her hands in his, squeezed them. 'We will hear no more from him.'

Catherine freed herself from his grip. 'I hope you're right,' she said, glancing instinctively along the footpath towards the town.

'I am,' he reassured. He paused, and she saw a different look appear in his eyes, a softer aspect. 'I love you,' he blurted suddenly. 'I love you, Catherine. I love you so much. I've missed you, our life together. I want… I want us to be together… for always.'

Catherine was disappointed. If he thought it was going to be that simple, he was sadly mistaken. 'Some bad stuff has happened, Alex. You can't come down here, rescue me from the baddie, like in some cheap "B" movie, and expect everything to be *hunky-dory*. It takes more than that. I'll be straight with you: I left you to be on my own, to plan a new life.'

He nodded solemnly, his eyes suddenly apprehensive in the moonlight. Catherine studied him. Her choice of words had caught him unawares, had cracked the shell of his temperament. 'When Brenda told me of the danger you were in,' he began, 'I was concerned, agitated, distraught… Oh, I don't know… an entire gamut of emotions…' He fell silent, became thoughtful, his eyes restless, scouring the area, as if searching for evidence to support his case. After a moment, he went on: 'I came down here because I care, because I love you… a whole lot. And I am not prepared to let you walk away. We have to talk, we have to discuss this…' His expression turned fraught, and he said: 'I love you, Catherine.'

He was pleading, desperate – he did not want to lose her.

Catherine appreciated that. But it amounted to the same old formula: a glib declaration of love, as if he thought that that would put everything right, would redress every wrong. There was no contrition, no apology. In her mind's eye, she saw herself being carried to their bedroom, being dumped on the bed... coerced. 'Love isn't the same thing as lust,' she snapped. 'They can't be swapped around regardless, manipulated to suit the occasion.'

He made a perplexed look. 'You're... you're right and that's why we should go home and talk.'

That he was stalling for time was obvious; he had no argument, no defence. He was dissembling. She wasn't even sure if he understood her point. But if she agreed to his wishes, Catherine knew that he would win, eventually. Once home, amongst the familiar, little by little, he would whittle away her resolve. 'What's wrong with here?' she shot back.

Seemingly still puzzled, he looked around the cliff-top austerity, at the stunted trees, the sparse gorse. 'Nothing,' he said at length.

Catherine scrutinised his expression. She sensed that her earlier manner, her sympathy, her concern, had made her appear open to persuasion. Unwittingly, she now realised, she had given him succour. He thought that a little flattery and a declaration of love were all that were required to win him a gullible lady. She decided to go in hard. That was her way in an argument, in dealings. Make the opening gambit decisive, gain the upper hand early – and keep it. 'You raped me,' she accused.

It was fortunate for Alex that he wasn't sitting nearer to the cliff edge. If he had been, Catherine thought that he might have toppled over it. As it was she observed him draw back, almost as if she had slapped his face, and a startled look came to his eyes. She decided to press home her advantage.

'Lust masquerading as love doesn't pardon that. It makes it worse: it's an abuse of trust.'

Alex got to his feet and wandered silently across the path. She watched him staring out over the sea. He seemed deep in thought, studious, contemplating. Was he ruing past events, finally regretting what he had done to her? Then a thought leapt into her mind, it was an irrational one inspired by fear: he wasn't going to jump... was he? If he did that, and Armstrong returned... perhaps with his friends, she would be done for. She started to get up. But at that moment, he turned round. Catherine sat down again.

He came back and sat beside her, on the grass. She noted that he had left a gap between them, a visible divide, as if not to threaten her personal space. His face was impassive; his temper hard to read. Surely he didn't intend to argue, to diminish her accusation? Just now he had appeared flattering, eager to declare his love. Then she heard him say: 'I didn't rape you.'

She stared at him, dumbfounded. His words were a declaration, served up as a statement of incontrovertible fact – like a judge delivering his verdict. It was as if he actually believed himself innocent. It was not the response she had anticipated. She had expected him to be contrite, penitent, begging for forgiveness. Catherine had not anticipated a flat denial of the obvious. He had changed his tactics. From being soft and pleading, he had gone on the offensive. 'Yes you did,' she said angrily. 'I said no; you didn't accept that; you attacked me; I tried to fight you off, but you overpowered me and threw me onto the bed and... and had your way. If that's not rape, I don't know what is.'

'That would be rape,' he said. 'But it wasn't like that, was it? Sure we argued and we were horsing around, and I admit that I was vigorous–'

'Vigorous, horsing around,' she interrupted. 'You're good with the euphemisms: you were forceful, and we were fighting.'

'Okay. But it wasn't real fighting, was it? There was plenty of snogging going on, that you enjoyed. You can't deny that. Oh, and by the way, I didn't *throw* you on the bed: I placed you there gently. Then you lay there, receptive, as if–'

'Well there wasn't much point in putting up further resistance then, was there. You were going to do it, whatever I said or did.'

'There was every point,' he said heatedly. 'If you had said no – and meant it – then that would have been that. But you didn't.'

Did he actually believe this rot, this fanciful rubbish? she asked herself. No, of course not. This was another dissemble, a smokescreen to hide his guilt. 'I did say no,' she retorted crossly, 'and more than once.'

'Yes, at first, when we were in the sitting room horsing... arguing, if you must. But later, when we were in the bedroom, you... you were different. And that's when our game started.'

'Your game, you mean.'

'Our game,' he said. 'Okay, I may have started it, but you played along. You didn't have to, but you did. I said... oh, something like, "You'll darn well enjoy it" and you said, "No I won't." It was a challenge – and a challenge accepted. I admit it was a surprise that you did, after the row we'd had – and that made me feel that everything would be okay in the morning, when we'd discussed it calmly.' He started to move his hands towards hers but then, noting her unchanging expression, withdrew them again. 'But, more important,' he continued, 'it was then that you should have made your position clear. If you had done that, none of this would have

247

happened.' His gaze became focused. 'I'm no fool, Kate. Sure it was only one of our games, but if you had won it, you wouldn't have left me, would you?'

'So it was my fault, then?'

'I didn't say that. Mostly, I… I misjudged your mood; I failed to see what was happening. It was our first real disagreement. I… I just didn't know. I truly didn't understand. And I apologise for that.' His face took on a suddenly resolute mantel, and he held her stare. 'But I am right.'

Catherine stood up and wandered across the path, thinking. He had made his point well – his game, their game, her participation in it. She watched the moonlight shimmering on the sea, listened to the lapping of the waves on the rocks. He was right: there was no denying that she was a bad loser. But if you wanted to achieve something in life, you needed to be competitive, and part of being competitive – an important part – was to abhor losing, losing at anything.

After a while she went over and sat beside him. 'All right,' she said quickly, 'I played along… and… and I would not have… if… if…'

'I know,' he cut in. 'Sorry, Catherine, but you can't accept coming second at anything, even a game.' His expression remained challenging, and he added: 'You can't even put it into words.'

'I don't think you would have held back in the bedroom,' Catherine said, shaking her head. 'Nothing that I said… or did would have stopped you. You were highly emotional at the time – you had lost control, unlikely to take no for an answer. You wanted sex… You wouldn't have stopped, would you?'

'You wanted it too,' he said evenly. 'Even after Anna's intervention, we were exchanging looks. Then, still later, when the row got heated, I felt that I was still picking up "come-on" signals. Obviously I was wrong, and that's my mistake and I have apologised for it.' He started to inch towards her. 'But we've been together a while now, long enough to know one another pretty well. Kate, you wanted me as much as I wanted you.'

He was still prevaricating. 'You're evading the issue,' she said dismissively. 'You didn't answer my question.'

'I didn't think it necessary to provide one. I thought you knew me better than that. However, if you insist – yes.' She saw his expression instantly transform into one of wide-eyed astonishment. 'But of course I didn't want to stop. Good God, it was your party, the announcement of our promotions, no the last thing I wanted to do was stop. I wanted more than anything in the world to celebrate by making love to the woman I love.' He paused, shaking his head. 'But of course I would have stopped. But let me say again: you wanted me as much as I wanted you.'

With hindsight, Catherine wished anew that she had been more forthright that night. If she had been, he would have no argument now; he would have nothing with which to cloud the issue. 'All right,' she began noncommittally. 'But why go into the bathroom and masturbate?' He started to speak but, raising her voice, she went on: 'Please don't deny it. I know you did.'

Alex sighed and pulled an embarrassed face. Catherine sensed that she had him cornered. 'I was angry, Kate. As I said, I'd looked forward to your birthday for so long, meticulous planning, our jobs in the States – and then it all went awry. And I blamed you.' His shoulders sagged. 'I'm sorry but I really did.' His shoulders slumped some more. 'I supposed I wanted... Oh, I don't know... to get my own back. It's infantile, I know, but that's how I felt, how it was. After planning so hard to please you I felt rejected, hurt… denied your gratitude.' He smiled lamely, glanced away. 'Yes, looking back on it from here, I think I even expected that. I know how that makes me sound, and I accept it.' He caught her gaze. 'Anyway, I did it. I'm not proud of it. And I apologise.'

'I can understand that,' she said. She noted a tweak of relief come to his face. 'But why call out Anna's name? Was that to sweeten your revenge? Or was it to humiliate me?'

'I didn't call out her name!' Alex shot back, at once angry. 'Christ, Kate. Why do you have to bring her into it? I feel bad enough about what I did without you making it worse.'

'You were fantasising about her and then… and then you shouted her name. I… I heard you.'

Shaking his head, Alex kept her fixed in focus. 'You're wrong – totally wrong.' He continued to shake his head. 'I swear to you, Catherine, I did not call her name. I admit to calling out… but it wasn't Anna.' His stare drilled into hers. 'You're right about one thing though: I did fantasise. I–'

'I knew I was right.' Catherine's words came out in a triumphant exclamation. 'I knew it all–'

'Don't prejudge me, Kate,' Alex cut back in. 'Please… not before you've heard me out.' His expression immediately softened. 'I imagined that our party went off as planned – as I thought it would. You were thrilled at my surprise, already chatting about America. We had a great time, celebrating, everybody applauding us, saying how hard we'd worked for it, predicting how well we would do out there, and then… and then we were in bed.' He paused to clear his throat. 'I saw us lying together, holding one another, you know, as we do, just talking, planning… Then we were kissing, caressing. I held you to me. We were pressed so close together – your arms round my neck. I told you that I loved you. You said you loved me too.' Alex paused, his eyes welling as he held her gaze. Catherine studied his emotion. 'Seeing how badly the evening had actually gone, when I heard you say those words in my fantasy, I felt so good, so wonderfully good. And then… and then it happened. Somehow in the bed, our eyes met. We had been looking at one another, talking, but now it was different… like in a dream. You know, where magical things happen and you accept them, without question. We were so close, closer than physically possible, and your eyes, those lovely green eyes… I said something silly, sentimental, that I would look after you. You smiled… it was one of your disarming smiles.' He fell silent, before concluding: 'And that was my fantasy.'

Catherine sniffed, turned away quickly to wipe away a tear. 'Didn't we make love?' she asked.

Alex glanced towards the sea, then returned his gaze to hers. Catherine could not read his expression. He seemed embarrassed. She nodded encouragingly. 'Well, no,' he said at some length. 'I thought we would. I intended it that way.' He shot her a hesitant look. 'But when you gave me that smile, that sort of… sort of ended things – prematurely. I wanted the fantasy to last longer… but it didn't. And that's when you heard me cry out.'

Catherine took a tissue from her bag and dabbed away another tear. 'You pervert,' she laughed.

'I know it was wrong to… to go into the bathroom and do that – and I apologise for it again.' He picked up her hands. 'The past week has been miserable. I've missed you. And I love you so much.'

Catherine wasn't entirely convinced that he would have been able to restrain himself in the bedroom. When he told her that he would, he had obviously thought he was speaking the truth. He was a decent person, trustworthy, in no way mendacious. Suddenly, she made up her mind; in truth, she had already done so. 'Prove it,' she said, gazing deeply into his eyes. 'Prove it, unless that big bad bully has knocked all the stuffing out of you.'

Even before the mischief of her challenge had left her mind, she saw that old familiar grin spread across his face. He was like a condemned man just told his sentence has been commuted. Then she experienced his lips on hers, strong hands guiding her on to her back, and his mouth moving on hers. She closed her eyes, wrapped her arms round his neck... and melted into his care.

In a little while she felt him start to unbuckle her belt, focused fingers pulling down the zip of her jeans. She saw the moon through hooded lids, its trajectory across the night sky made erratic by the wild beating of her heart. And then she experienced his hand dipping down, to cup, to caress – her reflexive gasp. He was outside her underwear, but all the more intimate for it, the softness of the material a cushion to focus the heat of his hand... and the drumming fingers. He knew her body; he knew her longings – and how to excite them.

All at once Alex propped himself up and gazed around, his eyes taking in the locale. Just for a moment Catherine thought that the big bad bully had indeed subdued him. But then she heard him say: 'We seem to be in some sort of a hollow. Shall we move to somewhere else?'

Catherine smiled secretly. He had noticed – for of course he knew. Despite their reconciliation, he was asking, seeking her permission. He did not want to trespass uninvited on her past. The decision was hers to make. And she made it. Unnoticed, she reached up to her neck and opened the locket. Catherine shook the contents into her hand, took one last look, whispered her farewell, and then scattered them on the grass beside her. There it was done. She had brought Christopher home, home to where he now belonged. She had said goodbye. She turned back to Alex. 'Oh, no,' she replied gaily. 'This is fine.' She raised her hips to allow him to remove her jeans. 'In fact, it's perfect.' A moment later she heard his contented sigh as his eyes took in the voluptuousness of her spilling flesh.

'Oh, dear God,' he moaned as he fell to caressing her rump. 'I thought I'd never do this again.'

In a little while he sat her upright and started to unbutton her cardigan. She held his stare, his eager stare. His passion was taking charge of their lovemaking. Oddly, though perhaps it was due to his rapt attention, she felt not unlike a gift, a birthday present, and he the birthday boy removing the wrapping, gleeful, his awareness of what was inside redoubling his pleasure.

He gripped her upper arms, returned her stare. 'I'm going to fuck you,' he told her. He repeated his assertion. 'I'm going to fuck you.'

At his words, Catherine experienced something not unlike the tingle of a mild electric shock occur between her legs. She liked it when he talked dirty to her during sex. It was a turn-on – an explicit narrative of what was going to be done to her. She nodded a submissive head. 'All right,' she said demurely.

And it was then that she heard the sound of voices.

Catherine froze. 'Listen.'

'I can't hear anything.'

'It's him.' She fell silent, then: 'Alex, it's him. It's Armstrong.' She strained her ears. 'He's coming... Let me put my clothes on.'

'I told you: he won't come back. But if he does, he will soon wish that he hadn't.'

'There is somebody with him…' Catherine shivered. 'It's his friends.'

'Well, they won't thank him for bringing them up here.'

'But my clothes…' Catherine scrambled around on the grass, gathering up items of hastily discarded clothing, her bra, her pants, her cardigan. The voices were coming along the path, getting closer. She mustn't, just mustn't be like this when Armstrong arrived. She started to guide a foot into her knickers…

'There's no time.' Alex's words were insistent. 'Here, keep as low as you can.' He shrugged off his jacket. 'Put this round your shoulders.'

Catherine did as she was told, squirming into the garment and pulling it shut as though it were a suit of medieval armour. Her face was white, drained – all her sexual feelings, so expertly roused by her lover, had evaporated.

Alex turned up the collar for her, smiled. 'Don't worry,' he said. 'Everything will be all right. I'll see to that… Anyway, it's probably not him.'

'It is…' Catherine felt her teeth chattering in the warm evening air. 'And he has brought his friends with him.'

'Then we'll have a party.'

She knew that he couldn't take on all three. That would be ridiculous. For while he was fighting one, another one would get behind him… She started to look around, her stare feverish, desperately trying to locate a large pebble.

'What're you looking for?' Alex asked. She told him her plan. Through a look of astonishment, he said: 'You just stay here, lie low. It'll be fine.' All at once, a grin spread across his face. 'But if you do feel inclined to join in, whatever you do, don't hit me.'

'I'm serious, Alex.'

'So am I,' he said. 'Now, keep out of sight.'

Catherine cowered into the hollow. The voices were now almost upon them. Please don't let it be them… Oh, please. She raised a cautious head, peered over the rim of their hideaway. The moon was waning but, by starlight, she could just make out the silhouette of two approaching figures… a man… a man and a woman. Her heart leapt. 'I don't think it's them.' She all but sang with relief. 'I think… Alex, I'm nearly naked.' Catherine experienced her heart pounding in her chest as a runaway of alternative unwelcome thoughts leapt into her mind. Caught like this, at her age, like a wayward teenager, compromised, bonking in the bushes. She blanched, saw the tabloid headline: *The Banker's Summer Bonus.* And then she felt his hand sliding down her naked stomach, down, down… all the way down and on to the mound of her sex. 'No, Alex, don't. They'll hear us.'

'It's all right. They'll pass by.'

But they didn't and, much to her chagrin, Catherine watched the couple, now no more than a yard or two away, step off the path and approach the cliff edge. She knew with all certainty that if one of them turned round, glanced in this direction, then they were bound to be seen. It was inevitable. The hollow was not deep enough to conceal them from somebody so close.

She remembered another time, two lovers lying here as voices passed by in the night. Then they had hardly dared to breath, had hardly dared to move a muscle. But still Alex's fingers teased her…

She reached down, grasped his wrist in her two hands, tried to prevent what was happening to her. But she wasn't strong enough, nowhere near strong enough. He was manipulating her unreservedly. Not only that but he had his leg over hers, wedged between her knees. He had her pinioned and candid; she could not even close her legs against his ministrations.

The couple were chatting, casting occasional glances across the sea, now and then turning to one another. They were not young. They looked middle-aged, respectable – holidaymakers taking a stroll after supper. He was wearing blue canvas trousers, fawn brogues, a plain white shirt – with a loosened tie; she a red floral print frock, scooped neckline, sandals with a cork heel. A rose tattoo embellished her right ankle. All these details etched themselves into Catherine's feverish mind. What would they say, if they knew what was going on just yards away, behind their backs? They would be shocked – scandalised.

'I'm going to make you come,' Alex murmured into her ear. 'I'm going to make you come so hard that your shouts will scare those two right over the cliff.'

Feeling herself already a-tingle, Catherine grasped the nettle. 'I think they're going to jump. Look, they are.'

'Nice try,' he whispered. 'But they're snogging, that's all. Now, try not to disturb them.' He held her gaze, smiled lightly. 'Please try hard, Catherine. You don't want their demise on your conscience, do you?'

It was another of those confounding cases where, simply because she didn't want to, she knew that she would. She noted the wicked twinkle in his eyes. 'No, Alex,' she said. 'Seriously, even a little noise would–'

'A loud one would do it for sure. That's why you have to be silent… and I know that you can be… when you want.'

She held his wrist, tried to stop him, redoubled her effort. But it was not possible. He was a monster, a leviathan –

unstoppable. It was like trying to retard the motion of a mechanical machine, a remorseless unrelenting machine.

'*Round and round the garden...*' His mischievous gaze... watching... waiting, synchronising. '*... like a teddy bear...*' And all the time his fingers... circling... lolloping... slowly teasing her swollen flesh. '*... one step, two steps... tickle you under there...*'

'You meanie. You...' She giggled as she realised her fight was lost, all propriety forgotten in the heat of the moment. 'You dirty rotten...' His hand came across her mouth, muffling her. Then, unable to hold back any longer, she screwed her eyes tight shut, spluttering mutely into his palm as he brought her to climax – the red mist, the flushing, hot, torrid, and the unbelievable pulsing of her sex, her entire insides seeming to flow from her.

After a little while he carefully removed his hand from her mouth. 'Are you okay?' His eyes examined hers. 'Sorry.'

Catherine nodded, unable to speak for fear her voice would be made loud by her erratic breathing.

A full minute passed before she was able to focus her gaze. From her spread-eagled posture, she peered up at him. Her heart was still going like a drum. 'Oh, Alex,' she moaned, gratefully watching the couple recommence their walk. 'I've missed you.'

He raised his head and gazed at her. She could see the overwhelming love in his eyes. 'You're really beautiful, you know.' He lifted her fringe, rubbed several strands of hair between his thumb and fingers. 'I like the new colour, by the way... Auburn suits you.'

'I didn't think you had noticed.'

'I saw it straightaway, when I was coming along the path.'

'Did you? I thought of going blonde.'

'Thank God you didn't,' he said, his face aghast.

'What would you have done if I had?'

Alex shrugged. 'Probably turned round and gone home.'

'What and left me at the mercy of Armstrong?'

He shrugged again. 'Yeah, sorry about that.'

She thumped his chest.

Alex let out a yelp. 'Bloody hell, Kate,' he complained. 'That was harder than Armstrong hit me.'

'Yes,' she laughed. 'I heard him call you a sissy.' Then she started kissing him. She was pleased that they could joke, tease one another, so soon after – it boded well for the future. Then Alex started kissing her back – and she quickly lost the ability to think about anything other than being fucked.

In a little while she helped him take off his clothes, item by item, until, like her, he too was naked. She caught her breath – for it was very much apparent that the big bad bully had not knocked the stuffing out of him.

Catherine closed her hand around him, gripped him. The heat came off in waves, like radiation from a nuclear rod. She ran her hand along the shaft to the bulb, tried to squeeze... and failed. She had never known him so firm before – there was no give. Neither had she known him so big – like a giant, a colossus. Her fingers would scarce encompass him. The skin felt taut, stretched with the need of his erection. It throbbed in her hand, alive – like an animal. The feeling was overwhelming, even a little frightening.

'I think I will need to be on my best behaviour tonight,' she teased.

Alex glanced down at himself, grimaced as he attempted to gain the upper hand over his passion. 'Me too, Kate.'

'Let me see if you can be,' she responded, taking him in both hands. 'Show me how disciplined you are.' Tensing her grip, she drew her hands down the shaft to his groin, held him there, so that he stood out like a missile, a rocket sitting on its launch pad – *primed for its Venusian mission.* Then she bent forward and kissed the glans. Alex responded with an inarticulate burble. She peeked up at him, mischievously, her eyes daring him to try and stop her. But his mind seemed somewhere else, his stare fixed on a star in some faraway galaxy. She knew he could scarce contain himself. Struck then with a sudden desire to redeem her earlier comeuppance, she kissed him again, lingered there for a second, tickling with her tongue, before parting her lips fully… to suck his bulb slowly into her mouth.

'For God's sake, Kate… No… No, I want…'

But Catherine took no notice. Licking the underbelly as one would a gobstopper, she glanced up at him again, her eyes twinkling with wicked intention. She reckoned him now grown like a pillar, a Corinthian pillar. But she could manage. Puffing up her cheeks, she bobbed her head, once, twice, then, elongating her neck, she performed a trick that Alex had taught her.

Like a man at his wit's end, Alex muttered more incoherent words in a colourful invective of exasperation.

His outburst told Catherine that he was approaching his point of no return. Deep down, she could sense him bubbling, like a simmering cauldron… that wasn't far off boiling over. But she knew what to do. She had been here before – brinkmanship was her forte. Gripping his scrotal sac in her hands, she pulled down gently, held him there. Alex spluttered. Catherine accepted that he was having a tough time of it, that his determination to hold himself back was all but exhausted. She needed to act – now. Taking the shaft partially from her mouth, she inflicted a sharp circumferential nip with her teeth just below his glans. Alex spluttered some more, placed uncertain hands behind her neck.

After a second or two Catherine repeated the operation, albeit with a touch more venom this time, then she took him wholly from her mouth. He was wet with her spittle, glossy in the starlight. She looked up, smiling impishly. 'You were almost a naughty boy,' she said.

'Oh, God,' Alex sighed, shaking a relieved head. 'Kate I would have choked you.' He shook his head again. 'I really would.'

She feigned affront. 'I have always managed before.'

'I know you have... But this is a whole new ball game.'

For a second or two they stared at one another, each seeming to dare the other to be the first to laugh. At length, Alex said: 'I'd like to rephrase that...'

But before he could Catherine put silent arms round his neck and drew him to her, and for a while they kissed. Her heart was soon going all out. Of all the things they did, kissing turned her on quickest.

Alex guided her onto her back, brought brief lips to hers, then, parting her legs, rolled on top of her. There was now an undeniable urgency to his directions. Catherine was aware that he would not be able to delay for much longer. Her foreplay had aroused him almost beyond reason – even a kiss was precarious. He needed to fuck; he needed to fuck now.

She felt him position himself, experienced him held against her lipped cunny, big, bulbous, and beautiful. Closing her eyes, she prepared to receive him, made ready to accept his love. She wanted him; she wanted him now, in this place, on the cliff top, in *their* place. And with that wish, she felt his mounting pressure, his hands pulling down on her hips, the transient resistance of her body, then the surrender of her flesh to the power of his penetration. Catherine took all of him. No, he had never been like this before – so large, so potent.

But neither had she felt so wanton. Their time apart had been a shared burden.

She slid her arms round his neck. 'I love you,' she gasped. She was bursting with joy. Her heart was bursting with passion. 'I love you,' she repeated.

'My darling,' he responded, pressing his pubis against hers in a full-body kiss.

For a little while longer, he held himself inside her, still and quivering – Tantric sex, the tranquillity of meditation. But not tonight: tonight demanded the vigour of reconciliation. And that was the thing he now commenced to give her. Over and over, again and again she felt the intensity of his thrusts, the pressure waves preceding his plunges, as he drove them towards their orgasm – and the rhythmic slapping of his sac against the softness of her under flesh, enhancing her pleasure.

In a moment she heard the groan, the groan that indicated he was approaching his climax. Nothing could stop him now. If the moon fell from the sky, if the planet spun from its orbit – not a thing. The touch paper was lit, the fuse was ignited… for them both. He was fucking her with meaning.

With a muted gasp, almost one of protest, Catherine entered pre-orgasmic tension. Her body clutched him, tightened round him. In dancing spikes of coloured light she experienced the first palpitation, deep inside her the gentle flapping as of a bird's wing… then clitoral engorgement, held like a treasure. Then the release of bliss… and the bliss of release – two bodies, two hearts as one. Too soon her shiver as her rapture ebbed; his moan, almost a death rattle, as he gave up the last of his love – and later, some untold time later, the breaking of his hardness and the melding of their flesh. He was still inside her, their flesh as one, love's umbilical cord.

At length Catherine opened her eyes. The stars had never seemed so bright, so near – light years crossed in the blinking of an eye. It felt as though she could reach up and pluck them from the sky, pluck them one by one… 'Gosh! I've just seen a shooting star,' she said.

Alex bent his head and kissed her. 'Listen,' he said, still out of breath, 'and we'll see if we can hear the hiss as it splashes into the water.'

Catherine laughed, then cupped her ear theatrically. 'I don't think we will,' she said. 'I think it's gone all the way across the ocean to America.'

'Then we shall just have to go over and see if we can find where it landed,' he replied.

'Yes, we will,' she said. She moved gentle hips, delighting in the feel of him inside her. Then she felt him stiffening again. 'Mm… Yes, we will,' she repeated. 'But first things first…'